THE BOOK OF
DOOM

AN AFTERWORLDS BOOK

THE BOOK OF
DOOM

BARRY HUTCHISON

HarperCollins *Children's Books*

First published in Great Britain by HarperCollins *Children's Books* 2011
HarperCollins *Children's Books* is a division of HarperCollins*Publishers* Ltd,
77-85 Fulham Palace Road, Hammersmith, London W6 8JB

The HarperCollins *Children's Books* website address is
www.harpercollins.co.uk

1

Text and illustrations copyright © 2013 by Barry Hutchison

The author asserts the moral right to be identified as the author and illustrator of this work.

ISBN: 978-0-00-744091-7

Printed and bound in England by
Clays Ltd, St Ives plc

To my auntie and number one supporter:
Jessie Corson MBE. (Sorry, couldn't resist.)

PROLOGUE

"Yes, Gabriel. What is it?"

"I bring news, sir."

"News? Of the book?"

"Of the book. We have tracked it down."

"You have? Excellent. Where is it?"

"It's... well, it's *down below*, sir."

"What? On Earth?"

"Somewhat further down below than that, sir."

"Oh. Right. Yes. Of course. The blighters. No surprise, I suppose."

"Not entirely unexpected, sir, no."

"Right. Well, now we've found it, what's happening? They going to send it back?"

"No, sir."

"No? What do you mean, 'no'? They're not playing silly sods again, are they?"

"They have requested that we send someone down to collect it in person."

"You must be joking! One of us? Down *there*? You must be joking!"

"Alas, no, sir. They're quite adamant about it. If we want the book back, we have to send someone to pick it up. They assure us it isn't a trap."

"It sounds like a trap."

"They assure us it isn't."

"If I recall, Gabriel, they're rather fond of lying. Rather adept at it too."

"Quite, sir. But if they refuse to send it back, I don't see that we have much of a choice in the matter. They have us over something of a barrel on this one. We need that book. What with the... current situation."

"Yes, yes. You're right, of course. Bless it all, we're going to have to send someone. But who?"

"I anticipated you might ask that, sir. If I may be permitted to make a suggestion...?"

"Speak freely, Gabriel."

"What if we didn't send one of us, sir?"

"What do you mean?"

"They didn't specify whom we should send. They just said we should send 'someone'."

"I don't follow."

"If it is, as we suspect, a trap, then it would seem unwise to send one of our own marching in. Better, surely, to send someone from down below?"

"A demon? How would that work?"

"Somewhat *less* far below than that, sir."

"A human. Hmm. He wouldn't like that."

"He isn't around to make the decision, sir. You are. With all due respect."

"True words, Gabriel. True words. But whom would we choose?"

"I have taken the liberty of choosing for you, sir, so that you may distance yourself from any subsequent... unpleasantness."

"Good thinking. Good thinking. Excellent. Off the record, though, who did you pick? No names, just the basics."

"Someone disposable, sir."

"Yes. Yes. Well, aren't they all? But capable, I trust?"

"Oh, my word, yes, sir. He's capable. He's most capable indeed."

CHAPTER ONE

BULLETS. HE HATED bullets.

He especially hated bullets that were travelling towards him at high speed, like the one that had just missed his head.

He kept low, zigzagging across the rooftop, his black outfit all but blending him with the night. There was a gap coming up, a space between this roof and the next. Three metres, he estimated. Three and a half at most. Not easy, but doable.

He sped up, straightened, threw himself over the opening. His shoulder hit and he rolled quickly, letting his momentum carry him back to his feet, and then he was up and running again.

He was halfway across the roof when he heard the

shooter clear the gap. Private security. It had to be. Police couldn't make that jump. Police would've given up long before now. Besides, the cops didn't have guns, and if they did, they probably wouldn't be aiming for his head.

The next roof was closer, but higher. He scrambled up the wall, caught the top ledge and pulled himself over. A chunk of stone pinged from the wall where his legs had been. He threw himself on to the rooftop, face-first, and a third bullet whistled by above him.

He raced forward, a dark shape against a dark background. The edge of the roof came up more quickly than he'd been expecting. He stumbled, tripped, then fell three metres on to the next roof.

The landing hurt, but there was no time to dwell on it. As he scrambled to his feet, something slipped from his pocket and landed with a clatter on the slates. He glanced up at the ledge he'd just fallen from, saw no one there, so wasted a second bending to retrieve the ornate gold cross he had dropped. When he stood up, a gun was in his face.

"You're fast. I'll give you that," puffed the man with the

gun. "You almost lost me back there. But that cross doesn't belong to you. It belongs to my boss, Mr Hanlon."

Behind his hood and mask, the figure in black remained silent. The gunman was in his early thirties, well built, with hair that was shaved almost to the bone. Ex-military, no doubt. Well trained and in good shape.

"Do you know what Mr Hanlon does to people who break into his home and take his property?" asked the man. "Or, let me put it another way, do you know what Mr Hanlon lets *me* do to people who break into his home and take his—"

The dark-clad figure leaned left and brought his hand sharply up, fingers together like the blade of a spear. The blow connected just above the gunman's right armpit. The man's finger tried to tighten on the trigger of the gun, but there was no strength left in his arm.

The right side of his face went slack. His right leg wobbled as his arm – and the gun – began to drop.

"What... what've you done to me?" he slurred as he folded down on to the rooftop.

"Don't worry, the paralysis is only temporary," the figure in black said. "But I'd consider a safer line of work in future. Tell your boss thanks for the cross."

The fallen gunman blinked. There was a rustle of fabric, and he was suddenly alone on the roof.

Five minutes later and several streets away, the shadowy figure clambered down a drainpipe into a narrow alleyway. Just beyond the alley mouth he could hear the hustle and bustle of the city. It was midnight, but the city, like him, rarely slept.

He took off the mask. The night air was cool against his skin. He let himself enjoy it for a moment, taking it in through his nose in big gulps, refilling his aching lungs.

"Zac Corgan?"

The voice came from behind him. The accent was New York – Brooklyn, maybe – but Zac didn't recognise the voice. He spun, already crouching into a fighting stance.

An overweight man in a brown robe stood in the alleyway. Moonlight gleamed off his balding head. Despite the hour, he wore a pair of designer sunglasses. Zac's reflection stared back from both lenses.

"Zac Corgan?" the man asked again.

"Sorry," said Zac, backing away. "I don't know who that is."

"Don't jerk me around, kid. You're Zac Corgan."

"No, I'm not."

"You're Zac Corgan, fifteen years old. Parents disappeared when you was eighteen months, so you live with your grandfather."

Zac hesitated. "I don't know what you're talking about."

The man in the robe gave an impatient sigh. "You wear size nine shoes. You eat mostly eggs and pasta, for the protein and carbohydrate. You're home educated. You got no friends. And you have a birthmark the shape of a smiley face on the back of your hand."

"No, I don't."

"Yes, you do," the Monk insisted.

"I haven't got a birthmark. You've got the wrong person."

"See for yourself, kid."

Hesitantly, Zac pulled off his gloves. A brown splodge he'd never seen before grinned up at him. He tried to rub it away, but the smiley-faced mark wasn't going anywhere.

"All right," Zac said, pulling his gloves back on. "You've got my attention. Who are you?"

15

"They call me the Monk."

Zac glanced from the man's bald head to his long brown cloak. He could just see a pair of sandalled feet poking out at the bottom.

"Why do they call you that, then?"

"Funny, kid. Real funny." The Monk took a step forward. Zac took a step back. "My... employer wants to talk to you. He's impressed with your work, see? Thinks maybe you can help us with a little problem we got."

"I don't do requests," Zac said.

The Monk's voice became cold. "We wasn't making one."

"I'd advise against threatening me," Zac warned. "Tell your *employer* I'm not interested."

The Monk smiled thinly. "I don't think that's so good an idea. You don't know it, kid, but you're in a whole heap of trouble. And that trouble's gonna come find you real soon."

"I can handle myself."

"What, you think just because you can sneak around all dressed in black that you're going to be able to avoid it? You think being stealthy is going to keep you safe? I got news for you – we can all do stealthy. Stealthy ain't nothin' special. Check this out: now you see me —" he stepped sideways into the shadows – "now you don't."

"Yes, I do," said Zac. He pointed to a shape in the darkness. "There you are."

There was a soft scuffing of sandals on concrete.

"OK. Well, how about now, Mr Smart Guy? Bet you can't see me now."

"You haven't moved."

There was more scuffing, louder this time.

"All right, big shot... how about now?"

Silence.

"Ha! I knew it. You ain't got the first damn clue where I am, do ya? C'mon, take a guess."

More silence. From the shadows, there came a sigh.

"You're gone, ain't ya, kid?" the Monk said.

And he was right.

CHAPTER TWO

"COME IN, CHUCK."

Zac edged open the door and stepped into a cluttered office. It looked like the back store at a pawnshop, with clocks and books and ornaments and other clutter stacked crookedly on shelves, on tables, or just piled up on the floor.

And in the middle of it all, like a spider in her web, sat Geneva Jones. She lounged behind a desk, her grey hair scraped back, a hand-rolled cigarette stuck to her bottom lip. It was two in the morning, but there she was, wide awake. Of course, Zac only ever visited at night, but the rumour was Geneva never slept.

"Zac." She smiled, revealing a smudge of red lipstick across her teeth. "Knew you wouldn't let me down."

Without a word, Zac reached into his pocket and pulled out the cross. It landed with a *thud* on her desk. Geneva's eyes gleamed as she picked it up.

"The Cross of Saint Alberic," she said in a half-whisper. "Isn't it flippin' gorgeous?"

"Bit bling for my liking," Zac told her. "But if you pay me, I'll leave you two alone together."

"Yes, yes, of course," Geneva said, setting the cross back down. "What did we say again? Two hundred, wasn't it?"

Outwardly, Zac didn't react. He'd been here too many times before.

"Two thousand."

Geneva's eyes widened in surprise. She took the cigarette from her mouth and stubbed it into an overflowing ashtray. "Two *thousand*? I don't remember offering that. That's a lot of money."

"The cross is worth ten times that, easy," Zac said.

Geneva held the artefact out to him. "Then maybe you should try selling it yourself. If you're so up on the market rates."

Zac didn't move to take the cross.

"Two hundred," Geneva said.

"Eight hundred."

"Three."

"Five."

"Deal!" the woman said. She spat on her hand, then held it out. Zac shook it, then covertly wiped his palm on his jacket.

Geneva slid open a desk drawer and pulled out a rolled-up bundle of notes. She unfolded the pile, counted five notes from the top, then put the rest back in the drawer.

"A pleasure doing business with you, as always," she said, grinning as she handed Zac the money. Her face took on a wounded expression as Zac held each note up to the light and checked it. "What's the matter? Don't you trust me? After all these years?"

"I don't trust anyone," Zac said, folding the money into his wallet.

"Very wise. That'll keep you alive, that will," Geneva told him. "Ta-ra then, chuck. For now."

Zac nodded, then reached for the door handle.

"Oh, I almost clean forgot," said Geneva. "There was someone in 'ere asking about you earlier."

"Asking about me? Who?"

"A monk, would you believe? Robe and everything. Proper Friar Tuck, he was."

"What? When?"

Geneva lit another cigarette, then drew deeply on it. "Not long. Few minutes before you got here."

Zac tensed. "Did you tell him anything?"

"No, no, of course not. What do you take me for?"

Relaxing a little, Zac pulled open the door.

"I told him he could ask you hisself."

A bald man in a brown robe stood in the hallway, blocking the exit. He stared out at Zac from behind his mirrored sunglasses.

"Hey, kid," said the Monk. "Surprise!"

"I told you, I'm not interested."

"Figured you might say that," the Monk said with a shrug. His hand rose at his side, until it was level with his waist. An old-fashioned revolver, like something from a Western, pointed at Zac's chest. "So you ain't leaving me no choice."

Zac swung his leg with the speed of a striking cobra. His foot caught the Monk's wrist and slammed it against the wall. There was a *bang*, deafening in the narrow space, and an antique clock in Geneva's office exploded into matchsticks.

"Hell's teeth! Watch what you're doing, chuck!"

Zac stepped in close to the Monk, using his body weight to keep the gun arm against the wall. The heel of his hand crunched against the bald man's chin, snapping his head back. Folding his fingers into the shape of a blade, Zac struck the Monk just above his right armpit. He stayed in close as he waited for the Monk to fall.

But the Monk had other ideas.

"Nice try, kid," he said. "My turn."

Zac could move fast, but the Monk could move faster. There was a blur of hands. Zac caught a glimpse of his reflection in the Monk's sunglasses, and then there was a strange sensation of weightlessness and motion, and Zac realised what was going to happen next.

The door shattered beneath his weight and Zac found himself outside, lying on his back on the road, pain stabbing the whole length of his spine. A moonlit shadow passed across him. He rolled left just as a sandalled foot slammed down.

The Monk stamped again and again, forcing Zac to keep

rolling. At last, he managed to scramble to his feet and threw himself forward into a sprint. His sudden dash had given him a head start, but the Monk was already right at his heels.

Zac dug deep and forced his legs to move faster. There was no way the Monk should be able to keep up with him. He had to be three or four times heavier than Zac, at least, and yet his footsteps were drawing closer.

A hand grabbed him roughly by the shoulder. Zac ducked and pulled free, stumbling as he made it to the junction.

A horn blared as a taxi swooshed narrowly by him, its headlights dazzling in the darkness. From behind Zac there came a screeching of brakes. Another cab bore down on him, the driver's face a mask of terror as she stomped the brake pedal down to the floor.

Before Zac could move, the Monk was in front of him. The man in the robe raised a fist above his head, then brought it down sharply on the bonnet of the car. There was a scream from inside the vehicle as the back end flipped up into the air.

Zac watched, frozen, as the car somersaulted above his head. It landed, right way up, with an almighty *crash* behind him. He watched, dumbstruck, as all four wheels rolled off in different directions.

When he turned back, the Monk was looking at him, arms folded, a self-satisfied smirk on his face.

"What the Hell are you?"

"Trust me, Hell ain't got nothin' to do with it," the Monk replied.

"What you did... the car... it's not possible."

"Not possible for *you*, maybe," the Monk said, shrugging. They began to circle each other, Zac tense, the Monk a picture of tranquillity. "Me? I can do lots of things."

"Oh, really?" Zac said. "Well, you're not the only one."

He had seen the night bus approaching from the corner of his eye. He darted across in front of it as it sped by, narrowly avoiding being hit. The Monk hung back, waiting for the bus to pass before he gave chase.

It swept by in a gust of wind and a whiff of diesel. Behind his mirrored lenses, the Monk's eyes scanned for any sign of the boy, but Zac was nowhere to be seen – not on the road, not on the pavement...

The bus. The Monk turned his head, following the vehicle as it spluttered away from him. A black-clad figure stood at the back windscreen. Zac smiled and waved. The Monk pulled the gun from within his robe, but by the time he took aim, the bus was round a corner and out of range.

"H-help!" came a shaky voice from inside the wreckage of the taxi. "Help, I... I need help!"

The Monk didn't look round. "Yeah, yeah. You know what, sweetheart?" he said quietly. "You an' me both."

CHAPTER THREE

ZAC GLANCED OVER his shoulder to make sure he hadn't been followed, then slipped into his house through the back door. He closed the door and turned the key without a sound, then jumped as the kitchen light clicked on.

"Zac?"

"Granddad, it's you," Zac breathed. He looked at the old man standing in the doorway in his striped pyjamas. He held a green and blue stress ball in one hand, squeezing it gently between his fingers. "What are you doing up?" Zac asked.

His grandfather, Phillip, passed the stress ball from one hand to the other and back again. "I was hungry," he said. "Or... thirsty? I forget which. Where have you been?"

Zac crossed to the window and drew the blinds. "Working, Granddad, remember?"

"Until three in the morning?" Phillip asked. "Who eats hamburgers at three in the morning? I hope they paid you overtime."

"Yeah, well..."

"I mean, eating hamburgers at three in the morning. They need their heads examined."

"It takes all sorts, Granddad," said Zac, not meeting the old man's eye. He took a glass from the draining board and filled it with water. "Here, have this."

Phillip frowned. "What for?"

"You're thirsty."

"Am I?" He took the glass and gulped down some of the water. "Oh, yes, so I was." He licked his cracked lips. "Catriona's very worried. *Very* worried."

"Is she?" Zac asked. He glanced past his granddad into the darkened hallway, checking for any sign of movement. "What's she worried about?"

"Oh, everything. You know what Catriona's like!"

Zac filled himself a glass from the tap and sipped on it. The coppery tang of blood swirled around inside his mouth. "Well, no, not really," he said. "Who's Catriona?"

Phillip paused, his own glass halfway to his lips. "Catriona? She's..." His eyes seemed to dim as he struggled to remember. He squeezed hard on his stress ball. "You know. Catriona."

"Oh, you mean *Catriona*. Of course. Now I remember," lied Zac. "Yeah, she's a worrier, that one."

A relieved smile lit up Phillip's face. "Catriona," he laughed. "Fancy not remembering Catriona. She's asked me to help her out, but, I mean, what can I do?"

"You can do lots of things, Granddad," Zac said, patting the old man on the shoulder, "but I think it's time Catriona learned to stand on her own two feet. Stop worrying about her. She'll be fine."

Whoever she is, Zac added silently. Phillip spoke about people like Catriona all the time. People who snuck into his head at all hours of the day and night and told him their problems. People who, as far as Zac could tell, didn't actually exist.

"Where have you been all night?" Phillip asked.

"Work, Granddad. I told you, remember?"

"Is that a bruise?" Phillip said, peering at his grandson. Zac pulled back before the old man could get a closer look at his face.

"Oh, yeah, I walked into a door," Zac said. "Nothing serious. Anyway... I'm going to head to bed. Will you be OK?"

"I'll be fine," said Phillip, putting his glass in the sink. "If I can't sleep I might do some reading. Or listen to music. Or I might even watch some television."

"We don't have a TV, Granddad."

"Oh, don't we? Well, bang goes that idea. Maybe I'll just feed the goldfish, if I can get it to stay still for long enough. Anyway, I'll be fine. You go. You go. You need your beauty sleep."

Phillip shooed Zac out into the hallway, where an orange shape was zipping around inside a glass bowl. They both watched it for a few moments, moving so fast it was almost a blur of speed. Phillip had owned the same goldfish for as long as Zac could remember. In all that time, Zac had never once seen it stop moving.

Zac tore his eyes away from the darting fish and made

for the stairs. He stopped to check the front door was locked, then turned to his granddad. "Listen, if anyone comes looking for me... I mean, if anyone calls round..."

Phillip frowned. "Expecting someone? At this time of night?"

"No. Maybe. Probably. If anyone comes to the door, tell them I'm not in."

"Are you heading out?"

"No, I'm going to sleep, so tell them I'm not in."

"You're not in. Got it," said Phillip. "Where is it you're going?"

"I'm not going anywhere, Granddad. Just sleeping, remember?"

"Sleeping. Right." The old man tapped a finger against the side of his nose. "Say no more."

"You be OK?"

"I'll be fine, Zac," said Phillip. "Which is more than I can say for poor Bill."

Zac made an admirable attempt to contain a sigh. "Bill?"

"Lost his job, apparently. In a lot of financial trouble. He doesn't know what to do." Phillip shook his head sadly.

"Keeps asking me to sort it out for him, as if I can do anything about that kind of thing."

For a moment, Phillip seemed to drift away. He gazed into space, a fog descending behind his eyes. Eventually, he gave himself a shake and looked over to his grandson.

"Now, where were you going again?"

"Nowhere, Granddad," said Zac. He smiled weakly. "I'm just going to go bed."

"Right you are!" said Phillip, and he turned back to the goldfish bowl as Zac bounded up the stairs.

The door to Zac's bedroom was old and heavy. He closed it firmly and pushed his bookcase in front of it, just to make sure he wasn't disturbed. He needed time to think, to figure out who the Monk was, and why he was trying to kill him.

He sat on the end of his bed, facing the window. The adrenaline that had been pumping through him for the past few hours was wearing off, and he could now feel all the cuts and bruises he'd earned on his way through Geneva's front door.

A car. With a single punch, the Monk had flipped a moving car. It had to be a trick of some kind. It had to be.

Like the birthmark on his hand, which had vanished again by the time he'd got home. Those things weren't possible.

He looked through the window, along the leafy suburban street lit up orange by the glow of the streetlights. For a moment he thought he saw something glint on a roof at the other end of the street – a reflection of moonlight off a lens, maybe. He jumped up and quickly drew the curtains, suddenly unable to shake the feeling that he was being watched.

He was agitated. That was new. He never got agitated. Whatever the situation, he was a master at keeping his cool.

But a car. The Monk had flipped a car.

"Get a grip," he told himself. "You're being paranoid."

He turned from the window. A figure in brown stood against the wall near the corner of the room.

"See, kid?" said the Monk. "Told ya I was stealthy."

The roar of a gunshot echoed through the house.

CHAPTER FOUR

Z AC OPENED HIS eyes and instinctively grabbed
for his stomach, where he expected the gunshot
wound to be. He had felt the impact of the bullet
hitting him. The brief but overwhelming agony as it had
torn up his insides.

The last thing he remembered before the world went
dark was the Monk's voice, soft in his ear: "Don't worry,
kid, I'll stick your body in the cupboard."

And now...

And now...

Nothing. There was no pain. No blood. He hadn't yet
sat up, but he could tell he wasn't in his bedroom, and he
wasn't in the cupboard, either. He was... somewhere else,
lying on his back with something soft and fluffy below him.

"It's awake," said a gruff voice.

"*He's* awake, Michael, please," said another. It sounded friendlier than the first, but with the sort of upper-class lilt that Zac had never been keen on.

The smiling face of a youngish-looking man leaned over him. "Why, hello there," the face said. "You must be Zac."

Zac tried to leap to his feet, but the ground was squishy, like plumped-up pillows, and it took him longer than he would have liked. He stared, first at his surroundings – bright blue sky, fluffy white ground, with an imposing gate standing off to one side – and then at the two men he had heard talking.

They looked similar, and yet different, like twins whose lives had taken them down very different paths.

The one who'd spoken to him – the smiling one – was still smiling. He had long blond hair, hanging in curls down to his shoulders, and eyes that sparkled a brilliant shade of electric blue. He wore a long white... Zac hesitated to use the word *dress*, but he couldn't think of a more appropriate one. It was plain in design, and reached all the way down to the floor. The sleeves looked to be a little on the long side, with gaping cuffs that hung several centimetres from the man's wrists.

The other man – Michael, was it? – was facially very

similar. Same blue eyes, same blond hair, but there the likeness ended.

Instead of a gown, Michael was dressed like a Roman soldier. He wore a tunic of red leather, decorated with golden trim. On top of this was a breastplate, also the colour of gold. It wasn't real gold, Zac guessed, because real gold would make useless armour. It would be steel, painted to look like gold. Unless the wearer had no intention of actually using it in battle, of course.

A sword hung in its scabbard at Michael's side. The first man appeared to carry no weapon, although he could've probably hidden a bazooka up those sleeves if he'd wanted to.

"Please don't be alarmed," he said. "My name is Gabriel. It's a pleasure to—"

"What's going on? Where's the Monk? Where am I?"

"The Monk is on Earth," said Gabriel. "You, on the other hand, are not."

Zac's gaze went between the two men. "What? What do you mean I'm not on Earth? What are you talking about?"

"I thought you said it was smart," Michael grunted. "Doesn't seem so smart to me."

"*He is* smart. He's just a little... jet-lagged," said Gabriel, not taking his eye off Zac, and not lowering that smile. "It's a lot to take in, isn't it, Zac? Take a moment. Look around, and then tell me where you are."

For a long time, Zac kept watching Gabriel. The man's voice, like his smile, was as insincere as a politician on the campaign trail. Despite Michael's sword and demeanour, something about Gabriel made Zac suspect he was the one to watch out for.

"Go on," Gabriel urged. "Look. See."

Zac shifted his eyes to the left. The swirling mist that covered the ground stretched out in all directions, extending far beyond the limits of his vision. There were no hills, no buildings, just an endless plane of wispy white, and a dome of bright blue sky overhead.

Then there was the gate. It was, Zac realised, actually two gates, fastened together in the middle. They stood fifteen metres high, an elaborate tangle of silver and gold. There was no fence, just the gates themselves, standing proud and alone.

And a small desk. He hadn't noticed it at first, but there it was, right at the foot of one of the gateposts. It was fashioned from dark oak, with faded gold-leaf gilding decorating the carved legs.

A rectangle of cardboard had been propped up on the desktop. On it, someone had written:

GONE TO LUNCH
BACK IN 20 MINS

"Well?" asked Gabriel, seamlessly shifting his smile from *friendly* to *encouraging*. "Any ideas?"

"I'm in a coma," Zac said. "That's the only explanation."

Michael made a sound like the growl of a wild animal. "This is a waste of time."

Gabriel's smile faltered, just briefly. "No, you're not in a coma, Zac. Would you like to try again?"

"Not really," Zac said, with a shrug. "Because the only other explanation is that I'm dead, and this is Heaven."

"Aha!" began Gabriel.

"And I don't believe in Heaven."

"Oh." Gabriel's smile fell away completely, but rallied well and came back wider than ever. "Well, believe in it or not, that's exactly where you are. Or on the outskirts, at least."

"The outskirts?"

"Yes. Heaven itself is beyond the gates. This –" he gestured around them – "is sort of the suburbs. *Outer* Heaven, if you will."

"No," said Zac. "It's not. That isn't possible."

"The Monk tells us you evaded him. Twice," said Gabriel. "Congratulations. That's two more than anyone else ever has."

"His boss," Zac muttered. "He said his boss wanted to see me."

"Correct. That would be me," said Gabriel. Michael gave another growl. "Or rather, *us*. We have need of your... talents."

"So you had me killed? Couldn't you have, I don't know, phoned or something?"

Gabriel ran a hand through his golden locks. "I suppose, when you put it like that, it does sound a touch drastic."

Zac shook his head. "No, this is all nonsense. I'm dreaming. This can't be real."

"I assure you it is real, Zac," Gabriel insisted. "I'm afraid you have to face facts, my boy. You are dead."

"You killed me," said Zac quietly. "You had me killed."

He took a sudden step towards Gabriel, his hands balling into fists. Gabriel didn't flinch.

There was a sound like silk tearing. A sudden pressure across Zac's throat stopped him moving any further. The blade of the sword felt uncomfortably warm against his skin.

"Make another move and I slice," Michael warned.

"What difference does it make if I'm already dead?"

"Oh, there are many worse things than death," Gabriel said, still smiling. "I can think of at least a hundred off the top of my head." His smile widened and his blue eyes seemed to darken. "Would you care to pick a number?"

He waited a moment, until he was sure his point had been understood, before gesturing to Michael to step back. The man in the golden armour hesitated, then removed the blade from Zac's throat and slid it back into its sheath.

"And the whole *fate-worse-than-death* issue is precisely why we wanted to talk to you, Zac," Gabriel continued. "You see, what with all your exploits – stealing and whatnot – I'm afraid you've booked yourself a place in Hell."

Zac rubbed his throat. He could still feel the heat where the sword had touched his skin. "Hell?"

"Yes. You know, fire and brimstone; demons poking spikes

into places you'd really rather they didn't; etcetera, etcetera. It's one of the Four Suggestions, see? 'Thou Probably Shouldn't Steal'."

"Four Suggestions? What are you talking about?"

"The Four Suggestions," Gabriel said again, as if that explained everything. When he saw it didn't, he continued: "That God gave to Moses on Mount Sinai."

"You mean the Ten Commandments?"

"Ah, of course, I forgot. You're a human," said Gabriel, giving himself a tap on the forehead. "That was an error in translation. Much of the Bible's spot-on, of course, but sometimes the authors took a few liberties, or just missed the meaning completely. God doesn't give out commandments. What would be the point in that? Ordering people around all the time? No, it's not His style. He's quite laid-back, really."

"But He does make *suggestions*," Michael added. "And if you don't follow them, you'll burn for ever in the fires of Hell."

"Doesn't sound very laid-back," said Zac.

"I said He was *quite* laid-back," Gabriel replied. "I didn't say He was a pushover."

"If I'm going to Hell, how come I'm here?"

"We decided to intervene," Gabriel told him. "We snatched you away before Hell could claim you. We wanted to offer you a chance to—"

A smaller gate, built into the frame of the larger one, swung open. A man in a grey robe, with matching grey hair and beard, strolled through, whistling below his breath. He had a newspaper under one arm and carried a takeaway coffee cup.

The man walked towards the desk, then stopped when he realised he wasn't alone.

"Oh, erm, hello," he said. "I just popped out for a quick bite to eat. Wasn't gone long." He looked from Gabriel to Michael. "Nothing's happened, has it?"

"Nothing you need concern yourself with, Peter," said Gabriel, turning the full force of his smile on the newcomer. "Be a good chap and give us another five minutes, would you?"

The man in grey looked like he couldn't believe his luck. "Well, I suppose I could find some paperwork to be getting on with," he said, playing it cool. "Filing an' that."

"Wonderful. That would be splendid," said Gabriel.

Peter backtracked towards the gate he'd come through. "Right you are, then. I'll just go and eat some... I mean *file* some, um..."

Michael growled and fixed Peter with a furious glare. Peter's face reddened and his brow became shiny with sweat. "I'll go file some... some... sandwiches," he blurted, then he bit his lip.

"Very good, Peter," said Gabriel. "Peace be with you."

"Peace be with you," said Peter, bowing ever so slightly. "Peace be with you, Michael."

Michael growled again. Peter gave a final bow, darted through the gate, and let it close behind him. Zac couldn't see the man through the gaps in the metalwork, even though common sense said he should be able to.

"So, that was Saint Peter?" he asked.

Gabriel gave an approving nod. "For a non-believer, you know a lot."

"I'm an atheist, not an idiot," Zac said. "And you're Gabriel and Michael, the archangels, right? So where are your wings?"

With a sound like a flag flapping in a hurricane, a pair of wings unfolded suddenly from Michael's back.

"Satisfied?" asked Gabriel.

Zac blinked. He felt he should've had some sort of snappy and sarcastic comeback, but for the life of him he couldn't think of one. He just nodded instead, and Michael's wings tucked back in out of sight.

"As I was saying," continued Gabriel. "Your decision to ignore the Third Suggestion means you are – alas – doomed to an eternity of pain and suffering in the fires of Hell."

"Unfortunate," said Michael.

"Most unfortunate," Gabriel agreed. "However, we may be able to, let us say, pull some strings."

"And why would you do that?" Zac asked.

"Because we have need of your unique talents, Zac Corgan, and I believe we may be of mutual benefit to one another. If you were to scratch our backs, then we would gladly scratch yours." Gabriel folded his arms and rocked on his heels, his smirk wider than ever. "So, shall I arrange for someone from down below to come up and collect you? Or would you care to hear what we have to say?"

CHAPTER FIVE

H E WAS TAKEN by car – a long white limousine that made no sound as it rolled through the streets of Heaven. There was no other traffic on the road, but the pavements heaved with pedestrians, all decked out in white. They chatted and laughed as they strolled along in the sunshine, their worries long since forgotten.

Zac sat on the back seat of the car, looking out through the tinted windows. The two angels were sitting across from him. Michael looked a little more relaxed. His angry scowl had become merely an irritated sneer. Gabriel's smile, on the other hand, looked to be just hitting its stride.

There was a darkened screen between the back of the car and the front, meaning Zac couldn't see the driver. Then again, with everything that had happened in the past hour, he couldn't even be sure there was one.

Zac tried to take in the sights of the city around them. Every building was like a palace, each having more marble columns than the one before. The striped lawns in every garden were a vibrant, almost neon, green. The flowers too were more vivid than any Zac had seen. It was as if they had been coloured using crayons from a child's art set, where reds were *red* and blues were *blue*, and pastel shades didn't get a look in.

"The streets," said Zac, as they passed another palace. "They're proper streets. They're not wispy like at the gate."

"Ah, yes, the cloud effects. That's just for the tourists," Gabriel said. "Costs us a fortune in dry ice, but then where would we be if we didn't keep up appearances?" He gave Zac's black clothing a very deliberate glance. "Wouldn't you agree?"

There was a soft knock on the other side of the dividing screen, and the vehicle began to slow. Michael peered out through one of the side windows for a moment, before announcing, "We're here."

The car whispered to a stop and the doors opened automatically. "We're where?" Zac asked.

"See for yourself," suggested Gabriel.

Zac stepped out of the car and found himself outside an enormous, sprawling citadel. He'd thought the other buildings they'd passed had been palaces, but compared to this place they were little more than shacks.

A thousand white pillars stood by the smooth walls, each one carved to resemble a giant kneeling angel with wings fully unfurled. They all had their hands raised, supporting the overhang of a domed roof that was made up of intertwining bands of gold and platinum.

Light seemed to emanate from within the dome, bright enough to make a dull ache throb at the back of Zac's eyeballs.

There was sound too. It wasn't quite music; it was something more, or something less. Like the music that existed before music. A prototype version of music that bypassed the ears and launched a full-scale assault on the emotional centre of the brain instead.

Zac didn't notice Gabriel step out of the car behind him. He didn't even pull away when the angel's hand patted him on the shoulder.

"Nice, isn't it?"

"Not really my cup of tea," Zac said, pulling himself together. "What is it?"

"This? This is the house that God built," said Gabriel. He stepped past the boy and gestured towards the building's ornate front door. "Shall we step inside?"

Zac sat at one end of a long narrow table in a long narrow room. The table was made of dark wood, polished to a mirror-like shine. There were twelve leather office-style chairs positioned round it, evenly spaced. Filing cabinets and bookshelves lined one of the room's shorter walls. Over in the corner stood a water cooler. Every few minutes, it gave a loud *glug* and bubbles rose lazily inside the bottle.

Compared to the outside of the building, this room was relatively dull. There were windows, but Gabriel had closed the blinds as soon as they'd entered. A pot plant stood by the largest window, five completely different types of flower blooming from its stalks. Zac didn't recognise any of them.

At the far end of the table, directly opposite Zac, Gabriel lowered himself into one of the leather chairs. He leaned forward, his elbows on the tabletop, his fingers steepled in front of his mouth, his blue eyes sparkling.

Michael had been right behind Zac as they'd entered the room, but he hadn't followed the others in. There were only the two of them there now – the boy and the angel.

"Well?" said Zac. "You wanted to talk. I'm listening."

Gabriel waited a few moments before speaking. "We've misplaced something," he said, choosing his words carefully. "We would like you to help get it back."

"Why me?"

"Because we believe your unique talents and your... past exploits make you the perfect choice for the job. We need someone fast. Someone who can think on their feet and who is not afraid to fight dirty, should the need arise."

"Then why not send the Monk? He beat me."

"Alas, the Monk is well known to those who have taken the item. He would not, I fear, last two minutes."

"Why?" Zac asked. "Where is it?"

"Hell," Gabriel said. His chair creaked as he leaned back, not taking his eyes off Zac. He was watching for some kind of reaction, Zac knew. A look of shock, or fear, or something. But Zac wasn't about to give him the satisfaction.

"Right. And what was taken?"

One of Gabriel's eyebrows rose a few millimetres in surprise. "Did you hear what I said?"

"It's in Hell, yeah. I heard. What was taken?"

"A book."

"What book?"

"It is a book with many names," the angel said. "Down there they call it the *Book of Doom*. Up here we prefer the *Book of Everything*."

"Sounds like a children's encyclopedia," Zac said.

"Oh, I assure you, it isn't. The *Book of Everything* tells us... well, it tells us everything. Every shift of every grain of sand. Every movement of every cloud. Every thought inside the minds of every living creature, from the very beginning of time until the very end." Gabriel paused a moment, to let his words sink in. "It is omniscience. In paperback form."

"I can see why you'd want that back."

"Indeed. With the book in the hands of our enemies, there is nothing they could not do. No one they could not corrupt. Nowhere they could not conquer. Knowledge is power, and the *Book of Everything* contains all the knowledge in existence.

In the wrong hands, it is the deadliest weapon in all of creation."

Zac whistled through his teeth. "So, that's why they call it the *Book of Doom*."

"Correct," said Gabriel. "In their hands it could indeed doom us all."

"If the book tells them everything, won't they know I'm coming?"

"Almost certainly," Gabriel admitted. "I never said it was going to be easy. There's every chance you will not make it back."

"You're not really selling the idea," Zac said.

"I am nothing if not honest," Gabriel said, although Zac seriously doubted that. "And you are dead, remember? Either way you are going to Hell. At least our way there's a chance, however slim, that you will be able to return."

Zac found himself thinking about his grandfather, all alone in that big house with only a hyperactive goldfish and the voices in his head for company.

"Right. So, what does it look like, this book?" he asked, forcing himself back to the matter at hand.

"We don't know."

Zac frowned. "Well, when was it taken?"

"We don't know that, either," Gabriel said, giving a shrug of his slender shoulders. "It's all rather complicated, I'm afraid."

"Apparently I've got plenty of time on my hands. Uncomplicate it."

Gabriel gave a single nod. "Of course." He stood up and rolled his chair into position beneath the table, then rested his hands on the chair's leather back.

"The *Book of Everything* can take many forms," he began. "I, for example, may see it as a small, compact paperback. You may see it as a leather-bound tome. Some may look upon the book and see a carving on a stone tablet, or scribbles in a spiral-bound notebook, or – Lord help us – one of those awful electronic reading devices. Or even something else entirely. The branch of a tree, perhaps. Or a small flan. Nobody knows how they'll see it until they see it."

"Then how am I supposed to find it?" Zac asked.

"Because you *will* know it, when you see it. We shall grant you that ability. There will be no glimmer of doubt in your mind."

"Fair enough. You said you didn't know when it was stolen," Zac prompted.

"Yes, I did say that, didn't I," said Gabriel. He walked over to the pot plant and cupped one of its leaves in his hands. Another flower burst into bloom further along the stalk. The angel bent, sniffed the flower's yellow and pink petals, then nodded his approval.

"OK, well, let's narrow it down," said Zac, when he realised no more information was forthcoming. "When did you last see it?"

"Yesterday."

Zac felt himself frown again. It was becoming a habit. "So... obviously someone took it in the last twenty-four hours."

"Not necessarily," Gabriel explained, turning back to face him. "The *Book of Everything* exists outside of time. In many ways, I suppose, you could say that it *is* time. I saw it yesterday, but that doesn't mean it wasn't taken a thousand years ago. Or tomorrow."

"I don't understand," admitted Zac.

"No. It's not an easy one to get your head around, is it? We tried explaining it to Albert Einstein once, shortly after he got here. He's been having a lie-down in a darkened room ever since. Whimpering into a pillow, by all accounts."

Gabriel flashed his politician-smile again. "So let's not go into too much detail. Suffice to say the book has been taken at *some point* and that *right now* it is in the possession of Hell and all its minions."

The door opened and Michael strode in. Zac saw a subtle look pass between the angels, and the briefest of nods from the one in the armour.

Gabriel took his seat again, while Michael remained standing behind him. Both angels looked expectantly at Zac.

"Our offer is this," said Gabriel, clasping his hands together. "You find the book and bring it to us, and we wipe the slate clean. A fresh start. You are returned to life, and all your sins are forgiven."

"And if I say no?"

"Then you will still go to Hell, but as a prisoner of Satan, not as an agent of God. There you will be roasted, flayed, impaled and so on and so forth, for the remainder of time."

Zac didn't flinch. He held Gabriel's gaze. The angel shifted in his seat slightly, then leaned back and placed his hands behind his head.

"And then, of course, there's your grandfather to think about."

The tiny hairs on the back of Zac's neck stood on end. He almost reacted to that, but he bit down hard on the inside of his bottom lip to stop himself.

"He's how old now? Ninety-six? Ninety-seven?" Gabriel asked, not expecting an answer. "Old for a human. All alone down there. Defenceless. How is his health these days? The mind can start going at that age, can't it? Wouldn't it be a shame if you could never go back to him? Never even got the chance to say goodbye?"

Zac's voice was like the rasp of a saw. "OK," he said. "You win. I'll do it."

"Excellent. Excellent," said Gabriel. He spun his chair in a full circle, then stood up suddenly. "Michael will accompany you on the quest."

"No, thanks," Zac said.

Gabriel raised both impeccable eyebrows. "I beg your pardon?"

"I don't want him with me."

"Why ever not?"

"I don't like him. I'll go alone."

"I'm afraid that's quite impossible. Without him, you would not be able to cross over the barriers between realms."

Gabriel gave a dismissive wave. "Michael will get you out of Heaven, and Michael can bring you into Hell. You could not do these things on your own."

"Then I'll take someone else," Zac said. He met Michael's furious glare and shot it back at him. "Preferably someone who hasn't held a sword to my throat. In fact, preferably not an angel at all."

Gabriel laughed a hollow laugh. "This is Heaven. I'm afraid angels are all we have. But I don't understand – why don't you want an angel to accompany you?"

"Because an angel in Hell is going to stand out, I'm guessing. I want to get in and out without making a scene," Zac said. "Also, I'm still an atheist, so technically I don't even believe in angels. You two included."

"Well, I'm afraid there's nobody else," Gabriel said. He tapped a manicured fingernail against his flawless teeth. It made a sound like footsteps on marble. "Unless…"

"Unless what?"

"There is one who may be able to help, although he has nowhere near the strength or experience of Michael."

"I don't need strength or experience, I just need a guide," Zac shrugged. "Is he an angel?"

Gabriel shook his head. "No."

"What's his name?"

"His name? It's... ah... yes. His name is Angelo."

"Angelo?" said Zac flatly. "And he's not an angel?"

"No. Yes. Well he's *half* angel. But he's the closest thing to a human that we have."

Zac jumped up and pulled the drawstring of the closest blinds. They lifted, letting a flood of sunlight into the room. He gestured at the busy city-centre plaza beyond the glass, and the hundreds of people who milled about there, all happily going about their business.

"Humans," Zac said. "Dead ones, maybe, but humans. What about one of them?"

"Send a *guest*?" Gabriel gasped, his eyes widening. "We couldn't possibly do that. Think of the paperwork. No," he said, shaking his head. "It is Angelo, or it is Michael. The choice, Zac Corgan, is yours."

"Angelo, then," said Zac. It wasn't a difficult decision. He'd met Michael less than an hour ago, but already he wanted to stay as far away from him as possible.

"Very good," said Gabriel. "Michael, would you be so kind as to fetch young Angelo for me?"

Michael nodded, shot a final glare at Zac, then pulled open the door. A look of exaggerated surprise crossed his face. "Oh, now would you look at that," he said. "What are the chances?"

He let the door open all the way. Gabriel looked past the other archangel and then he too reacted with shock. "Angelo? Just walking past at that very moment! What a stroke of good fortune."

Michael stepped aside. Zac saw the figure framed in the doorway.

"Oh, come on," he sighed as Angelo shuffled into the room. "You have *got* to be kidding me."

CHAPTER SIX

I T WAS THE T-shirt the boy was wearing that had first caught Zac's eye. It was white, with yellow print on the front in the style of the *Baywatch* logo. The text read:

MY LIFEGUARD WALKS ON WATER

And then, underneath, for those struggling to work it out:

(BECAUSE HE'S JESUS)

The rest of Angelo wasn't much more promising, either. He was a good fifteen to twenty centimetres shorter than

Zac, and about half the width across the shoulders. The T-shirt hung loosely from his skinny frame, reaching down almost to his knees.

The knees themselves were on full display, knobbly and ever-so-slightly grass-stained. His legs were also bare, and Zac really hoped the boy was wearing some kind of shorts beneath the trailing shirt.

On his feet, Angelo wore flip-flops with I Love Majorca printed in jolly lettering across the plastic strap. They were the most violent shade of fluorescent green Zac had ever laid eyes on.

Zac's gaze went from the feet to Angelo's face. The boy looked young – eleven or twelve, at a guess – with eyes that seemed cartoonishly large. His hair was blond, like the angels', but it was a dirty, brownish blond, cut into an uneven bowl shape round his head.

Angelo smiled nervously. "Good King Wenceslas walks into a pizza shop," he said. His voice was wobbly and unbalanced, as if he were still learning how to use it.

"What?"

"It's a joke," Angelo explained. "Good King Wenceslas

walks into a pizza shop, and the assistant asks, 'How do you want your pizza?' And Good King Wenceslas says, 'Deep pan, crisp and even.'"

The boy's huge eyes blinked several times. He watched Zac, waiting for a reaction.

"You know? The song," he added. He began to sing. "*Good King Wenceslas looked out...*"

Zac nodded. "Yeah."

"Deep pan, crisp and even."

"Yeah."

There was silence. Somewhere close by, Gabriel coughed gently.

"You don't get it, do you," Angelo said. "Deep *pan*—"

"No, no. I get it," Zac cut in. He looked back at the archangels. "It's not too late to change my mind, is it?"

Gabriel smiled his politician-smile and clapped Zac on the shoulder. "Oh, I think you two are going to get along like a house on fire."

There was no mistaking Angelo's room. It was like a bricks and mortar version of the boy himself.

The walls were a dull white, but decked out in brightly coloured posters. One picture showed an electric guitar with the words JESUS ROCKS! emblazoned across it in blue writing.

Keeping with the guitar theme, the next poster featured a large, gold-coloured plectrum. I PICK JESUS! was carved into the plectrum's surface.

There were two or three other posters too, but the one that caught Zac's eye was a full-length picture of Christ himself. It reminded Zac of a painting he'd stolen once, but this was no painting. It was a photograph.

Jesus was standing in a wheat field, with the sunlight casting a halo behind his head. With one hand he held a lamb, tucked up under his arm. With the other hand he was giving a thumbs up to camera, while flashing a smile so sincere it could've shattered concrete at a hundred paces.

"That's Jesus," Angelo said. He was sitting on the edge of the room's narrow bed, his feet swinging a few centimetres off the bare wooden floor. "He's my hero."

Zac scanned over the other posters. "So I see."

"Well, him or the Incredible Hulk. It's hard to choose," Angelo said. "I mean, Jesus is the son of God, and sacrificed himself for the sins of all mankind and everything, but the

Hulk can punch a tank into outer space. So I don't know who to pick."

"Yeah," replied Zac absent-mindedly, "it's tricky."

"I love the Hulk. I mean, I love all superheroes, but the Hulk is the best. Everyone thinks he's a monster, but he's not. He's one of the good guys. He just wants people to stop trying to hurt him. He just wants a friend." Angelo blushed and squeezed out a bashful smile. "Have you ever read any Hulk comics?"

Zac shook his head. "No. Not lately."

"I've got loads of them here, if you want to borrow them," Angelo said. "That's... that's what friends do, isn't it? Lend each other stuff."

"I'm fine, thanks," Zac said. He strolled over to Angelo's bookcase. The room was tiny, so it didn't take long. He cocked his head to the side and studied the shelves. It was mostly Bibles on there, all different shapes and sizes. Down on the bottom shelf, though, were several different versions of Robert Louis Stevenson's *The Strange Case of Dr Jekyll and Mr Hyde*, half a dozen superhero graphic novels, and a book full of diagrams of the *USS Enterprise*. There were also seven different editions of the *Star Wars* trilogy on

DVD, each one only marginally different to the ones before.

"Have you ever met him?" Angelo asked.

"Jesus?"

"The Hulk."

Zac looked back over his shoulder at Angelo. The boy was still perched on the bed, his huge eyes filled with hopeful expectation.

"No," Zac said, turning his back on the bookcase. "Never met him."

"He moves around a lot, that's probably why," said Angelo. "If you do ever meet him, whatever you do, don't make him angry. You wouldn't like him when he's angry."

"Right," said Zac, with only a momentary pause. "I'll keep that in mind. You like Jekyll and Hyde too, I see."

"Not really," Angelo shrugged. He shifted uneasily. "Gabriel keeps bringing them to me. He thinks it's good for me to read them, with the whole half-blood thing. He got me into the Hulk to begin with too."

"Right." Zac looked around the room again. It was small and windowless, with just one door. There were only the two of them there, and they had only been in the room a few minutes, but already he was beginning to feel claustrophobic.

"So," he began, looking Angelo up and down again. "Why you?"

Angelo smiled anxiously. "What do you mean?"

"They had you come and wait outside the door. They knew I'd say no to Michael coming with me, so they had you lined up. Why?"

"I don't..."

"What did they say to you? Why did Michael tell you to wait outside?"

Angelo smiled bashfully. "They said they'd found me a friend. He said we could be friends. You and me. So, um... Can we?"

"No," said Zac. "We can't."

Angelo's smile stayed fixed, but he looked away from the boy in black. "What? Oh. Right. What? I mean, yes. OK." He wriggled uncomfortably on his bed. "It's just, see, I don't have many friends."

"I don't have any. Suits me just fine." He saw the hurt behind Angelo's fixed smile and softened slightly. "I mean, look, I'm sure you're a great kid and everything, but... you're

64

too young to be my friend. That's it. Too young. It'd be weird."

"I'm nearly a thousand years old in human years," Angelo said curtly.

"Really?" asked Zac after a pause. "You're bearing up well. What's that in angel years?"

Angelo scratched his ear. "Um... about twelve."

"Right," said Zac. "That's what I thought."

There was a rhythmic knock on the door, then the handle turned and the door swung inward. Gabriel stepped through, his smile still frozen in place.

"Apologies for the slight delay. I trust you two have been getting to know each other?" the angel said.

Angelo looked quickly to Zac, then down at his flip-flops. Zac folded his arms across his chest and leaned on the bookcase. Neither of them spoke.

"Splendid," said Gabriel, not faltering. "Splendid. I have a gift for you, Zac. Put this on." He held up a cheap-looking digital watch.

Zac took the watch and turned it over in his hands. It was made of flimsy black plastic. He had found a similar watch in a Christmas cracker once, and it had gone straight in the bin.

"What does this do?" he asked.

"It tells the time," Gabriel replied.

Zac looked at the watch again. "Is that it?"

"No. Angelo has one too. It will allow the two of you to stay in contact if you become separated. It will also allow you to get in touch with us when you have the book. At which point, we'll be able to retrieve you."

He watched Zac secure the strap across his wrist. "Splendid. It has other functions too. Angelo will explain."

"Right," said Angelo, holding up his wrist and pointing to his own watch. It was identical to the one Zac wore. "You see this button here?"

"Later, Angelo," Gabriel said with a hint of annoyance. "Explain later. There's no time now."

"Oh," said Angelo, deflated. "Right. Later."

Gabriel looked down at Zac and lowered his smile a few calculated notches. "Are you ready?"

"As I'll ever be," Zac nodded.

"Very good. We have reason to believe the book is being held by a demon named Haures. A Duke of Hell, no less. We're informed he's keeping it in the tenth circle. You will have to find your own way in, I'm afraid."

"Tenth circle? I thought there were only supposed to be nine circles of Hell."

Gabriel's eyebrows knotted above his nose. "Yes. So did we. I have no idea what you will find waiting there, but I do know that if you fail, then everything – the very existence of the cosmos itself – will be in grave peril. The book is the ultimate weapon, Zac. Do not forget that."

"No pressure, then."

The angel smiled thinly. "Quite." He stepped aside. Angelo hopped down off the bed and stood next to Zac. He pulled his long T-shirt up and tucked it untidily into the white shorts that Zac was relieved to see he was wearing beneath it. Then he held out a hand. Zac peered at it.

"You have to hold my hand," Angelo said. "Or it won't work."

Zac sighed, rolled his eyes, then locked his fingers with Angelo's. Gabriel gave a single nod.

"Peace be with you," he said.

"Peace be with you," replied Angelo automatically.

"Oh, and rest assured, Zac, I shall ensure your grandfather is well looked after in your absence."

Zac felt his muscles tense. His grip on Angelo's hand tightened, making the boy gasp.

"Right. Whatever," he growled. "Can we just—"

There was a blip of light, like the flash of a camera. Zac's stomach heaved, as if he were looping the loop on a roller coaster, and then everything was plunged into sudden darkness.

CHAPTER SEVEN

H E WAS STILL in the dark, even after the world stopped lurching. He was lying on an uneven surface, his legs twisted at awkward angles. Somewhere above him, he could hear breathing, and he realised he was still holding Angelo's hand.

"Are we there?" he asked quietly. "Are we in Hell?"

"Um, no, not yet," Angelo replied. "Not unless I've really messed up. I've just jumped your soul back into your body."

Zac pulled his hand free and felt around on the floor beneath him. Shoes. He was sitting on shoes.

"The cupboard," he said. "We're in my cupboard."

He untwisted his legs and kicked open the door, revealing his bedroom. The curtains were still closed and the bookcase was still in front of the door, but there was no sign of the Monk anywhere.

Zac stood and looked down at his stomach. A round hole had been torn through his T-shirt. He reached round and felt his back. There was another hole there, slightly larger than the one on the front.

The material round both holes was slick with blood, but his body itself was gunshot-wound free.

"So... what? I'm alive?"

"Sort of. I mean, no, not properly," Angelo said. "Your soul's just temporarily back in your body. So you're not alive, but you're not dead, either. I suppose you're sort of like a zombie." He held his arms out in front of him and groaned. "Uuuuh. Braaaains!"

"Stop that."

"*Braaaaaaains!*"

"Cut it out!"

Angelo lowered his arms. "Anyway, you can still be hurt, and your body can still be destroyed, so be careful." He stepped past Zac and stood in the middle of the room, turning slowly on the spot as he looked around. "Is this your bedroom?"

"What? Yeah," replied Zac absent-mindedly. He was looking at a rectangle of card that had been pinned to his T-shirt. The card was black with white writing that read:

YOU WERE KILLED BY THE MONK.
THANK YOU FOR YOUR BUSINESS.

Beneath that was a phone number. Zac ripped the card in half before dropping it into his wastepaper bin.

"Where are your posters?" asked Angelo.

"I don't have posters," Zac answered.

"Why don't you have any posters?"

"I just don't."

Zac pulled off the long-sleeved T-shirt and tossed it into the corner of the room. Then he crossed to his chest of drawers, pulled out another identical piece of clothing, and slipped it on.

"Posters help cheer up a room," Angelo continued. "Your room doesn't look very cheerful. It's gloomy. It's a gloomy roomy." He laughed. "*Gloomy roomy*. I bet it's not easy to say that five times fast."

"What are—?"

71

"Gloomyroomy gloomyroomy gloomyroomy gloomyroomy gloomyroomy," Angelo blurted. "Oh no, it is quite easy, actually." He looked around the room. "Anyway, you should definitely get some posters."

"Will you stop going on about the posters?" Zac sighed. "I don't like them, OK? They're childish."

"Gee whizz, OK. I was only saying," Angelo mumbled. His eyes fell on the bookcase, which Zac was now shoving out of the way of the door. "Got any Hulk comics? Or are *they* childish as well?"

"No, I don't, and yes, they are," Zac said. "I'm going to make sure my granddad's OK. Wait here."

"Why do I have to—?"

"Just... just wait here, OK?"

Angelo opened his mouth, closed it again, then sat down on the bed. "I'll wait here," he said. "But don't be long. I get panic attacks."

"Surprise, surprise," muttered Zac, as he left the bedroom and pulled the door closed behind him.

He met his grandfather halfway down the stairs. Phillip was walking up slowly, an iron poker held in his withered hands.

"Oh, you're all right," the old man said, visibly relieved. He lowered the poker to his side. "I heard a bang; what was that bang?"

"When?" asked Zac.

"A few seconds ago. Loud, it was. *BANG!* Like a gunshot."

A few seconds? Zac thought. So, he must've come back just moments after the Monk had shot him.

"Didn't hear anything," Zac said. "Maybe it was something outside. Come on, let's go downstairs."

"Are you sure you didn't hear anything?" Phillip asked, allowing himself to be led back down into the hall. "Because it sounded like a gunshot..."

"Car backfiring, probably," Zac said with a practised shrug. "Nothing to worry about."

They reached the bottom of the stairs and Zac ushered his granddad through into the sitting room. It was a mess of mismatched furniture that had been accumulated over decades, with no attempt made to tie any of it together.

"Sit down, Granddad, I need to talk to you," Zac said. He took a seat on a red-and-green floral patterned sofa, while Phillip creaked down into a beige armchair.

"What is it, Zac? Is... is something wrong?"

Another voice spoke before Zac could. "Sorry. I had to come down."

Zac and his grandfather looked over at the door. Angelo stood there, chewing on a fingernail and bouncing uncomfortably from foot to foot.

"I told you to wait," Zac said.

"I know, but, well... I think I need the toilet."

"You *think* you need the toilet?"

Angelo nodded. "Yes. But I'm not sure. I've never needed the toilet before. It must be to do with being on Earth." His hopping became more frantic. "Yep, I'm almost sure I need the toilet."

"Well go, then!"

There was a pause. Angelo stopped hopping. Zac watched in slowly dawning horror as Angelo's white shorts turned slightly yellow at the crotch.

"Wow. That helped *a lot*," Angelo said. "That's much more comfortable. Thanks!"

Zac got to his feet. "I didn't mean go right there! I meant go to..." He saw only puzzlement on Angelo's face. "I meant *go to the bathroom*, not *wet yourself*."

"Oh."

Zac sighed. "Jesus."

"Where?" asked Angelo, his eyes widening with excitement.

"No, not... not..." Zac pinched the bridge of his nose. "Look, never mind, just go back upstairs and we'll find you more clothes."

"OK," said Angelo brightly. He moved to leave, then hesitated. "Oh, by the way, your goldfish is going crazy."

"Yes. It does that."

"Hello," said Phillip, who had been trying to follow the conversation that had just taken place, but failing miserably. "Are you Penelope?"

"No. I'm Angelo."

Phillip looked disappointed. "Oh. I thought you were Penelope. She's been banging on at me all night, telling me her cat's sick, but what's that got to do with me? What do I know about cats? Nothing. Hear that, Penelope?" he said, raising his voice. "I don't know the first thing about cats."

"OK, then!" said Angelo, shooting Zac a glance. "I'll just go and get changed. Nice meeting you, sir."

"Nice meeting you too, Angelo," Phillip replied. He waited until the boy had left the room, before adding: "He seems nice. Who is he?"

"No one," said Zac hurriedly. "He's just... a friend."

"I heard that," came a voice from the hallway. They listened to Angelo beatboxing happily all the way back upstairs.

"A friend, eh? That's good. I always thought you should have more friends," said Phillip. "Or, you know, one, at least."

"Yeah, well. He's more a colleague, actually," Zac corrected. "But listen, Granddad, I need to talk to you."

"You're going away, aren't you."

"How did you...?" Zac began, then he nodded. "Just for a little while."

"Is it dangerous?"

"What?" He forced a laugh. "No, why would it be—"

"Come on, Zacharias. I'm an old man, not an idiot. I know you didn't pay for this house working in a hamburger shop. You think I don't hear you sneak in and out every night? You think I don't notice your cuts? Your bruises?"

Zac stayed silent. He was used to seeing a fog behind his grandfather's eyes, but that fog had lifted now. He'd never noticed how blue the old man's irises were before.

"I don't know what you do out there, and I don't ask. You're young, but you're a man now, Zac. You make your own decisions, and I don't pry. I don't pry, I let you make your own choices, don't I?"

Zac nodded.

"So, I'm going to ask you again, and I want you to tell me the truth. Wherever you're going, whatever you're doing – is it dangerous?"

A pause... a brief one... then, "Yes."

Phillip gave a single nod, like the answer had confirmed what he already knew. "And do you have to go?"

"Yes."

The old man leaned back in his chair and looked towards the corner of the room, as if seeing some Autocue there telling him what to say next. "I'd rather you didn't," he said at last. "But you know me, I'm a big believer in free will, and I won't try to stop you if you think it's something you have to do."

"It is," Zac said, realising that he hadn't given his grandfather anything like the credit he'd deserved over the years. "But I'll be back, I promise."

Phillip tore his gaze from the corner and looked back at Zac. Tears swam in those piercing blue eyes. "I hope so."

"Will you be OK?"

"I've lived a long time, Zac," Phillip replied. He stood up and motioned for Zac to do the same. "I think I can cope on my own for a little while. When do you leave?"

"Um, well..."

"Now?"

"Pretty much."

Phillip stepped forward and wrapped his arms round his grandson. Zac returned the hug and tried to control the shake he could feel taking hold of his limbs.

"Be careful," Phillip said. "And if you ever need me, just shout."

Zac smiled and hugged a little bit harder. "I will, Granddad. I will."

"I think your grandfather might be a total nutjob," said Angelo as Zac returned to the bedroom. "No offence."

"Watch your mouth," Zac snapped, shooting the boy a glare. "He isn't a nutjob. He just... hears voices sometimes."

"I wasn't talking about that," said Angelo. "I read his aura and it was all jumbled up. All different colours, swirling together. I've never seen one like that."

"I don't believe in auras," Zac said. He pulled open his wardrobe and began rummaging inside. "I don't believe in tarot cards or healing crystals or the power of prayer, or any of that stuff. And my granddad is *not* a nutjob."

"You don't believe in crystals?" scoffed Angelo. "Next you'll be telling me you don't believe in star signs." He watched Zac's face. "*You don't believe in star signs?*" he gasped. "You're so cynical. I bet you're a Scorpio, aren't you?"

"I have no idea."

"When's your birthday?"

"Look, here." Zac tossed a bundle of black fabric to Angelo, who fumbled clumsily, then dropped the pile on the floor.

"What's this?" Angelo asked, bending to retrieve the garments.

"Clothes. Put them on."

"But I've got clothes," Angelo said. He pointed to his lifeguard T-shirt. "See? Exhibit A."

"OK: one – you look ridiculous," Zac told him. "And two – you've wet yourself. Either one of those would be reason enough to change. Pick your favourite."

Zac turned his back as Angelo reluctantly changed into the black outfit.

"No looking."

"Just hurry up," Zac said. He listened to the sound of zips being undone and the clothes being pulled on. "So, you can just teleport us into Hell, right?"

There was a momentary pause. "Yeah. Course. No problemo. I'm ready now – you can turn around."

"Right, so we should get going and—" began Zac as he turned back to Angelo. He stopped when he saw the clothes. "What... what have you done to them?"

"It's not my fault," Angelo said defensively. "I'm part angel. Angels can't wear black."

The clothes, which had been the very definition of black, were now a faint grey. As Zac watched, even the grey began to disappear. It sank in a swirling vortex pattern towards the bottom of the trousers, like murky water trickling down a drain.

Zac looked down and saw black dye dripping on to his bedroom carpet. When he looked up again, the clothes were a shade of white usually reserved for washing-powder adverts.

"I can do white or yellow," explained Angelo sheepishly.

"Light blue at a push." He glanced at his feet. "Sorry about your carpet. If you get me a cloth, I'll clean it up."

"Forget it, it's fine," said Zac.

"Are you sure? Maybe I could just..." He rubbed the wet stain with a bare foot. "Oh no, that's just made it worse if anything."

"I said leave it, it's fine. We've got more important things to worry about."

Angelo blinked. "Have we?"

Zac stared.

"Yeah, yeah, right. Of course. I forgot," Angelo said. He slipped his flip-flops back on. "How do I look?"

"You look –" Zac hunted for something complimentary to say – "marginally less ridiculous," was the best he could do in the circumstances.

"Really?" said Angelo brightly. "You're not just saying that?"

"No, you look... good," Zac said, but that last word came out much higher than he'd intended. "So, are you ready to do this?"

"Before we go, I should warn you. Watch out for the demons. They're horrible. And I mean *really* horrible."

"Seriously?" said Zac. "And here I thought they were going to be a right old barrel of laughs."

"Well, you'd be wrong," said Angelo with absolute sincerity. "So it's lucky you've got me to keep you right."

"Oh, yes. I'm a lucky guy," Zac said. "Now, you ready?"

Angelo took a few quick breaths. He held out his hand. "I'm ready."

"Then let's do it." Zac slipped his hand into the boy's.

Angelo grinned nervously. "Here we go, then. Bowels of Hell, here we come!"

CHAPTER EIGHT

ONCE THE WORLD had stopped spinning, Zac looked down at his legs. They were buried in snow up to the knees.

A light flurry of flakes continued to fall from an otherwise bright blue sky above. Beside the boys, smoke curled lazily from the chimney of a large stone building with a thatched roof. Muted laughter and singing squeezed out through gaps in the shuttered windows and heavy oak door. It all sounded quite jolly, really.

"So," said Zac, "this is Hell, is it?"

"Yes," said Angelo.

Zac shot him a withering look. "Are you absolutely sure?"

"Yes. I mean, no. I mean... it might be."

Zac blew a snowflake off the end of his nose. "I'm going to go out on a limb and say it isn't."

"You might be right," Angelo admitted. He smiled shyly. "I'm a bit of a novice when it comes to teleporting."

"A novice? How often have you done it?"

"What, including the two times with you?" Angelo asked. He began counting up on his fingers. "Twice."

"Twice," Zac said. He shook his head. "Can you take us to Hell? Honestly?"

"Yes!" said Angelo enthusiastically, then, "Maybe..." Then his shoulders slumped and he admitted, "Probably not. It's trickier than it looks. I might send us somewhere really dangerous by mistake."

"What, more dangerous than Hell?"

"You never know," Angelo said in a half-whisper. "There could be worse places out there. It's not like Heaven and Hell are the only afterlives, is it?"

Zac frowned. "Isn't it?"

"No!" Angelo laughed. "They're all real."

"What do you mean? What's all real?"

"You don't know?"

"Know what?"

"You really don't know, do you?"

Zac gritted his teeth. "Know *what*?"

"That every religion in history has been right. Although," Angelo added quickly, "Christianity is *more* right than the others, obviously. There are thousands of afterlives out there. Xibalba. That was the Mayan underworld. Then there's, let's see... Olympus, home of the Greek Gods. Adlivun..."

"What's Adlivun?"

"It's where Sedna the She-Cannibal lives," Angelo explained. "But I wouldn't recommend going there. Everyone says she's a right cow. Besides, it's underwater, so we'd get wet."

Zac rubbed his temples. "This is nuts," he said. "This is too nuts."

He straightened and looked around them. The stone building they were next to stood at the top of a high hill. A number of other large buildings stood close to one another down the snowy slopes, as if huddling together for warmth. They all gleamed in the faint sunlight, each one a palace of silver or gold.

Beyond them, the snow extended miles into the distance until it met a wall that stood several hundred metres high.

Clearly someone wanted to keep whatever lay on the other side of the wall out.

A kilometre or so in the other direction, the land stopped like a shore meeting the sea. There was no water there, though, just blue sky and a bank of cloud and, if Zac looked hard enough, the beginnings of a rainbow leading away from the edge.

"So, where are we now?" asked Zac. Despite the mounting evidence, he was still finding it hard to believe any of what he was being told. "Santa's grotto?"

"Haha, very funny. Of course it isn't." Angelo gave Zac a playful nudge on the arm. "Santa's grotto's got a green roof. I don't know where this is."

Zac looked at the door. The wood was dark, and the metal handle had been sculpted into the shape of a gargoyle-like head. An iron ring was gripped in the creature's unmoving mouth. The place may have sounded quite jolly, but it didn't look particularly inviting.

"Only one way to find out," he said; then he turned the handle, pushed open the door and stepped inside.

A moment before, the bar had been filled with the sounds of cheering and laughter and the loud-mouthed gloating of a hundred drunken men. Tankards had clattered against tankards, ale had been quaffed, food had been scoffed and the din of it all had been deafening.

That all stopped when Zac and Angelo stepped into the Great Hall. The laughter died. The cheering ceased. And an amusing ditty about ritual disembowelment came to an abrupt, scratchy halt. A sea of horned helmets turned as one in the direction of the door.

An enormous wooden table filled the hall. It groaned beneath the weight of the feast spread out upon it. If you could call it a feast. It looked to be light on food and heavy on alcohol.

Standing in the corner closest to the door, a bearded man who had been juggling six short swords lost his concentration and then, a moment later, lost several of his toes. He didn't scream. He didn't so much as gasp, and as the echo of the clattering swords faded, silence filled the vast room.

Zac felt Angelo step close behind him. He surveyed the faces that looked back at him. Their expressions were a blend of surprise, confusion and annoyance, all tied up in bristly beards and long, matted hair.

The silence was broken by the sound of chair legs scraping on the flagstone floor. At the far head of the table, a man stood up.

At least, Zac assumed he was a man. He was man-shaped, certainly, but looked to have been scaled up somewhere along the way. He stood taller than anyone Zac had ever seen, with shoulders broader than the average family car. Across those shoulders he wore a cape lined at the edges with white and grey fur.

On his head was a helmet with three horns – one each side, and a third sticking up from the front like a unicorn's. A grubby white patch covered one of his eyes. On it, someone had drawn a cartoon eye in black marker pen. It was surprisingly effective.

The man's beard was Father-Christmas white. His long hair hung in pigtails, dangling down over the top of the metal breastplate that was strapped across his chest. Unlike Michael's armour, this stuff had been well used, and was now dented in more places than it was smooth.

Both the real eye and the hand-drawn one glared at Zac and Angelo as, somewhere in the beard, the man's mouth began to speak.

"Who dares enter the Hall of Valhalla?" he demanded. It was a strong, commanding voice. The type of voice that could rouse sea serpents from the deep, and make avalanches change their minds and head back uphill.

"It's Valhalla," Angelo whispered.

"Yes, I heard," replied Zac below his breath.

"Where dead Vikings go."

"I can see that."

"Thou art trespassers in this place," boomed the one-eyed man. "In the name of Asgard I shall pierce your innards with mine axe and rend your guts asunder! Then I shall summon my wolves to feast upon your quivering innards, unless thou reveal to us who thou art."

Zac smiled broadly. "Hi, I'm Zac. This is my... colleague, Angelo."

Angelo poked his head out from behind Zac's back and gave a shy wave. "Hello."

The giant glared at them, but looked a little surprised that, despite his threats, they hadn't made any effort to run away.

Zac fixed him with a cool glare. "And you are?"

There was a muttering then that rippled through the

hall. At the far end of the table, the man's face turned a blustery shade of red.

"Dost thou not know?" he growled.

"Nope," Zac said. He took a step towards the table. A hundred hands reached for a hundred swords. "Should I?"

"Impudent dog!" spat a Viking who was sitting halfway along the table. He rose to his feet and slammed one fist angrily down on the tabletop.

After a moment, when he realised Zac hadn't flinched, and that no one else was paying him the slightest bit of attention, he quietly sat down again.

"I am the Allfather," the one-eyed man boomed. "Lord of the Aesir, Ruler of the Gods—"

"Um... just the *Norse* Gods, sir," said a helpful Viking who sat a few seats along the table. "We wouldn't want to step on anyone's toes by claiming you were ruler of *all* gods. Remember what happened last time? With the Romans?"

"*SILENCE!*" boomed the Allfather. The sheer force of his voice toppled tankards all along the table and forced Zac to take a pace backwards.

"S-sorry, sir, I was only trying to—"

"Wilt thou *shut up*!"

"Shutting up now, sir."

The Allfather squeezed the bridge of his nose between finger and thumb and muttered below his breath. Only after that did he look back at Zac.

"Now. Where was I?"

"Lord of the Aesir, Ruler of the Gods," Zac reminded him.

"Norse Gods," said a voice quietly.

The Allfather's glare was one of pure malice. "I swear," he told the interfering Viking, "another word and I will punch thine mouth loose."

Nobody, least of all the man who was the focus of the Allfather's gaze, uttered a word.

Only when he was absolutely certain the Viking wasn't about to speak again did the Allfather turn back to Zac.

"Right," he said, a little flustered. "So... Where was...? Yes. Allfather, Lord of the Aesir, Ruler of the *Norse* Gods, if thou wants to get picky about it. I am the all-powerful Odin!"

A chorus of cheers went up around the hall. "Hail, Odin, Master of the Runes!"

"Odin?" said Zac.

"Hail, Odin, patron to the skalds!" went the cry.

"Yes," said the Allfather. "Odin."

"Hail, Odin, sole creator of magical songs!"

"For the love of Thor, will ye *shut up*!" Odin bellowed. "Thou doesn't have to go through all that every time someone says 'Odin'."

"Hail, Odin, delighter of—"

"Cut it out! I'm warning thee." Odin's aged brow furrowed. "Warning thou... Warning *ye...*?" Odin threw up his arms and sighed. "Oh, who actually talks like that anyway? It's ridiculous."

The Ruler of the (specifically Norse) Gods turned back to Zac. "So, yes. In answer to your question, I am – and I don't want to hear another bloody word out of anyone here – Odin."

Around the hall there was the sound of a hundred Vikings chewing their bottom lips. Zac took another step closer.

"Never heard of you."

The assembled audience gasped as one. Those hands already gripping sword handles gripped them tighter.

"What are you doing?" Angelo whimpered. "Don't upset him. Look at the size of him!"

"Relax. I've got a plan," Zac whispered.

"Have you?"

"Well, no, not really," Zac admitted. "But I'm sure something's going to pop right in there any minute now."

There wasn't the explosion of temper from Odin that Zac had expected. The Allfather simply stared for a long time, as if trying to get to grips with the idea that someone didn't know who he was.

"Haven't you?" he asked at last.

Zac shook his head. "Nope. Should I have?"

"Of course you should!" boomed Odin. Then a flicker of doubt crossed his broad face. "Well, I mean... I suppose it *has* been a long time. And Baldr knows, things have changed over the years." Slowly, he lowered himself back down into his chair. "Maybe... maybe people don't know who I am any more. Maybe it's—"

"Wait," said Zac. "Did you say Odin? *The* Odin?"

Odin's eyebrows rose hopefully. "Yes."

"Lord of the Aesir? Ruler of the Norse Gods?"

"Yes," nodded the Allfather, suddenly perking right up. "Yes!"

"Father of..."

"Thor," whispered Angelo.

"*I know*. Father of Thor?"

Odin was standing again. He nodded encouragingly. "Yes. Yes. Go on. Go on!"

"Of course I've heard of you! Everyone's heard of Odin. I thought you said you were *Wodin* to begin with. My mistake. Sorry about that."

The Allfather laughed loudly enough to shake the rafters. "Aha! I knew you would know of me! Apology accepted, mortal," he said. He raised his hands and the assembled Vikings cheered on cue.

"Come. Sit by my side," insisted the Allfather. "Stop a while in the Great Hall, Valhalla, and share what tales you know of Odin, Ruler of the Gods!"

"Just, uh, just the Norse Gods, sir."

Odin sighed. "Right, that's it. Get out."

"What? But, but, Allfather..."

"I've warned you already. Out!"

Zac turned to Angelo and gave him a curt nod, just as the scolded Viking shuffled past on his way to the door. "See? Told you I'd come up with a plan," Zac said.

"Pretend you don't know who he is. That was your plan?" Angelo said.

"I never said it was a great plan," Zac admitted.

"How did you know he wasn't just going to get angry and cut your head off?"

"I didn't. But I wasn't really worried," Zac replied.

"Why not?"

"Because I'm pretty sure I can run faster than you can. Now, I'm going to sit with Odin and see if he can help us."

"Help us do what?"

"Get to Hell. Since, you know, you can't take us there."

"Right," said Angelo. "Good thinking! What should I do?"

"You?" Zac said. "Nothing. Do absolutely nothing at all. Understood?"

"Nothing; right," Angelo nodded. He smiled. "We make a good team, don't we?"

"If you say so," replied Zac, then he turned his back, walked to the head of the table and took his seat beside the Allfather.

CHAPTER NINE

THERE WAS ANOTHER round of clapping, cheering and fists thudding on tables when Zac sat down, and then the Vikings got back to the business of eating and drinking, as if the last few minutes hadn't actually happened. Only Odin paid him any notice.

"Ale!" the god cried, pushing a dented metal tankard into Zac's hands. "Drink!"

Zac set the mug down on the table. "No, thanks," he said.

Odin looked at the tankard, then back at the boy. "Ale!" he insisted. "Drink!"

"I'll just have some water."

There was a sound like thunder as Odin hurled back his head and laughed. "Ah, young Zac, thou dost make me laugh!" he boomed, reverting back to character. "Ale it is!"

He pushed the tankard closer to the boy's hand. Zac pushed it back. "Water will be fine."

Odin frowned and gave his beard a stroke. Up close, the Allfather didn't quite look real. His scaled-up size and the way he exaggerated his movements gave him the appearance of an animatronic puppet from a low-budget children's movie.

"Water," the Allfather mumbled. He rolled the word around in his mouth, as if tasting it. "*Water*. Very well."

He gave two claps of his hands. Something large immediately dropped from the ceiling and landed beside him. Zac twisted in his chair, tensed, ready to fight, but instead of coming face to face with another Viking, he found himself looking at a tall, slender figure in a black leather bodice and matching leather trousers.

She was a girl, if you ignored the wings. Around his age, he'd say, although he'd been several centuries out with Angelo, so he wasn't committing to anything at this point.

Her hair was long and dark, tied back behind her head in a functional ponytail. The girl's white feathery wings folded in against her back with a sound like rustling velvet. She focused her gaze on Odin, not so much as glancing in Zac's direction.

The girl's mouth smiled, but her eyes weren't really in on it. "Yes, Allfather? How may I be of service?"

"Ah, young Herya," he boomed. "Meet Zac. Zac, Herya here is a—"

"Valkyrie," said Zac. "You retrieve the souls of Vikings killed in battle and bring them to Valhalla."

Odin clapped Zac on the back. It was like being slammed across the spine with a shovel. "Very good, Zac! Ye are not as dim as I first suspected!"

"I read a lot."

"Herya, fetch our guest some…" Odin turned back to Zac. "What was it again?"

"Water."

"*Water*," Odin repeated. He gave a bemused chuckle. "Drinkable water. What will they think of next?"

"Will that be all?"

Odin looked along the table. "Who's for another round?"

The Vikings' cheers almost lifted the roof. Shouts came from all corners of the table at once.

"Down here, love."

"A few more flagons at this end, sweetheart."

"Ale! And be quick about it!"

Herya reached into her pocket and produced a small notepad and pencil. "All right, keep your helmets on," she said, fixing her smile in place. Zac watched her hurry along the table, scribbling furiously as drunken orders boomed at her from all directions.

Odin saw Zac watching her. "Terrible shame," he said. "Poor girl. Born too late."

"Too late?"

"Didn't arrive into the world until after the age of true Vikings had passed." The Allfather shook his head sadly. "Never got the opportunity to soar above the battlefield. Never got to carry the fallen back here to Valhalla. Never got to fulfil her destiny."

"Oh. Right. Not a happy Valkyrie, then?"

"Quite the opposite," Odin said. "What could be more fulfilling than an eternity of service in the Great Hall, Valhalla?"

Zac looked along the table to where Herya was frantically scrawling orders in her notepad. "Yeah. What could be better than that?" With a flap of wings, the Valkyrie flew up towards the roof once again. Zac watched her clamber between the rows of circular golden shields that lined the rafters, before she slipped out of sight behind them.

"So, Zac, what bringst thou to Valhalla?"

"I'm looking for a book."

"A what?"

"A book," Zac said. "It was stolen. I'm trying to get it back."

"A book?" Odin frowned. "What, one of them jobbies with the squiggly lines and whatnot?"

"Writing," Zac nodded. "Yes, one of those."

The Allfather gave a snort. "Good luck finding one around here."

"I know where it is, I'm just not sure how to get to it. I was hoping—"

An impromptu song explaining why you should never become romantically involved with a giantess erupted around the table. Odin's face lit up with glee and the room shook as he lent his voice to the choir. It reminded Zac less of a sing-song, and more of an ugly mob at a football match, chanting about the less desirable qualities of the opposing team.

The roar was so loud Zac failed to hear the footsteps on

the floor behind him. He jumped as another dented tankard was set down in front of him.

"There," Herya said, shouting to make herself heard over the din. She balanced a tray on one hand. A dozen or more tankards were stacked on top of it. "Water."

"Thanks," Zac said.

"Second verse, same as the first!" bellowed Odin, and the song rose further in volume. "*Oh, a giantess don't look the best, whatever you do don't peek up her dress...*"

Zac glanced at the Allfather. Clearly he knew nothing about the book, and was going to be no help whatsoever. He turned to the Valkyrie.

"Can I talk to you?" Zac asked.

"You're talking to me already. Mission accomplished," Herya said. She moved to walk away, but Zac stood and blocked her path.

"I meant can I ask you some questions?"

Herya stuck out a hip and placed a hand against it. "Do I look like I have time to answer them?"

"Get a shift on, Valkyrie!" shouted someone along the table. The rest of the crowd jeered in agreement, then got stuck into the sing-song again.

"You're standing between a horde of dead Vikings and their booze," Herya said. "You want my advice? Move."

Reluctantly, Zac stepped aside. "Maybe later, then."

Herya flashed her false smile. "Keep dreaming, mortal." Her leather outfit *creaked* softly as she moved along the table, dispensing drinks as she went.

Zac sat back down and leaned his elbows on the table, watching the Valkyrie go. She moved confidently through the crowd, taking their abuse with that smile fixed in place.

"*Oh, a giantess, her face is a mess, she's got a big arse and a hairy chest...*"

Further along the table, Angelo was sandwiched between two bear-like Vikings. They had their arms round him and were swaying him back and forth in time with their singing. Angelo's eyes were wide with horror. They darted anxiously left and right, before he realised Zac was watching him.

Help me, Angelo mouthed silently.

Not now, Zac mouthed back. *Don't panic.*

Don't panic? Don't panic? I'm being manhandled by two dead Vikings. What do you mean, don't panic? mimed Angelo frantically, but Zac didn't catch a word of it, and replied with a double thumbs up.

A sudden crash broke up the singing just long enough for a jeer to go round the room. Zac looked in the direction of the sound and saw a particularly hairy Viking pulling Herya by the arm.

"Stupid Valkyrie," the man snarled. "Spill ale on me, will you?"

Herya's tray was on the floor. The Viking who held her had an upturned tankard hooked on to one of the horns of his helmet. The Valkyrie pulled at her arm, but the man's grip was proving difficult to break.

Zac turned to Odin. "I think Herya's got a problem customer," he said.

Odin grunted. "Huh? Oh, right. Not to worry."

Zac watched the Allfather knock back another tankard of ale, then burp loudly.

"Let go, Jurgen," Herya said. "It was an accident."

Jurgen's free hand clenched into a fist the size of a boulder. "Well, now it's time for you to have a little accident of your own, Valkyrie."

"I really think she's in trouble," Zac said.

"Well deserved, no doubt," Odin said. "Don't worry about it, lad. Valkyries heal quickly."

The Allfather scooped up another tankard and clanked it against one held by the Viking next to him. They both cheered drunkenly.

Zac looked back to Herya. Jurgen was towering over her, his clenched fist raised. The other Vikings were all chattering and laughing, paying the Valkyrie no attention whatsoever. The girl was on her own.

"I'm more or less dead," Zac shrugged. He climbed on to the table. "What's the worst that can happen?"

He began to advance, slowly and deliberately, along the table. "Hey, Jurgen!" he yelled. Jurgen and a few of the other nearby Vikings looked up. "She said it was an accident. Let her go."

Jurgen's eyes narrowed. Herya's widened. Down at the far end of the room, Angelo's face went pale. Nobody quite knew how to react as Zac continued along the tabletop.

"You dare tell me what to do?" Jurgen growled.

"I'm not telling you. I'm asking you nicely," said Zac as he arrived next to them. Even standing on the table, Zac was barely the same height as Jurgen. The Viking's ginger beard seemed to bristle with agitation. "Please. Pretty please with sugar on top. Let her go."

The laughter and cheering had choked off into silence, and now you could've heard a pin drop in Valhalla. All eyes were on Jurgen, waiting to see what he would do next. Zac could feel the tension in the air. Any moment now, the crowd could turn ugly. Or *uglier*, at least.

"I could rip you in two, boy," Jurgen said.

Zac held his gaze. "You could try."

A low *Ooooh* went round the table. Jurgen's eyes darted to the other Vikings around him.

"Or you could be the bigger man and let her go, then get back to enjoying the party," Zac suggested.

Jurgen ground his rotten teeth together. "Very well," he said at last. His hand opened and Herya pulled free. "She is free to go."

"Thank you," said Zac.

The big Viking cracked his knuckles. "I'll make *you* pay for her stupidity instead."

"Hey!"

The voice from the end of the table was shrill and

high-pitched. All eyes turned to Angelo, still sandwiched between the two Vikings. The angel swallowed nervously.

"Let's do that song again. What was it?" He began to clap out of time. "*A giantess... she, um, wears a vest...?*"

A roar of approval went round the room and the tension immediately lifted. Muscular arms came up and pulled Jurgen down into a happy bear hug, and soon he was singing along with the rest of them, his anger all but forgotten.

Zac jumped from the table and landed beside Herya. The Valkyrie eyed him suspiciously. "Why did you do that?"

"Do what?"

"Interfere," Herya said. "I could have handled him myself."

"I'm sure you could have," Zac conceded.

"Why did you help me? What do you want?"

"Nothing, really," Zac said. "Although now you're free, maybe I could ask you those questions? It'll only take a few minutes."

For a long time she said nothing. Eventually she gave a sigh. "Fine. You've got two."

"Great. Is there somewhere we can go that's less –" Zac gestured around at the Viking horde – "that?"

"Outside," Herya said, and she began walking in the direction of the door. Zac followed close behind her.

Two minutes, he mouthed as they passed Angelo.

Angelo's lips moved in reply. *Hurry up. These two are squashing me. And they smell. And I'm pretty sure I need to go to the toilet again.*

But Zac once again had absolutely no idea what the angel was trying to say. He gave another thumbs up, then hurried outside after the Valkyrie.

The door closed shut and the racket within was muted just a little. Herya turned to face Zac, her hands on her hips. "Two minutes," she said. "Starting now."

"I'm looking for a book," Zac began, not wasting any time. "You... um... you know what a book is, right?"

"Yes," she said, and the temperature seemed to plummet a few degrees further. "I know what a book is."

"Right, good. Well, this one has been taken from... Well, it doesn't matter where it was taken from, but it's now in Hell."

"Single or double L?"

Zac hesitated. "What?"

"Is the book in *Hell*, double L, or *Hel*, single L?"

"What's the difference?"

"Double L's a place. Single L's the daughter of Loki."

Zac tutted quietly. "Well, the place, obviously. How would the daughter of Loki have a book in her?"

Herya shrugged. "She's a big lass. You're eating into your two minutes," the Valkyrie advised. "Get to the point."

"I need to find a way into Hell, and I thought someone here might know something."

Herya's gaze was witheringly cold. "Here? In Valhalla?"

"Yeah. Well, we sort of ended up here by accident," Zac said. "I suppose it was a bit of a long shot."

"Yes," agreed the Valkyrie. "It was a bit."

Zac nodded. Suddenly he felt very stupid. "Yeah. Daft idea, really." He turned and pulled open the door. Roars of laughter rushed past him. "Sorry for wasting your time. Thanks for the water."

"Wait."

Zac turned back.

"I said it was a long shot," the Valkyrie said. "I didn't say you were wrong."

CHAPTER TEN

ANGELO WATCHED THE door close again and felt his heart sink. The din in the hall was deafening. The smell of stale Viking sweat was all around him. The singing had degenerated into drunken slurring, and flecks of foamy spit felt like scattered showers all along the table.

He was alone in a room filled with godless heathens. OK, technically not godless. They had plenty of gods. Too many, if anything. There was only one God as far as Angelo was concerned, and you wouldn't catch Him singing about what lurked under a giantess's skirt.

A tankard of ale was slid in front of him. He gave it a quick prod, nudging it away. A rough, scarred hand swooped and grabbed the tankard and it was downed in one noisy *schlurp*.

The song reached some sort of shambling conclusion. The Vikings all cheered at this, but then Angelo was beginning to suspect they'd cheer at pretty much anything.

"More song!" shouted someone along the table who was apparently too drunk to even have a bash at full sentences. As expected, everyone cheered. Everyone, that is, except Odin.

"No, no, no!" he bellowed. "Enough singing. Let's dance!"

A roar of delighted agreement made Angelo cover his ears. All around the table, Vikings began to shout out the names of their favourite dances.

"The Filthy Hag!" cried one.

"Too slow," said Odin. "We need something upbeat."

"The Shepherd's Daughter," suggested another of the Vikings. He stood up and threw his hands above his head. No one was quite sure why.

"And who's going to be the daughter?" Odin asked. "You?"

The standing Viking thought about this. He lowered his arms and sat down.

"The Deathly Hallows?" volunteered someone else.

Odin shook his head. "No, no. Far too long and complicated. We'd be here all bloody night." He clicked his fingers and pointed along the table. "You," he said. "What's your name again?"

Angelo swallowed nervously. "Um... Angelo."

"Umangelo, right," said Odin. "What about you, Umangelo? What dances do you know?"

"I, uh, I don't really know any."

Odin banged a fist on the table. Angelo jumped in time with all the dishes and plates. "You must know one dance," Odin insisted. "Everyone knows one dance. Come on, boy, think."

Angelo thought. With the eyes of a hundred dead Vikings and their god burrowing into him, he thought harder than he had ever thought in his life until – at last – a single word popped into his head.

He stood up. He cleared his throat. "OK," he said. "I've got one."

Zac looked at Herya expectantly. "So... what? You do know something?"

"I know a lot of things," Herya said. She gave a short snort of laughter. "You don't think this is all I do, do you?

Serving drinks to meatheads? I travel. I go on adventures. I see things."

"Right," said Zac. "Well, good for you. But what about the book? Do you know about the book?"

"Maybe. Where exactly is it?"

"I already told you, it's in Hell."

Herya sighed. "Yes, I know that, but where *exactly* is it? What circle is it on?"

"The tenth."

"There is no tenth."

"There is now."

The Valkyrie's eyebrows rose in surprise. "They've built a new circle in Hell?"

Zac shrugged. "Looks like it."

"Must be an important book."

"It is. Hell calls it the *Book of Doom*. It's also got the potential to be the most powerful weapon in existence. Or so I'm told."

Before Herya could respond, the door at Zac's back was yanked open. Angelo staggered out. His face was red and slick with sweat. Odin stood behind him, bending down so he could hold on to the boy's hips. As Angelo and the

Allfather emerged, Zac realised there was a whole train of Vikings following in single file behind them.

"Conga, conga, *cong-a*!" they hollered, as Angelo led the line out into the snow. "Conga, conga, *cong-a*!"

Angelo met Zac's unblinking stare. *Help me*, he mouthed, then he was off leading the conga in a wide circle round the Great Hall.

"Conga, conga, *cong-a*!" chanted the horde, kicking up clumps of snow on every third word. By the time the end of the line came out through the door, the front was making its way back in again.

Now would be a good time, said Angelo silently, but Zac just watched as the long snake of Vikings danced their way back inside Valhalla, and closed the door behind them.

Zac and Herya stood in the near silence, listening to the soft *pitter-patter* of the falling snow.

"Well," said Zac at last. "There's something you don't see every day."

Herya gave a shrug. "You'd be surprised. You want Argus."

Zac frowned. "Who?"

"Greek demon. He sees everything. If Hell's had an extension built, he'll know about it."

113

"Where will I find him?"

"You won't," Herya said. "You can't find him."

"Oh."

"But I can. I'll take you to him."

"Right. Well, thanks – but no, thanks," said Zac. "I work alone."

Herya glanced at the door through which the conga had just passed.

"Yeah, except him. I'm sort of stuck with him," Zac said. "Long story."

The Valkyrie folded her arms. "Well, that's the deal on the table. You want to find the book, you need to find Argus. You want to find Argus, you need to bring me." She shrugged. "Your choice, mortal."

Back in the hall, the conga line had broken up. Everyone had staggered and stumbled back to their places at the table, clapping Angelo on the shoulder and cheering as they passed his spot on the bench.

"Thank you, Umangelo," boomed Odin, "for introducing

us to this *conga* of yours. It is a gift we shall treasure always here in Valhalla."

Angelo smiled. Despite his initial reservations, he was beginning to have fun. "No problemo."

"And now more singing," the Allfather commanded. He clapped his hands together. "Suggestions?"

"'My Old Man's a Viking!'" cried one of the men.

"'Loki Tried to Poke Me in the—'" began another.

"No, no, no!" Odin shouted, his voice cutting through the din like a sledgehammer through warm butter. "We've done all those. We should let Umangelo choose."

"Um..." said Angelo.

"Go on, give us a song, Umangelo. And by Bragi's balls, make it a good one."

"Well, I'm not a very good singer," Angelo said shyly.

"Come on, Umangelo!" another Viking yelled. "You can do it!"

"Let's hear it!"

More voices went up, demanding that he perform. Soon the hall was a chorus of "Umangelo! Umangelo! Umangelo!"

chanted over and over again, as fists banged repeatedly down on the tabletop.

Slowly, shakily, Angelo got to his feet once more. The crowd went wild as he cleared his throat, then the cheering became an expectant hush as all eyes fixed on the boy in white.

Angelo looked across the sea of horned helmets, then he adjusted his glasses, took a deep breath, and in a high, reedy voice, he began to sing.

"*He's got the whole world in His hands; He's got the whole wide world in His hands; He's got the whole world in His hands; He's got the whole world in His hands.*"

Along the table, several dozen of the Vikings began to sway back and forth. Odin nodded along in time with Angelo's warbling.

Encouraged by this, Angelo sang more loudly. He pointed at one of the closest Vikings as he continued:

"*He's got you and me, brother, in His hands; He's got you and me, sister, in His hands...*"

The Viking Angelo had pointed to on the word *sister* stopped swaying and muttered unhappily to his neighbour.

"*He's got all of us together in His hands; He's got the whole world in His hands.*"

The atmosphere in the room had very subtly begun to change. Only a handful of the Vikings were swaying now, and Odin was no longer nodding along.

But Angelo was just hitting his stride. He drew in a deep breath before launching into the next verse with renewed vigour.

"*He's got the thunder and the lightning in His hands...*"

As one, every Viking in the hall gave a gasp of shock.

"*He's got the thunder and the lightning in His hands...*"

The tankard Odin was holding crumpled into a metal ball, spraying ale in all directions.

"*He's got the thunder and the lightning in His hands...*"

Like a sea monster rising ominously from the deep, Odin stood up. Plates and mugs were blown off the table and scattered across the floor as the Allfather's voice came like a hurricane.

"That... is... ENOUGH!"

It took Angelo a few seconds to register what Odin had said. He squeaked out a final, "*He's got the whole world in His...*" before the words died in his throat. He glanced at the angry faces around him, then he coughed gently and sat down.

"Who is this *he* you sing of?" Odin demanded. "Who claims to have the thunder and lightning in his hands?"

Angelo's mouth had gone dry. It clicked strangely when he spoke. "It's... it's... God," he managed to rasp.

Odin placed the knuckles of his clenched fists on the table and leaned forward. "*Which* god?"

"Um, just... just, you know, God," Angelo said. "The real one," he added, and immediately wished he hadn't.

"*WHAT?*"

"The Christian one!" Angelo yelped. "That's what I meant!" He looked around desperately. "Not... I didn't mean..."

"He said you weren't real, Allfather," said one of the Vikings at the table.

"He claims Thor does not rule the thunder!" said another. "And he does. He bloody does, I've seen him."

"He rules it like nobody's business," agreed yet another.

Angelo suddenly felt very hot. He shifted uncomfortably in his seat, all too aware now of the pressure building inside his bladder. He looked up into the faces of the Vikings on either side of him. Their rotten teeth and pockmarked skin grimaced down.

"Seize him!" barked Odin, and Angelo felt vice-like grips clamping down on his shoulders. Odin flipped up his eyepatch. There was another patch beneath it. The eye drawn on to this one was narrow and angry-looking. His real eye blazed with something between fury and madness. "And let us show him just what a *real god* can do."

"So, what's your decision, mortal?" asked Herya. "Do you want my help, or don't you?"

Zac considered the offer. Having one partner was bad enough, but having two would make him part of a trio. He'd never been part of a trio before. He had never wanted to be.

"I don't know if I'd be able to protect you," he said.

"Ha!" Herya snorted. "Protect me? I don't need protecting. We Valkyries are born warriors. I can look after myself. Besides, people know me out there. If anything, I'll be the one protecting you."

"Well, I'd hate to put you in that position," Zac retorted. "So how about you just tell me where Argus is and save us both the bother?"

"Hello?" said Zac's wrist. It sounded worried. Both he and the Valkyrie looked at it in surprise.

"Hello?" said the voice again. There were other noises in the background too – cheering and yelling and what sounded like the sharpening of a blade. "Zac, are you there?"

"What sorcery is this?" Herya whispered. She tried, but she was unable to hide the shake in her voice.

Zac raised his arm and peered at the watch, just as Angelo spoke again. "I hope you can hear me," crackled the voice from the tiny in-built speaker, "because I really need your—"

"HEEEEEEEEEELP!

The last word screamed out through the wood of the door leading back into the Great Hall.

"Great," Zac sighed, pushing the door open. "What now?"

He froze, half in and half out of Valhalla. Behind him, the snow swirled and danced. Before him, Odin raised an ornate battleaxe, as the rabble of Vikings whooped and hollered with delight.

"I could be wrong," said Herya's voice in Zac's ear, "but it looks like your little friend is about to lose his head."

CHAPTER ELEVEN

"WHAT'S GOING ON? What are you doing?" Zac demanded, stepping into the hall.

Only Odin's eye moved. "Ah, young Zac. You are just in time."

Zac looked at the axe, then down at the spot in front of the Allfather. Angelo was on his knees, his arms folded up his back by a brawny Viking with a thick black beard.

Tears were trickling down Angelo's cheeks and dripping on to the cobbled floor. He was muttering incoherently below his breath, his body trembling with fear.

"Just in time for what?" asked Zac, stalling for time.

Odin's laugh was a boom of delight. "I shall give ye three guesses," he grinned. "And the first two don't count."

"Look, I know he can be irritating," Zac said. "Really *incredibly* irritating, and I don't know what he's done to upset you, but don't you think beheading him's a bit... harsh? Can't we talk about this?"

He flicked his gaze down to Angelo. The boy's whole body was shaking uncontrollably now. The Viking holding him seemed to struggle for a moment. He grimaced as he forced the arms further up Angelo's back.

"Do not worry, young Zac," the Allfather said. "This is Valhalla. No Viking can ever truly die in Valhalla. He'll be up and about again in no time."

Zac heard Herya's voice in his ear once again. "He's not a Viking."

"Yes, thank you, I know that," Zac hissed. He took another step closer to the group. Behind Odin, the rest of the dead Viking horde watched on, barely able to contain their excitement. "He doesn't belong here, though," Zac said. "He's not a Viking. Cut his head off and it won't grow back. You'll kill him."

"Really?" asked Odin. For a moment, he seemed to have second thoughts, then his face lit up in a broad grin. "Ah well, not to worry!"

The Allfather's muscles twitched and the axe began to swing. With a cry of panic, Angelo twisted and the Viking holding him was pulled into the weapon's path. The blade cut the unlucky Norseman across the shoulder, splitting him from neck to ribcage.

The Viking looked down at his arm as it hit the flagstone floor with a damp *splat*. A fountain of blood erupted from a vein in his neck. "Oh... *come on*," he tutted.

"Whoops," said Odin. "Sorry about that."

"No, no. My fault, Allfather, my fault," said the Viking, smiling apologetically. He released what was left of his grip on Angelo and picked up his fallen arm. His blood continued to pump out in a wide arc. "Permission to fall unconscious, sir."

Odin nodded. "Yes. Yes, of course. Do whatever you must, man."

"Hail, Odin, most gracious giver of—" the Viking began. And then he blacked out on to the floor.

The Allfather turned to the other Vikings and flashed a *silly me* face. Then his expression darkened and he stabbed a finger towards Angelo. "Hold him!" he bellowed. "He will pay for what I just did to... um... what's-his-face."

Angelo twisted on to his back. He kicked out, scuttling across the floor as half a dozen Vikings moved to grab him. "Stop it, stop it," he wailed. "Leave me alone, you... you... *big bullies!*"

Zac put himself between the boy and the men in the horned helmets. "I can't let you do that," he said. "I need him. And his head. Together."

Odin's eye widened with surprise. He flipped up his eyepatch, revealing a third one below. The cartoon eye drawn on it shared the surprise of the real one. "You dare defy a god?" he asked.

Zac held his gaze. "*Defy* is such a strong word. It's just, you know, beheading a guest seems like bad manners."

"What are you doing?" Herya hissed, but Zac didn't reply.

Odin gave a curt nod, as if coming to a decision. "Very well," he said. "You are indeed our honoured guests here in Valhalla. Both of you."

With two fingers he gestured for more Vikings to step forward. "As such, we will kill you both. Together."

Despite Zac's lightning reactions, he couldn't move quickly enough. Two of the Norsemen caught him by the arms and forced him down on to his knees. He watched helplessly as Odin let the axe clatter to the floor and wrapped his fingers round Angelo's throat. The god lifted the boy smoothly into the air.

"Allfather, this is wrong!" protested Herya. "Let him go. In the name of Baldr, let them both go."

"Do not defy me, Valkyrie," the Allfather warned. "Lest you be punished too."

There was the sound of applause from high in the rafters. It took a moment for Zac to realise he was listening to the beating of feathery wings. Eight Valkyries – larger and older than Herya – alighted around Odin and the Vikings.

"Herya," growled the largest Valkyrie. "Know your place!"

"But, *Mother*—"

"Know your place!"

"But this is not right! They're just travellers. They don't know the rules."

The head Valkyrie took two large paces forward. There was a noise, sharp and sudden like the cracking of a whip, as the back of her hand struck Herya's cheek, sending the girl spinning to the floor.

"Apologies, Allfather," the Valkyrie said, bowing

respectfully. She lifted the squirming Herya with one hand. "My daughter shall be severely reprimanded for her insolence."

Odin grunted and nodded. Zac struggled against the arms holding him, but he was pinned too tightly. He could only watch as Herya was dragged back up to the ceiling and devoured once more by the shadows.

"Now, where were we?" the Allfather asked. "Oh, yes, I was about to tear your head off." He chuckled merrily. "Any last words?"

Angelo was fighting for breath, digging his fingers in between his throat and Odin's hand. His legs kicked uselessly, as if he were riding an invisible bicycle that was going nowhere.

"Well?" Odin demanded. "Anything you would like to say?"

With some effort, Angelo managed a nod. The assembled Vikings leaned in to listen. This was the best entertainment they'd had in centuries, and they didn't want to miss a moment.

Angelo's voice was little more than a wheeze. Zac groaned when he heard the boy's words.

"P-please d-don't make m-me angry," he said. "You w-wouldn't like me when I'm a-angry."

There was silence for a moment, and then the room was filled with the raucous laughter of a hundred dead Vikings and one Viking god.

"Good one!" cried Odin, when he was finally able to compose himself. He wiped away a tear with the back of his hand, still chuckling. "You are bolder than you look, Umangelo," he said. A flicker of discomfort crossed his face. "Heavier too," he said more quietly.

All eyes were on Odin and Angelo now. Zac tried to stand, but the Vikings pushed him back down.

A fit gripped Angelo and his whole body started to shudder and convulse. His arms dropped to his sides, shaking wildly along with the rest of him.

Odin's arm hadn't lowered at all, but the tips of Angelo's toes were now scuffing against the floor. The Allfather's face was turning red, as if the effort of holding the boy aloft was taking all his strength. The soles of Angelo's feet touched the ground, although Odin still hadn't moved a muscle.

That was when Zac realised – he was growing. Angelo

was growing. In that moment, something inside Zac's head went *click*.

Jekyll & Hyde. A whole shelf full of *Jekyll & Hyde*. Gabriel had said Angelo was only half angel.

But he never said the other half was human.

Zac shuffled a few centimetres backwards on his knees, until he could retreat no further.

One of the Vikings beside Odin pointed at Angelo's face. He laughed, but the sound was nervous and uncertain. "He's going an awfully funny colour, Allfather," he said.

"Is anyone hot in here all of a sudden?" asked another of the Norsemen.

And at that, all Hell broke loose.

CHAPTER TWELVE

Angelo's fingers balled into tight fists, then opened again suddenly. Smoke trailed from his blackened nails.

The T-shirt he was wearing split down the back as the boy's frame filled out. A jagged row of blood-red spikes tore through his skin along the length of his spine. He hurled back his head and screamed, spewing fire in a mushroom cloud above him.

As one, the Vikings shuffled back. Odin tried to maintain his grip, but Angelo was growing exponentially, and soon his neck was too broad for the Allfather to hold on to.

There was another *rip* as the sleeves of the shirt surrendered to Angelo's bulging biceps. His toes distended, sprouting curved black claws. The plastic straps of his flip-flops snapped as his feet rapidly outgrew them.

His skin too was changing. It wasn't just the colour – now a reddish-brown, like dry desert mud – it was the texture too. Rough, coarse scales covered his flesh, like a fish with a bad case of psoriasis.

Odin's eye swivelled up and down as he examined the creature that now towered above him. "A dragon!" he announced.

"A demon," Zac corrected. The Vikings holding him had loosened their grip. He pulled free and jumped to his feet, but they were too startled to try to catch him.

At the sound of Zac's voice, the Angelo-demon whipped round. Fire burned in the hollows of his eyes, and Zac knew in that instant that Angelo wasn't at home any more.

"A challenge!" Odin bellowed. He stooped to retrieve his axe. "How long have I waited for a moment such as this? I say we battle. What say you, dragon?"

Angelo's jaws opened, revealing several hundred needle-like teeth. He let out a deep, guttural roar, and a blast of flame hit Odin in the face.

The Allfather blinked. "Right, then," he mumbled, patting

down the embers in his smouldering beard. "I'll take that as a yes."

The thing that had been Angelo was still transforming. The spikes down his spine now continued along a twisting tail. It tore through the back of Angelo's trousers – which miraculously were still more or less in one piece – and flattened into an arrowhead point at the end. The tail gave a faint *boing* as it reached its full impressive length.

Odin, who had mere moments ago seemed enormous, was now dwarfed by the demon. Angelo's head hung low and his broad, scaly shoulders were stooped, but even hunched over he was at least four metres tall. Taller, if you included the horns jutting up like elephant tusks from the top of his head. His ears were pointed and elf-like. His nose was flat, spread across his face like a clumsy boxer's.

"Right, then, Dragon!" Odin bellowed. "What say we—?"

The sole of the Angelo-demon's foot slammed against Odin's armour. Vikings were scattered like skittles as the flailing form of the Allfather cannoned backwards across the hall. Those still on their feet watched as Odin was driven clean through the wall and into the snowy wilderness beyond.

131

For a moment, there was no sound, save the falling of plaster and the swirling of wind through the newly formed hole. Then, from somewhere in the crowd, there came a battle cry. It was hesitant and uncertain, but it was a battle cry all the same. Others soon followed.

"Slay the dragon!"

"Cut off its head!"

"Stop talking about it!" roared one of the Norsemen. "And just kill the thing!"

He and some of the Vikings nearer the back of the crowd began to push forward. They shoved with an enthusiasm reserved for those who know full well that there are several dozen other people between them and anything dangerous.

Those Vikings who were unfortunate enough to be near the front were much less gung-ho. They had seen the full horror of the creature, they had felt the searing heat of its breath and they had decided that while they might already be dead, this thing could almost certainly make them deader.

The crowd heaved, half of it pushing forward, the other half pushing back. Those pushing forward had managed to seize the element of surprise, though, and the throngs quickly began to tighten round Angelo.

With an inhuman screech, he swung a scaly arm, batting half a dozen Vikings into the air. Even before they landed, he was sweeping his other arm out in a wide arc. Ten, twenty, thirty Norsemen crunched down across the room.

Those pushing from the back did some quick mental calculations and realised they didn't have nearly the number of human shields they'd had a moment ago. They hesitated, their swords no longer waving so enthusiastically, their shouting now barely audible over the cries of their kinsmen.

Roaring, Angelo smashed both enormous fists down on to the floor. The ground quaked, yet more Vikings fell, and for the first time since they had been erected, the walls of Valhalla began to tremble.

Over the sounds of the screaming and the roaring, Zac heard another sound. It was a high-pitched whistling, like something slicing through air. He looked up to see one of the shields from the ceiling zipping towards him, and leaped sideways in time to avoid being sliced cleanly in two.

With a metallic *ba-doing*, the shield embedded itself several centimetres into the stone floor. It was a decorative piece, too large for even Odin to wield in battle, and as Zac looked up he thought he saw Herya scuttling away from the space where the shield had been hanging.

Cupping his hands round his mouth, he shouted to the Valkyrie lurking somewhere above. "Oi, watch out! That nearly hit me!"

Another shield began to fall. It flipped over, mid-plunge, and landed face down on the stone right beside Zac. The *clang* rang out like the tolling of a church bell. The echo lapped the hall half a dozen times, before fading away.

"And again!" Zac shouted. "What are you doing? Trying to kill me?"

Zac felt a gust of warm breath breeze over him. Angelo had turned away from the Vikings and now stood glaring down at him, shoulders hunched, fists clenched.

"Oh... hi," Zac offered as brightly as he could. The fire danced higher in the demon's hollow eye sockets. It opened its wide jaws, and Zac saw something spark at the back of the cavernous maw.

He swore then, loudly and creatively, but the words were drowned out by the crackling of the flames from Angelo's throat. Zac dived and tucked himself in behind the upright shield just as the inferno hit. He felt the metal go red-hot; coughed as his lungs filled with the tang of fire and brimstone.

There was a hiss from the floor. Zac looked down to see drops of molten gold pooling together on the cool stone. He looked up. The flames were still licking over the top and round the edges of the shield, melting his defences away.

"Stop!" he wheezed. "Angelo, stop."

But Angelo was no longer listening, because Angelo was no longer there. Only the demon remained, scaly and sizzling and – Zac hated to use the word – *hulking*.

Gold flowed in rivers round his feet. The shield was little more than a gleaming wafer now. Zac's time was up.

"*DRAGON!*"

The word raced round Valhalla, deep and booming and oh-so-very angry. With a *whoosh* of inrushing air, the fire stopped.

A moment later, what was left of the shield became a shimmering sludge on the floor, and Zac saw a demon turn to face a god.

Odin was standing at the far end of the long wooden

table, axe in hand, several centimetres of snow piled up on top of his helmet. His white beard was dark with soot, but his expression was darker still. He flipped up the patch with the surprised eye drawn on, revealing a fourth and final patch beneath. The eye drawn on this one scowled furiously, with flecks of red painted at the centre of the pupil.

With one hand he swung the axe down on the table. The wood split along its entire length, and the two halves fell neatly in opposite directions. Odin began a slow march along the newly formed path, and with each step the god took, Zac felt his ears go *pop*.

"I welcomed thee into my home, Dragon, and you repay me thus?" Odin growled. He ground his teeth together and tiny blue sparks spat from his mouth. "You attack my Viking brothers. You destroy the Great Table."

"Um, actually, I think that was you, Allfather," whimpered a voice from somewhere beneath a pile of groaning Vikings. "To be fair."

"And you defy the all-powerful Odin," continued the god, ignoring the interruption. "Here in Valhalla. Here in *Asgard*, you defy *me*!"

Odin was halfway to the demon now. The handle of the axe creaked as he tightened both hands round it. "I, who have slain giants in my sleep. I, who created all of Midgard from the blood, bones and flesh of my fallen enemies."

He stopped just a few metres away from the monster. "I, who has a dirty great axe and a very short temper."

The few Vikings who were still intact and fully operational gave a cheer at that, but it was a cautious one, as if they weren't completely sure that Odin was going to win. The last thing they wanted was to get any further into the demon's bad books.

"Thou hast put a right bloody dampener on an otherwise fine afternoon, Dragon. And for that thou shalt die!"

CHAPTER THIRTEEN

THE THING THAT had until just a few moments ago been Angelo, vomited Hellfire in the Allfather's face. The flames licked hungrily across the old god's weathered skin, turning his eyepatch black and melting the snow that had been balanced on his head.

Although he was several metres away, the heat forced Zac to draw back. Odin growled with pain, but otherwise didn't flinch. He raised the axe before him, using the flat of the blade to block the worst of the fire.

Angelo's tail flicked around like a striking cobra and his clawed fingers curled into fists as, step by agonising step, Odin advanced.

Zac kept his distance and just watched. For the first time

in as long as he could remember, he had absolutely no idea what to do. He'd spent a lifetime thinking on his feet, finding solutions to problems before they even happened. Now, though, standing in a mythical land, watching a Norse god fight a transforming angel-demon, he was fresh out of ideas.

As he drew close to the demon, Odin swung the axe in an upwards curve. The blade clipped the brute on the chin, snapping his head back and making him shriek and howl furiously.

The Vikings cheered, but Odin's brow knotted when he saw the blade hadn't cut through the scaly skin. He swung again, hacking this time at the demon's barrel-like ribcage. The blow struck like a battering ram smashing against rock. The Angelo-thing staggered, but the axe had failed to draw blood once again.

"What manner of creature art thou?" Odin wondered, before four jagged knuckles crunched into his nose, splattering it across his face. With a roar as savage as any the demon had made, Odin hurled himself forward, letting the axe fall to the floor.

The demon lashed out with its arms and tail. It opened

its mouth to cough up more flame, but Odin's hands clamped round its jaws, pinning them shut.

"Let's see you do your fire trick now, Dragon!" cried the Allfather. Fury was etched into every line of his face, but there was something else there too, beneath the blood and the beard – a bloodthirsty joy. The Allfather was loving every minute of this.

Thrashing wildly, the monster stumbled, a fireball stuck somewhere near the back of his throat. Zac moved quickly from their path, as god and demon crashed towards the wall, then carried on crashing right through it.

There was a *hiss* of steam as the demon's fiery hide hit the snow, and then both combatants were sliding down the hill, each raining blows on the other as they ploughed a trench through the melting slush.

Zac rushed to the hole in the wall and looked out. Angelo and Odin were twenty metres away already, and they were still picking up speed. He looked ahead of them, down the slope. There, just beyond where it levelled out, Asgard dropped sharply off into nothingness. They were hurtling towards the edge, and they didn't even realise.

"Angelo, look out!" he shouted, but they were too far

away to hear, and there was no saying the demon could even understand a word he was saying.

There was a soft *whoosh* and Herya appeared beside him. "We have to get out of here," she said.

"Stopped dropping shields on me now, have you?" asked Zac, still watching Odin and Angelo sliding down the hill.

Herya caught him by the arm and pulled him away from the wall. "I was saving you from the demon's fire."

Zac's feet splashed through the puddle of melted gold. "OK, I'll give you that one."

She bundled him towards the second shield, which sat like a wide plate on the flagstone floor. "This one's for our escape."

"Escape?" said Zac, then he realised that Jurgen and the other Vikings were closing in round them, weapons drawn. They looked far from happy. "Oh, yeah. Escape."

"There will be no escape for you," Jurgen growled.

"We were having a lovely time until you showed up," snarled another of the warriors.

Jurgen glared at Herya. "And as for you, Valkyrie, stand with us or face the—"

"Oh, shut up, Jurgen," Herya said. She shoved Zac into

the bowl of the shield. "And just so you know, when I spilled that drink on you earlier? So not an accident."

Zac looked beyond the edge of the shield to the deep trench in the snow. It was already refreezing, the sides now smooth and slick like polished glass. The shield scraped across the flagstones as Herya heaved it over towards the hole in the wall. Zac finally understood her plan. He gripped the shield's edge as Herya shoved the makeshift sledge on to the polished ice.

"Hold tight!" she said, jumping in behind him.

"Yeah," he replied, as the front of the shield began to dip and the back rose up into the air. "I kind of worked that one out for myself."

There was a bellowed, "Stop them!" from the hole in the wall as the slow-witted Vikings realised what was going on. But there was no stopping them now. As gravity took hold and friction gave up, the shield began to hurtle headlong down the hill.

A blizzard hit Zac in the face. The icy winds tore at him, forcing him to screw up his eyes until they were almost closed. The snow swished past beneath the shield as it raced like a toboggan along the trench cut by Angelo and Odin.

"They're getting away!" said one of the Vikings as they watched the shield slice down the hillside.

"Not for long," said Jurgen. He crammed two thick fingers in his mouth and whistled. Eight winged shapes clambered from the shadows by the ceiling and plunged screeching from the rafters. "Right, then," said Jurgen as the Valkyries alighted around him. "Think they can ruin *our* party, do they?"

Zac ducked his head and gulped down a breath. The wind was impossibly cold. It snapped at his skin like a thousand biting insects, making his eyes water and his face go numb.

"I'm free. I don't believe it – I'm free!" Herya said, but the whistling of the wind stole her words away.

"What?" Zac asked, straining his ears.

"Nothing," Herya said, raising her voice to be heard above the storm. "Uh-oh."

"*Uh-oh?* What do you mean, *uh-oh?*"

"We've got company," she said as eight winged figures swooped across the sky behind them.

Zac squinted ahead through the snowstorm. He could see the writhing shapes of Angelo and Odin, still locked in battle, still unaware of the drop into nothingness that lay ahead of them. The sound of each thunderous punch and kick rolled across Asgard. It was surely only a matter of time before the other gods emerged from their palaces to find out what all the racket was about. Zac tried not to think what would happen then.

"Go right!" Herya barked, snapping him back to the present.

"What? Why?"

"Stop asking questions and *go right*!"

Zac threw his weight sharply to one side. He heard a short, sharp scream, followed by a *crunch*. He risked a glance back and saw a Viking lying face down on the hard-packed snow, unmoving.

"What the Hell—" he began, before a cry of "*Geronimo!*" and a loud *whumpf* cut him off. Another Viking plopped into a soft snowdrift just off to the left of the trench.

Zac looked up and saw the eight Valkyries cutting through the sky above them. Six of them carried Vikings, who dangled from the Valkyries' grip, wildly waggling their weapons at the world below.

As Zac watched, one of the Valkyries dropped the man

she was carrying. He screamed as he fell, only stopping when he smacked down on to the compacted snow, just a dozen or so metres ahead of them.

"Hold on!" Zac warned, leaning sharply left. Herya gave a yelp of shock as she was thrown off balance. Not looking back, Zac reached round and grabbed her leg, steadying her.

"Thanks," she said.

"Don't mention it."

They swept past the groaning Viking and Zac snatched up the Norseman's sword. It clattered into the bowl of the shield between him and Herya.

"Might come in handy," he explained, biting his lip and leaning his weight towards the front of the shield. It immediately sped up until the snow around them became a streak of blurry white.

They were drawing closer to the god and the demon, but they in turn were now only thirty or forty metres from the edge. The slope was levelling off, slowing their descent, but there was no way they were going to stop in time.

"How *dare* you!" screeched one of the Valkyries above. "How dare you defy the ruler of the gods!"

"Just the Norse gods, actuall-*eeeeeeeeeeeeeeeee!*" said the Viking she was carrying, and then he hit the ice in front of the shield with a *thud*. There was no way to avoid him. Both Zac and Herya heard a faint *crunch* as they slid over the top of him.

"Ooh, that had to hurt," Zac winced. He very deliberately didn't look back.

"Four more coming in low," Herya warned. There was a *splat* from somewhere back up the slope. "Make that three."

"We're almost there!" Zac shouted. Over the sounds of the storm he could hear Odin's voice now, cursing and swearing as he wrestled with his 'dragon'. The hissing and screeching he could also hear was Angelo, Zac guessed. Only something truly demonic could make those sounds.

"Left, left, left!" Herya cried. They both leaned left just as Jurgen hit the ground beside them. He landed on his feet, skidded frantically for a few wild-eyed moments, then his legs went in opposite directions and he did the splits on the ice.

"Right, right, right!" They leaned again, narrowly avoiding a seventh Viking bomb. His fingers clawed for the edge of the shield, but they were sliding too fast for him to hold on.

"One more," Herya said.

Zac gave a curt nod, keeping his gaze fixed ahead. They were barely fifteen metres from Angelo and Odin now, and they in turn were barely fifteen metres from the drop.

"Here he comes," Herya warned. Her eyes followed the falling Viking as he plunged harmlessly into a snowbank several metres to the left. "*Aaaand* there he goes."

Herya turned. "Right, I think we're in the clear," she said, and then something hit the back of the shield and the world gave a sharp, sudden lurch. Zac's chin smashed against the ice as the shield flipped over. The ice hit him like a wall of raw cold, frost biting him as he slid head first down the slope.

He clawed at the polished ice, trying to get a grip to slow his descent, but his fingers found no purchase on the slippery surface. Behind him, also sliding, Herya was pinned beneath her mother. The older Valkyrie was shouting, screaming, but Zac couldn't hear her over the howling of the wind and the high-speed thudding of his own racing heart.

Odin and Angelo were nowhere to be seen. All that lay ahead now was the edge, and beyond that, the abyss. Too fast. He was going too fast. The sword slid by him. One chance, only one chance.

He stretched out and found the sword's handle. The edge was five metres away now. Four. Three. Gritting his teeth, he drove the blade into the ice.

At once, he began to slow down. Those behind him didn't. Herya crashed into him, her momentum carrying them all the way to the edge of the drop. There was a panicked fluttering of wings and Herya's mother flew clear, just as the bottom dropped out of the world and Zac felt his legs sliding off into nothingness.

With a sharp jerk, the sword stopped. A grunt burst from Zac's lips as every muscle in his arms stretched to tearing point. The pain was like fire. It burned through him, making his head go light. But he hung on, his frostbitten hands locked round the handle of the sword.

There was a weight on his legs, pulling him down. Craning his neck, he was able to see Herya clinging to his feet. Beneath her was nothing but grey mist, lit up every few seconds by a crackle of lightning.

He was about to tell her to let go and fly them to safety when he saw her left wing. It drooped at an awkward angle, the white feathers dark with blood. An ornate-handled knife was embedded into the wing just by her shoulder. There was no way she was flying anywhere.

She looked up and met Zac's gaze. "I know," she said. "Worst. Mother. Ever."

"Ah, young Zac. Fancy seeing thee here."

Zac looked to his right. Just a few metres along the cliff face, Odin was clinging by his fingertips. The Allfather's face was a rash of bruises. His white beard was matted with blood, and one of the horns on his helmet was pointing the wrong way. He grinned broadly, and appeared to be missing some teeth.

"I hoped we might have the opportunity to *hang out together*," the Allfather said, then he hurled back his head and laughed long and hard at his own joke.

"Where's Angelo?" Zac demanded. His arms were shaking now, both from the cold and the effort of holding on to the sword.

"The dragon? Gone. Down there," Odin said, nodding into the cloudy abyss. "Unfortunate, really. I would have enjoyed seeing his head on a spike. Not in a nasty way, you understand? All in good fun."

There was a commotion up on the ledge above them. Four Valkyries touched down by Odin's hands. They took hold of his arms, two to each one, and dragged him back up on to solid ground.

"My thanks, ladies," the Allfather said. "Thy loyalty is commendable." He glared down past Zac to where Herya dangled. "A shame the same cannot be said for all thine number."

"I do not know what has come over her, Allfather," said Herya's mother, stepping up to join Odin at the edge of the cliff. They were both standing close to the sword. Worryingly close for Zac's liking. "She always was... headstrong, even for a Valkyrie."

Odin nodded sagely. "She is a disappointment."

"No," spat the older Valkyrie. "She is a disgrace."

Zac's muscles screamed at him as he tried to pull himself and Herya back up. But the cold was too biting and the pain was too great, and it was all he could do just to hold on.

"H-help us up," he pleaded. "We're going to fall."

Odin squatted down. He examined the sword, then he

turned to Zac and smiled kindly. "That's right, young Zac," he said. "Thou art."

Still smiling, the Allfather tapped a finger against the ground. The sword shuddered, then sliced through the last few centimetres of ice. Zac felt his stomach do a flip and then he, the sword and Herya were sucked down into the swirling mists of the abyss.

CHAPTER FOURTEEN

ZAC WAS LYING on something. It was sharp and uncomfortable and was digging into his back. His eyes were closed and they were in no mood for opening just yet. His ears were probably working, but all they could hear was silence, so he couldn't be sure. His nose was definitely functioning, though. A cold swirl of decay and damp seeped up each nostril and whispered dark thoughts into his brain. They told him many things had died in this place, and that he would almost certainly be next, so it was probably best just to lie still and wait for it all to be over.

The sharp thing in his back begged to differ.

"Get off," it said, and Zac realised he was lying on Herya. More specifically, he was lying on her legs with the toe of her boot poking into his spine. The sudden kick she gave him was enough to jump-start his sleeping body. He rose quickly. His eyes opened. He could still see nothing.

To call the fog *thick* would be to do it a disservice. It looked almost solid, as if it had been painted on to the air in layers of white and grey.

"Where are we?" he asked. He heard Herya stand up somewhere nearby.

"The Nether Lands," she said grimly.

"The Netherlands?" Zac asked. "What, as in... beside Belgium?"

"No, not the Netherlands," she said. Her voice sounded muffled by the mist. "The *Nether Lands*. The void between the Afterworlds." Although he couldn't see her, Zac heard Herya shudder. Her voice became little more than a whisper. "The realm of the lost gods."

"Right. And I'm guessing that's not somewhere we want to be?"

"No," she said. "And *yes*. We can get to Argus from here. If we can find the way. And if we can avoid being eaten."

"*Eaten?*"

"There are other lost things in the Nether Lands," she explained. "Not just gods."

As if on cue, something howled in the distance. Zac turned to look in the direction of the sound, but all he saw were shades of grey.

"Great," he said quietly.

The fog around them was briefly lit up by a flicker of lightning. For a split second he saw Herya silhouetted in the mist. "How did we survive the fall?" he asked.

"Nothing dies in the Nether Lands," she said.

"But you just said we might get eaten."

"Yes," she replied.

It took a moment for Zac to realise her meaning. "Oh," was all he said.

"There are worse things than death."

Zac nodded. "Yeah. So everyone keeps telling me."

The howl came again, closer this time. A second later, another one answered.

"We should go," Herya said. "The things down here may not need to see us to find us."

"I should try to find Angelo," Zac sighed. "If he fell, he should be around here somewhere."

"Hello," said Angelo brightly. Zac and Herya both screamed in fright, then immediately pretended they hadn't.

"Where the Hell did you come from?" Zac demanded. He was grateful for the fog so no one could see that all the colour had drained from his face.

"Over there," Angelo replied. "Or was it over there? I'm not sure. Is it really foggy, or is it just me?"

"It's foggy."

"Oh, that's a relief. I was worried I'd gone blind. Phew!"

There was another crackle of lightning and Zac saw Angelo's outline through the mist. He was boy-sized again, and he no longer had a tail. Both good signs, but Zac wanted to be sure.

"Are you... OK?" he asked.

"Oh, don't you worry, I'm fine," Angelo said cheerfully. Zac jumped as the boy's slender arms wrapped round him in a hug. "But thanks for asking. I knew you cared really," Angelo said. "By the way," he added, "is anyone else naked?"

Zac leaped back as if he'd been electrocuted. He tried to push Angelo away without actually touching him, which proved to be just as difficult as it sounded. "Get off," he said. Reluctantly, Angelo stopped hugging him.

"It's funny. One minute I'm being strangled by Odin, the next I'm here. Where is here, by the way?"

"The Nether Lands," said Herya.

"What?" asked Angelo. "Beside Belgi—"

"No," said Zac before Herya could open her mouth. "A different one. And what do you mean? Are you saying you don't remember what happened in Valhalla?"

"Not really," replied Angelo. "I remember them trying to cut my head off. That's not something you forget in a hurry, let me tell you."

"Then what?"

Angelo thought. "Not much. I remember they grabbed you. I remember... I remember Odin picking me up, and not being able to breathe, and my head going all tingly and then... And then I woke up here."

"What about the bit in between?" Herya asked.

Angelo didn't reply.

"Well?" the Valkyrie pressed.

"Um, sorry," said Angelo. "It's just, you see, I've got no

clothes on. And you're, you know, a girl. And so, thinking about it, I probably shouldn't be talking to you."

"You are very modest for a demon."

Angelo snorted. "Demon?" he laughed. "I'm not a demon. Demons are big horrible ugly monsters. I'm an angel. A bit like you, but, you know? Proper."

"*Half* angel," Zac reminded him. "Half angel and half..." He left the sentence hanging.

"Well, *human*, obviously!"

There was stillness in the fog.

"Obviously," said Zac, after a while.

"He doesn't know," Herya realised.

"Know what?" asked Angelo. "What don't I know?"

A howl interrupted them. It sounded closer than ever, but it bounced around inside the mist, making it impossible to tell which direction it was coming from.

"Nothing," said Zac, remembering Angelo's earlier rant about how horrible all demon-kind was. "Doesn't matter. We need to move."

"Right you are. Should I put my trousers back on, do you think? They've got a bit stretched and ripped somehow, but they're not too bad. Maybe I can sort of tie the torn bits together so they stay up."

"Yes," said Zac. "Trousers. Definitely trousers."

There was a soft rustling of fabric. "I'm not very good at knots," Angelo said. "Can you help me?"

"Definitely not," Zac replied. "Figure it out." He turned to where he guessed Herya stood. "You said Argus is here somewhere."

"No, I didn't."

"You did; you said—"

"I said we could *get to* Argus from here," the Valkyrie clarified. "The Nether Lands connect all the Afterworlds, including the one where we'll find Argus."

"In that case, Angelo can take us to wherever he is. He can move between dimensions or... whatever they are. It'll mean holding his hands, but he's wearing trousers now at least."

"No, he can't. Not here. There are many ways into the Nether Lands, but only one way out. A portal."

"Where is it?"

"The portal can be found right at the top of the Mountain of Eternal Torment, in the Cavern of the Endless Damned."

Zac winced. "Oh, great. Really?"

"No, not really. Just kidding," said Herya. "It's in the middle somewhere. At the lowest point. The Nether Lands is like a big bowl with the portal at the bottom."

Zac scuffed a foot across the ground. It sloped slightly downward in one direction. "Right. Then we go this way." He reached out into the fog. "Grab my hand. Then we can all stick together."

"Yeah, in your dreams, mortal," said Herya. "I'll take the demon's hand and the demon can take yours."

"*Angel*, not demon," Angelo laughed. "You're such a Mrs Mix-up!"

"OK, fine, whatever," Zac sighed. He fumbled around until he found Angelo's left hand. Herya was already holding on to the right.

"This is nice, isn't it?" Angelo said, his broad smile wasted in the fog. "This is really nice. Three friends, just hanging out, holding hands."

"Just what I always wanted," said Zac. Then they all set off down the slope into the deepest depths of the Nether Lands.

CHAPTER FIFTEEN

THE GROUND WAS rough and uneven. They picked their way down it carefully, relying on their feet to feel the way. Zac took the lead; Herya's heeled boots were no good for testing the ground and Angelo... well, Angelo was just Angelo. Zac glanced in the boy's direction whenever another crack of lightning illuminated the fog, just to be sure he was still the same size and shape.

They had been walking for twenty minutes or more. The slope had become dangerously steep at several points, but they'd moved sideways until they'd found an easier route and carried on down that way instead.

Three times they heard a howl, each time further away than the last. But Zac remained focused, listening for any other movement in the mist. He wasn't keen on the idea of being eaten at the best of times, but to be eaten, digested and then *passed back out* in a place where it was impossible to die was, he reckoned, a definite no-no.

"*He's got the whole world in His hands,*" began Angelo. "*He's got the whole world in his—*"

"Please don't," said Zac, his voice clipped and gruff.

Angelo fell silent, but only for a moment. "*Give me oil in my lamp keep me burning,*" he sang. "*Give me oil in my lamp, I pray – Hallelujah! Give me oil in my lamp keep me burning burning burning; keep me burning till the break of day. I wanna sing Hosanna, sing Hosanna—*"

"Please stop," groaned Herya.

"What," protested Angelo, "just because it's not about... about... *a giant's knickers* it's not a good song all of a sudden?"

"Look, no one's singing anything," Zac said. "It makes too much noise. You'll attract attention."

"We should be safe to talk, though," Herya replied. "So talk to me. Tell me things."

Zac slid a few centimetres down a gravelly incline, paused, then sidestepped on to more solid ground before continuing downwards. "What sort of things?"

"I don't know. Isn't that what you do on Midgard? Just talk endlessly and never actually *do* anything?"

"Midgard?" said Zac. "That's what your lot call Earth, isn't it?"

"No. Earth is what your lot call Midgard."

"Ooh! Ooh! I can tell you something," said Angelo. If the others hadn't been holding them, he'd have raised a hand. "Me, me. I can tell you something!"

"Go on, then, demon."

"Angel," said Angelo automatically. His mind raced through the list of topics he knew about. The focus was narrow, so it didn't take long.

"I have two-hundred-and-nine Hulk comics, and the Hulk's real name is Bruce Banner," he announced happily.

Zac shook his head. "Jesus," he muttered.

"Where? Here? What's he doing here?" gasped Angelo. He shouted into the fog. "Jesus? Jesus, it's me, Angelo!"

A chorus of howls rose up, some far away, some not so much.

"Sssh, shut up!" Zac hissed. That settled it. He came to a decision. "As soon as we get to the portal, you're going home."

"What? But I can't," Angelo said. "They told me I had to go with you. I'll get into trouble if I don't go—"

Zac cut him off. "The decision's made. Herya will come with me. You'll go back to Heaven. No arguments."

"But—"

"*No arguments.*"

They trudged on without speaking for all of thirty seconds.

"My feet hurt."

Zac sighed. "They'll be fine. Keep walking."

"That's easy for you to say. I've got no shoes on. I bet you've got shoes on, haven't you?"

"Ha!" said Herya. "You think you've got problems? Try walking in these boots."

"What, can I?" Angelo asked.

"No."

"Oh, but I could just try them on for a—"

"Seriously, demon," the Valkyrie warned, "don't even think about it."

On they walked, in single file, hands locked, down through the soupy fog. For an hour they continued like that, in silence apart from the occasional comment from

Angelo. Once, he made a tuneless attempt to whistle what may have been 'All Things Bright and Beautiful', but which might just as easily have been 'Can't Touch This' by MC Hammer. He'd sighed heavily when Zac had told him yet again to shut up, and had remained quiet ever since.

Until now.

"Please don't send me back yet. I don't want to get into trouble."

"The fog's thinning," said Zac, ignoring the request. "I can see my feet."

"The area round the portal should be clear," Herya said. "The mist sits above it like a cloud."

Zac felt Angelo's hand tighten in his. "Are we nearly there, then?" the boy asked.

"Must be," replied Zac. "And, yes, you *are* going home. It's too dangerous to come with me. You could get killed."

"I don't mind that it's dangerous. I'm not scared of going into Hell," Angelo insisted.

"No, I meant *I* might kill you if you keep singing."

"Well... Well... OK. You can if you want, I don't mind. Seriously. Just, just please don't send me back. I don't want to get into trouble."

"Come on, it's Heaven. What are they going to do? Take away your harp privileges?"

"They might take away my posters. Or my comics. Or both," Angelo said. His voice shook. He took a deep breath. "Besides," he mumbled, "I'm having fun."

"Fun?" said Zac. "You call this fun?" He saw Angelo shrug through the final wisps of fog.

"It's more fun than sitting in my room all the time," he said. "That's all I ever get to do. No one else likes me, really, because I'm not a full angel. Even my mum doesn't come round. You two are my only friends in the whole Afterworld."

Herya snorted. "What? When did that happen, exactly?"

"Everyone says I can't do anything. They say I'm useless," Angelo said. He sniffed and blinked back tears. "And if you send me back, then that means they're right, doesn't it?"

"Oh, he's good," Herya said. "You've got to give him that."

But Zac wasn't listening. He was looking instead at a tattoo on Angelo's scrawny chest. The words HALF BLOOD had been inked on to it.

"Who did that?"

Angelo looked down at the tattoo. "Hm? Oh, that was Michael. He said it was for the best."

"Did he?" said Zac. The skin round the writing was red and raw. "Did it hurt?"

"I didn't cry," said Angelo, but he avoided Zac's gaze.

"Right, you can come," Zac said. "I mean, if you really want to."

"Whoopee!" cried Angelo, punching the air.

Zac rolled his eyes. *Whoopee*. Who actually used the word *whoopee*?

"But *don't* get in the way, *don't* sing and whatever you do, *don't* get angry." Zac turned and marched briskly down the hill. "We really don't like you when you're angry."

"This is it."

It had taken another hour or more of walking before they came to a ramshackle circular bandstand at the lowest point of the slope. It looked like it might once have been a grand, impressive construction, but now the red paint on the roof was flaking away, and the purple drapes that hung from each of the eight carved pillars were tatty and threadbare.

The curtains were all closed over the spaces between the

posts, but there were gaps here and there, through which Zac could see something moving.

"Are you sure this is it?" he asked quietly.

Herya gestured around them at nothing but emptiness. "No; maybe it's in one of these *other* places."

"All right, all right," Zac said. "So what do we do?"

A curtain gave a sudden *swish* and a face appeared round the edge of the material. The thing looked almost rat-like, with a long pointed snout and ears that stuck out like perfect triangles from the side of its head.

The nose crinkled as it looked at the three of them in turn. "Yes?" it demanded in clipped, nasal tones. "Yes? Yes?"

Herya stepped forward. "Hail, oh dweller of the Nether Lands," she began, "and Guardian of the Grand Portal."

She made a movement with her hands in the air, and Zac realised she was following some sort of official protocol or tradition.

"We have come to make use of the portal," she continued, "that we may leave this accursed place and gain passage to the Greek underworld, also known as Hades, also known as Erebus, also known as the Asphodel Meadows, also known as—"

"Well, you can't," sniped the rat-creature. "We're shut."

This took the wind from Herya's sails. "Shut?"

"Also known as *closed*," sniggered the creature. "Also known as *Bugger off, the lot of you*."

"Shut?" Herya said again. "What do you mean, you're shut?"

"I mean we're shut. Read the sign!" The rat-creature's eyes gestured left. The others looked and saw a notice fixed to one of the pillars. It read: WE'RE SHUT.

The face vanished as the curtain swished over again. "Come back tomorrow," said the thing on the other side. They heard it give a low, sinister chuckle. "Assuming, of course, you can survive that long."

From beyond the curtains there was a shimmer of green light. Zac bounded up the three wooden steps at the base of the bandstand and pulled the drapes aside.

A large wooden hoop stood inside. It was around three metres high and attached to an ornate base. The final flickers of an eerie green glow sizzled across its surface, then the hut fell dark and silent. Aside from the hoop, the place was empty.

And the rat-creature had gone.

CHAPTER SIXTEEN

GABRIEL SAT BEHIND a long walnut desk, writing neatly in the hardback notebook he used as a journal. With a final flourish, he finished the day's entry, and carefully set the quill pen down on the desktop.

He blew softly on the ink to dry it, then closed the book and slipped it into a drawer. Finally, he laced his fingers together in front of him and looked towards the door. A moment later it opened and Michael entered.

"Good afternoon, Michael," Gabriel said. "What may I do for you?"

"He's been asking questions," Michael barked.

"Who?"

"The Metatron; who do you think?" Michael stopped in

front of Gabriel's desk. His entire body was vibrating with barely contained rage. "He's looking for a progress report."

Gabriel leaned back in his leather chair. "Is he? And did you give him one?"

"Course I didn't. I'm not an idiot," Michael spat. "But he knew we'd sent the half-blood down with the human."

A flicker of concern crossed Gabriel's face. "Did he? And how did you respond to that?"

"I told him he volunteered to show the mortal the way. Told him he was only going as far as the entrance, then he was leaving him to it and coming back up here."

Gabriel gave an approving nod. "Quick thinking."

"Don't patronise me," Michael snarled. "Do you know what the Metatron will do if he realises we're lying to him?"

"He won't," Gabriel said. "Besides, even if he does, I'll have the book by then."

"*We'll* have the book."

"Quite. And once *we* have the book then we will have the knowledge, and when we have the knowledge, we will have the power. And when we have the power –" Gabriel rose to his feet – "we shall be gods."

CHAPTER SEVENTEEN

THEY SAT ON the floor, their backs against different pillars, listening to the distant howling of the things in the fog. It wasn't cold in the hut – no colder than it was outside, anyway – but even Zac felt a shiver travel the length of his spine as a flash of lightning briefly made the curtains glow purple.

"What time is it?" Angelo asked. "I've lost my watch somewhere."

Zac looked at the watch Gabriel had given him. "It says *twenty-seven*," he said. "So make of that what you like."

"It's local time," Angelo explained. "The watch adjusts to the right time wherever you are."

"Right," Zac said, then he shrugged. "Well, it's twenty-seven o'clock, then."

Angelo looked around the hut and nodded approvingly. "So now we know what twenty-seven o'clock looks like. How many people can say that?"

"You should get some sleep," Zac urged. "Both of you. I'll stand guard."

"I don't need sleep," Angelo said. "So I'll stand guard too."

"Nor do I," Herya said.

"Great!" cheered Angelo. "All three of us can stay up! It'll be like a sleepover, but without any sleeping. Just talking for hours and hours and having a laugh."

Zac's heart sank. "Great."

"What should we do to pass the time? Oh, I know, let's play I Spy!"

"No, let's not—"

"I spy with my little eye, something beginning with –" Angelo looked around the cramped hut – "curtains. No! Wait, I mean C. Something beginning with C!"

"Curtains," said Herya.

"Well done. Herya got it. Your turn."

"I spy with my little eye—"

"Seriously?" sighed Zac. "You're really going along with this?"

"Well, what else do you suggest?" asked the Valkyrie. She shifted her weight and a flicker of pain crossed her face.

"You should let me look at that," Zac said, nodding to the wound on her wing.

"Forget it, it's fine."

"It might get infected."

"It's fine," she said.

"Suit yourself."

The Valkyrie's leather outfit creaked as she shifted again, trying to avoid putting her weight against her wing. "Tell me about this book," she said. "What's so important about it?"

"It's the *Book of Everything*," Angelo said.

"What's it about?"

"Have a guess," said Zac. "There's a clue somewhere in the title."

"It's about *everything*," gushed Angelo. "Everything that has ever happened, everything that's going to happen and everything that's happening *right now*."

Herya thought about this. "So what? Are we in it?"

Zac shrugged. "Probably."

Herya looked pleased. "I've always wanted to be in a book."

173

"It's really dangerous," Angelo said. "If baddies get their hands on it, then they'll know everything in the whole world. There's no saying what they could do then. They could manipulate world leaders into starting a nuclear war, or kill all the good people before they were even born, or, or—"

"Get the winning lottery numbers?" Zac suggested.

Angelo's eyes widened. "I hadn't even thought of that!"

"Have you ever seen it?" Zac asked.

"Just once," said Angelo.

"What did you see it as?" said Zac. "Wait, let me guess. A comic book?"

"Come off it, I'm not *that* geeky," Angelo replied.

"What did it look like, then?"

"A DVD boxed set of *Star Trek: The Next Generation*."

"That's not a book."

"It doesn't have to be a book," Angelo said. "It can look like anything."

Zac rested the back of his head against the pillar. "What I don't understand – and I don't believe I'm about to say this... Why doesn't, you know –" he took a deep breath – "like, *God*, or whoever, just magic it back?"

"Oh, no," Angelo said, "he can't do that."

"Why not?"

"God quit."

Zac stared. "God quit?"

"That's right."

"What do you mean, *God quit*? How can God quit?"

"God can do anything. That's why He's God. He got fed up of it all and just jacked it in."

Herya gave a hollow laugh. "That's the trouble with modern gods. No stamina."

"*Jacked it in?*" Zac said. "What do you mean he *jacked it in*? How can God jack it in?"

Angelo scratched his head. "It was about a hundred years ago, I think. Maybe a bit less. He decided He'd had enough of Heaven and was going to go and live as a human on Earth instead. People weren't happy about it, but what can you say? He's God. You can't really argue with Him. No one knows where He ended up. No one's heard from Him in yonks. The Metatron's in charge now."

"The who?"

"The Metatron. He's been around from the start, sort of like a spokesman for Heaven. Whenever burning bushes start speaking to people in the Bible, that's the Metatron talking. He's the official Voice of God," Angelo explained. "He also does a very good Shirley Bassey, if you catch him in the right mood."

Zac's head was spinning. Yesterday, he hadn't believed in God. Any god, for that matter. For a few hours today he had been reluctantly forced to accept that a supreme being might exist after all. And now he was trying to come to terms with the fact that God not only existed, but that he'd taken early retirement.

Through it all, though, a thought bothered him.

"So, if God quit, who's to say he didn't just take the book with him? That's what I'd have done if it's really as dangerous as everyone keeps saying. What if he didn't want anyone else to have it?"

"Oh, no, it's in Hell," Angelo reminded him. "Gabriel said so."

"What if Gabriel's lying?"

"Angels can't lie."

"And who told you that?"

"Gabriel did."

Zac nodded slowly. "Funny, I thought you might say that." He leaned back against the pillar again, deep in thought.

Maybe Gabriel was telling the truth. Maybe the book really was in Hell. But something about the whole set-up stank, from the way they had threatened his granddad to the way they had teamed him up with the ticking time bomb that was sitting beside him now.

Gabriel hadn't lied about Angelo, exactly. He'd never claimed he was half human, but he'd omitted the fact he was half demon, and Zac couldn't help but wonder what else the archangel had neglected to mention.

"Why are they sending you?"

Zac turned to Herya. She was staring at him intently. "If the book is so important, why did they pick you to get it back? You're just a mortal."

"Because I'm good at that sort of thing," Zac said, suddenly defensive. "I break into places and steal things. That's what I do and I do it well. Really well. Better than anyone."

Angelo shook his head. He made no effort to hide the disappointment in his voice. "That's terrible. Stealing's wrong."

"Yeah, well," began Zac. He felt a pang of something in his chest. Was it guilt? That would be a first. But then he'd never discussed his career choice with anyone before. "I steal from private collectors. Gangsters, usually, or worse. Most of the stuff I nick, they've already nicked from someone else, so I reckon it balances out."

"It doesn't. Two wrongs don't make a right," Angelo said with a sniff.

Zac opened his mouth, then closed it again. Why was he trying to justify himself to this boy? He did what he did, and that was that.

"So why did you agree?" Herya asked. "You're willingly going to walk into Hell. That's not normal."

"I'm not sure about *willingly*," said Zac. "From my point of view I didn't really have much of a choice. They had me killed, told me I was going to Hell anyway. At least this way I'd have a chance of getting back out."

"They wouldn't do that," Angelo gasped. "No way. They wouldn't kill anyone."

"Yeah, well, they did," Zac said. "You think I stuffed my own body in that cupboard?"

Angelo shifted uncomfortably, but didn't reply.

"So let me get this straight," said Herya. "In order to avoid going to Hell, you agreed to go to Hell?"

"Pretty much," confirmed Zac. "Also, if the book's as dangerous as they say it is, someone has to get it back, right? And I've got a better chance than most."

He got up and walked over to the wooden hoop in the centre of the room. He passed his arm through the space in the middle. Nothing happened. "How long before it starts up again, do you think?"

"No idea," replied Herya. "What time is it now?"

Zac looked at his watch. "Just turned a hundred and nine, apparently," he said, then he crossed to the furthest pillar from the others and slumped down with his back against it.

The numbers on the watch flicked over to a hundred and ten.

It was going to be a very long night.

CHAPTER EIGHTEEN

Z AC WAS NOT wrong. Once the Nether Lands had darkened, the night had passed like slow treacle, the hours – or whatever the numbers on the watch represented – oozing lazily towards the dawn.

When the watch reached the high six hundreds, it reset to zero. The moment the display ticked over to four, green sparkles had illuminated the centre of the wooden hoop. The sparkles began to spin like a giant Catherine wheel until the entire hoop was alive with a shimmering jade glow.

The three of them stood together watching the swirling light, expecting the rat-creature to step through at any moment. It was a different figure who emerged in the end, though. An old woman with a cheerful cardigan and silvery-blue hair stepped from the portal, supporting herself on a walking stick. When she saw Zac and the others she screamed with fright.

"Ooh, you near scared the life out of me," she said, once she had regained her composure. She looked them up and down. "Who are you?"

"Three travellers, oh dweller of the Nether Lands," began Herya, but the woman quickly shushed her.

"We don't bother with all that these days, dearie," she said. "Too much effort. It's all much more relaxed now. Where you headed?"

The Valkyrie looked a little put out, as if she'd wasted months rehearsing a speech she wasn't getting a chance to deliver. Which, as it happens, was precisely what she had done.

"The Greek underworld," she said. "Also known as—"

"Yes, yes, Hades, Asphodel Meadows, I know the one." She waggled her crooked fingers in the vague direction of the portal. Nothing appeared to happen. "There you go, then. That's you," she announced.

Zac eyed the green circle suspiciously. "Are you sure?"

"Of course I'm sure, dearie," said the old woman. "I've been doing this for as long as I can remember. Look."

She raised her walking stick and pushed the end of it into the glow of the portal. A moment later, she pulled it back. An egg-shaped green blob was clinging to the end of the stick, gnawing furiously on the wood with its jagged teeth.

As the blob came through the portal, it stopped chewing. It raised its eyes and stared at the old woman. The old woman stared back. Slowly, she popped the stick back through the portal and gave it a flick. When it came back through, the green thing was gone.

"Let's try that once more," she said, then she waggled her fingers again. This time, the light dimmed briefly, then brightened again. "That should be it now," she said, smiling sheepishly. "What can I say? It's still early."

"Herya, why don't you take the lead?" Zac suggested. "You know your way around better than we do."

"What?" mumbled the Valkyrie. "I mean, yes. Of course. Plus I'm the best fighter, so it's safest if I go first, so I can protect you from... things."

"That's good of you," said Zac.

Herya stepped up to the swirling vortex. She glanced back at the old woman, who nodded encouragingly. Then, with just the briefest moment's hesitation, she stepped through the portal and vanished.

"I'll go next," said Angelo, bouncing excitedly from foot to foot.

"Wait!" yelped the woman. She had a pair of spectacles on a string round her neck. She pulled them on and looked Angelo up and down. "Whatever happened to your clothes, dearie? You'll catch your death."

With a bit of effort she wrestled off her brightly coloured cardigan. It had a rainbow knitted into it, and a picture of a kitten. Zac recoiled when he saw the lump sticking out of the woman's stomach. He recoiled even further when he realised the lump was a face.

"Oh, come on," Zac groaned. "That's just weird for the sake of it."

"Didn't think I'd be seeing you again," grimaced the extra head. Its rat-like features pulled into a sneer. "Thought you'd be well dead by now."

"Oh, don't mind him," the woman said. She handed Angelo the cardigan and he slipped it on gratefully. The darker colours – the reds and greens – faded slightly, but they didn't drain away like the black had in Zac's room.

"Thank you," Angelo said, fastening the cardigan. "It's very nice."

"Think nothing of it, dearie," the woman smiled. She stepped aside, leaving the way to the portal clear. "Now off you pop to Hades, and thank you for visiting the Nether Lands," she beamed. "We look forward to welcoming you back soon."

Zac's senses went into shock when he stepped through the portal behind Angelo. The green light filled his head like a flash grenade, blinding him and making his ears ring loudly.

A wall of cold hit him as he stepped out of the vortex. Dazzled, he stumbled, fell, and landed with a *splat* in a puddle of foul-smelling mud. He shook his head and blinked several times, until the glare behind his eyelids faded back to black.

He stood up and wiped away as much of the dark sludge as he could. His vision had cleared, but a piercing shriek still overwhelmed his ears. He'd emerged from the portal beside a wide river. A black, bubbling liquid babbled between its banks. It looked like tar or burned oil, but smelled like sewage. Whatever it was, he had no plans to go swimming in it any time soon.

The ringing in his ears was beginning to ease off, and he could hear another sound now. It was a low steady thumping, over and over again, three or four times a second. *Dum-dum-dum-dum.* There was a *tss-tss-tss* mixed in with it, faster than the thuds, but still somehow matching their rhythm. *Dum-dum-dum; tss-tss-tss.*

Zac turned to find Herya and Angelo standing just a few metres away. Like Zac's, Herya's front was smeared with wet dirt. Angelo, on the other hand, appeared completely clean, aside from his bare feet that were caked with squidgy mud.

"Is this it?" Zac asked. "Is this Hades?"

Herya looked around. A glimmer of doubt passed over her face for just a fraction of a second, but then was gone. "Yeah, this is it," she said. "I'd recognise it anywhere. Welcome to the Greek underworld."

Angelo was staring past them both, his gaze focused on a large skyscraper that stood on its own about half a kilometre away.

It loomed impossibly tall. Even at that distance, Zac couldn't see the top floor, which was lost in the high clouds.

He guessed there were around four hundred storeys below the clouds. How many were above that was anyone's guess.

In all the sparse, barren landscape it was the only building in sight, and it seemed to be celebrating that fact.

Rows of flashing lights ran up the side of it, stretching all the way from the bottom to where the clouds blocked his view. They lit up in time with the sounds coming from within; sounds that Zac now realised were music. Or an attempt at music, at least.

Down the front of the building were six letters, each around twenty or thirty metres tall. They glowed bright red and flickered slightly as the music continued to pump out.

"*Eyedol*," Zac read. "What's that?"

"A nightclub," explained Herya, with only a moment's hesitation. "The most famous nightclub in Hades. In all the underworlds, actually. And the most dangerous."

"You will never find a more wretched hive of scum and villainy," Angelo said, putting on an old man's voice. "We must be cautious." The others looked down at him blankly. "*Star Wars*," he said, grinning. There was still no reaction from Zac and the Valkyrie. "Oh, come on," Angelo sighed. "Not even *Star Wars*?"

"What have you brought us here for?" Zac asked Herya.

"You want to find out about the tenth circle of Hell? You ask Argus," Herya told him. "You want to find Argus? You go to Eyedol. He owns the place."

"How do we know he'll be there?"

"Well, because… he's always there."

"How do we know he'll see us?" asked Angelo.

Herya glanced at the mud-slicked grass and the withered trees all around them. A cool breeze tickled the back of her neck. "Trust me," she said. "He's seen us already."

"Have you been here before?" Zac asked.

"What? Yeah, I come here all the time," Herya said. "Like I told you, I get around."

"And you know Argus?"

Herya gave the briefest of nods. "Yep," she said quietly.

"Right, then you can lead the way."

The Valkyrie hesitated. "Of course," she said.

She took a step in the direction of Eyedol. Her fingers went to the sheath tucked up inside her leather bodice, and to her mother's knife that she had secured there.

She had a feeling they were going to need it.

CHAPTER NINETEEN

ZAC HAD BEEN expecting doormen at the entrance to the club, but he needn't have worried. The music had gradually become louder as they'd got nearer the building, and then become almost ear-shatteringly so when a set of double doors slid open at their approach.

"Welcome to Eyedol," chimed a mechanical voice. It had to be coming from somewhere around the door, but it sounded to Zac as if it were right inside his head. "You'll never want to leave."

He and Herya stopped inside the doorway, which swished closed unnoticed a few seconds later. Angelo hid behind them, mumbling a prayer beneath his breath. As far as he was concerned, they'd just entered his own personal Hell.

He found the noise overwhelming. Every beat shook his

bones, making his entire skeleton tremble a hundred and fifty times per minute. Red spotlights swept across the high ceiling and walls. Purple lasers painted pictures in clouds of blue smoke. Enormous flat-panel TV screens showing nothing but flames hung on every wall. The fires were only illusions, but Angelo could swear the heat from them was real.

A mass of heaving, sweaty bodies filled the dance floor, gyrating and twisting as if in the grip of madness. The dancers themselves took many forms, but the way they moved and thronged together gave them the appearance of a single living thing with too many limbs and heads to count.

The whole ceiling was designed to look like a bulging bloodshot eye, ogling endlessly down at the masses moving below. It was the single creepiest thing Angelo had seen in his life.

"I don't like this," he said.

"What?" asked Zac.

"I said I don't like this," repeated Angelo, raising his voice.

Zac pointed to his ear. "Can't hear you. What?"

Angelo's wide eyes darted around the cavernous room. The noise, the lights, the movement, they were all doing something to him, making his heart race and his head feel light.

Deep down inside the boy, something stirred.

"I said," he began, his voice cracking. The next few words came out as a deafening roar: "I don't like this!"

Zac ducked away, a hand clamped over his ear, a bubble of pain bursting on his lips. Down on the dance floor, a dozen heads glanced in their direction, before going back to thrashing and writhing around.

Angelo was trembling when Zac turned to look at him. His skin was slick with sweat, and in the dark centre of his eyes there was a dim red glow.

"It's OK. Relax," Zac said. He put his hands on the boy's shoulders, then recoiled from the heat. "Angelo, listen to me," he said more urgently. "Calm down, there's nothing to worry about."

"Don't like it. Don't like it."

"I know, but you have to calm down."

"D-don't like it." The words came as a strangled wheeze from Angelo's cracked lips. "Make... it... stop."

Herya elbowed Zac out of the way. She smiled down at

Angelo and pointed to the door. "Maybe you should wait outside."

Angelo turned to Zac. The boy's eyes were a shimmering haze of heat that flickered in time with the thumping beat of the music. "B-but..."

"It's fine, we'll call if we need you," Herya said. She looked to Zac. "Right?"

"Um, yes. Of course. We'll call if we need you," Zac said.

"O-OK," agreed Angelo, and there was a stench like sulphur on his breath. "I'll w-wait outside."

With a stuttered nod and a final glance around the inside of the club, Angelo backed towards the door. It slid open at his approach, making him jump. He waved gingerly at Zac and Herya, and then he was gone, leaving behind footprint-shaped scorch marks on the floor.

"That was close," Zac said, staring down at the footprints. He looked up at the door as it closed shut. "You think he'll be OK out there?"

"Better than he'd be in here," Herya shrugged. "This way's safer for all of us. He'll be fine."

"Yeah, I mean it's just the Greek underworld," Zac said. "What's the worst that could happen?"

"He could have his skin and flesh flayed from his bones by the—"

Zac raised his hands, cutting her off. "Yeah. I was joking."

Herya considered this. "Oh, right. I wasn't."

"I guessed that. So, how do we find Argus?"

The Valkyrie's gaze was sweeping like a spotlight across the room. There were a number of doors dotted along the walls. "He'll be on one of the higher floors."

"OK. So how do we get there?"

"Through one of those doors, I think."

"You *think*? I thought you knew this guy?"

"I do," Herya insisted. "But it's not like I track his every movement. One of these doors will lead us to him."

"That one," said Zac, pointing to a door set in the furthest corner of the club. He shoved past her and took to the steps leading down to the dance floor.

Herya was at his back almost immediately. "You're a mortal. How can you possibly know which door it is?"

"Because it says *Staff Only* on it. And because it's the only one being guarded," replied Zac, not looking back. He pushed through the crowds, avoiding arms and legs, and heads and tails, and other appendages he'd never seen the likes of before – and which he sincerely hoped he'd never see again.

Some of the dancers looked like demons. Not Angelo-grade demons, but demons all the same. The majority of them thrashed around and clawed at the air, as if re-enacting their favourite scenes from *The Exorcist*. Some of the others played air guitar, their faces contorted in concentration, their clawed fingers flying across an imaginary fretboard, joyfully oblivious to the fact that the pounding dance beat contained no whiff of guitar whatsoever.

There were other shapes in the crowd too. Something ogre-like with a dog's head. Something that looked to be part lion, part bird. In the middle of the dance floor a woman with a brown paper bag over her head gyrated along to the music's beat. Snakes wriggled up through holes in the top of the bag, and Zac realised she must be a Gorgon. He and Herya pushed on through the crowd until they reached the door and the man standing before it.

And he *was* a man, or close at least. He had exactly the right number of arms and legs and heads. Granted, he had one more mouth than was strictly necessary, but after everything he'd seen of late, Zac wasn't about to quibble over that.

The man wore a black bomber jacket and jeans that looked far too tight. His head was shaved and his arms were folded across his chest. He wasn't particularly big, but everything about him gave the impression that he was precisely big enough.

His two mouths sat one above the other. Both appeared perfectly normal, and if Zac just squinted a little, he was reassuringly human-looking.

"What do you want?" demanded the man's top mouth. His bottom one was chewing gum, like it was up against the clock.

"We... we want to see Argus," Herya said. The music was quieter away from the speakers, and she was able to talk at something like her normal volume.

The bouncer looked her up and down. His bottom mouth continued its frantic chewing. "Do you now?"

"Yes. So I'd advise you to let us through," the Valkyrie continued. She thought for a moment, then gave her knuckles a menacing crack.

"Would you now?" asked the bottom mouth, in a voice slightly higher than the first.

Herya hesitated. "Yes."

"Right," the man said, the top mouth taking control again. He stepped to the side. "Well, you'd best go through, then."

Another hesitation. "What?" Herya glanced at Zac, then rallied a little. "I mean, yes. Right." She reached for the door, but the bouncer was back in front of her, both mouths grinning.

"Nah, only joking." His expression turned serious. "No one sees Mr Argus."

"It's important," Zac said.

"Oh. Right. Is it?" asked the bottom mouth. The bouncer stepped aside once again. "Well, in that case maybe you *had* better go through, then."

"Yes, well... I should think so too," Herya said. She was midway through grabbing for the handle when the man blocked her again.

"Joking again," said the top mouth. "No one sees Mr Argus. I thought I'd made that clear?"

"You did," confirmed the bottom mouth.

"Thanks," replied the top.

"Look," said Herya firmly. "Get out of the way or I'll... I'll... kick your ass."

The bouncer laughed. "You know why I got these two mouths? It's so I can eat twice as quick." All four sets of teeth snapped the air just a few centimetres from Herya's nose. "Now fly away, little birdie, and take your mortal with you."

Zac caught the Valkyrie by the arm and pulled her away. She resisted, but only for a moment.

"What did you do that for?" Herya demanded. "I've fought bigger than him. I could've taken him."

"Well, maybe you could, but you don't have to," Zac told her. "There's another way through."

Herya reluctantly tore her gaze from the bouncer. "How?" she asked.

"The lock on the door. It's a five-pin deadbolt."

"And? What does that even mean?"

Zac reached into a pocket and pulled out a slim leather case. He unzipped it and showed Herya the tools wrapped within. "It means I can open it. I just need to get that guy out of the way."

"I could slice out his lungs," the Valkyrie said, "and, er, make him wear them as a hat."

Zac blinked. "Well, there's that, but I was thinking something a bit more subtle," he said. "Just cause a distraction. Get him to walk away. Thirty seconds, that's all I'll need. Do you think you can do that?"

Herya snorted. "Well, *yeah*. I cause distractions all the time."

"Do you?" frowned Zac. "Why?"

"What?"

"Why do you cause distractions all the time?"

Herya chewed her lip. "Practice," she said at last. "Now let me do my thing so you can do yours."

Zac nodded. "Fair enough." He took one of the tools from his bag. It looked like a thin screwdriver with a slightly hooked point.

Herya turned and slipped off through the crowds, cursing herself below her breath. *I cause distractions all the time*, she thought. *What in Thor's name did I say that for?*

Contrary to everything she'd said to Zac, she had never actually been in Hades before. The creatures dancing and gyrating around her were like images from her childhood nightmares, all twisted and misshapen and wrong.

As she sidled through the throngs, Herya felt her mouth go dry. Zac would be watching her, she knew, waiting on her making her move. But what move? She had no idea how she was going to lure the bouncer away. She had no idea about anything.

Maybe there was a fire alarm somewhere that she could activate. That might work. She changed course and set off in the direction of the nearest wall. With any luck, it would have a fire alarm button on it somewhere.

A flailing foot caught her on the back of the knee. She cried out in shock as she stumbled forward, before thudding into the back of someone standing by the edge of the dance floor.

There was a *crash* as the person she had collided with dropped their drink and the glass shattered into slivers on the dirty floor.

"Not again," Herya groaned. She looked up, past a washboard stomach and a bodybuilder's chest, and up to the bull-like head of a Minotaur. A hot swirl of steam snorted out from the creature's nostrils as his mouth pulled into a snarl.

"You spilled my pint," the Minotaur growled.

"Um, yeah," said Herya, her voice coming out as a squeak. She glanced over to the bouncer and took a shaky breath. "What you going to do about it?"

Even over the sound of the music, Zac heard the roaring of the Minotaur. There was a sudden commotion and a frantic scuffle as the creature swung its arms in a wide arc. Herya ducked out of the way. The Gorgon wasn't so lucky. The Minotaur's fists sent her sprawling to the floor, the brown paper bag slipping off as she fell.

There was a scream as several dancers who had been looking the Gorgon's way turned to stone.

"Sorry, everyone, sorry!" stammered the snake-headed Gorgon, but panic had already gripped the crowd. It surged away from the Gorgon, only to be battered back by the raging Minotaur.

Demons and monsters alike began to clash, and in seconds the club had become the scene of a full-scale riot.

Zac watched and found himself admiring the Valkyrie's work. The dancers who weren't yet fighting were now rushing to get involved. Revellers knocked one another over, then trampled across the fallen in their hurry to get stuck into someone. The club had been chaotic before Herya had done anything, but now it was a very specific type of chaos. One that was taking place well away from the guarded door.

"Oi! What's going on?" the bouncer's upper mouth demanded, as the bottom one bit down on another stick of gum. He pushed into the crowd, ducking something short and hairy and vaguely troll-like as it flailed by above his head. "Cut it out, the lot of you!"

Zac sidled along the wall to the now unprotected door. He didn't hear the faint sloppy *schlurp* the eyeball on the ceiling made, or see it slowly swivel to look at him as he knelt down beside the door handle.

After a quick glance over his shoulder to make sure the bouncer wasn't coming, Zac slid the pick into the waiting lock. Before he could find the first pin, the door opened with a faint *click*.

Zac gave it a cautious push. It swung inward, revealing a long dark corridor. A stale breeze breathed at him from deep within the darkness.

"Come, Zac Corgan," it said. "I have been expecting you."

CHAPTER TWENTY

NGELO STOOD OUTSIDE Eyedol with his back pushed firmly against it. The flickering neon glow of the sign washed the surrounding area in shades of red, but he'd discovered that if he pressed right up against the wall he could tuck himself up in a pocket of shadow, out of sight of the rest of the underworld.

His breathing was steady now and he was no longer sweating. He thought he could probably do with going to the toilet again, but it wasn't a pressing emergency quite yet.

He felt stupid. That was the worst part. He'd been scared by the sights and the sounds in the nightclub and he'd made a fool of himself in front of Zac and Herya. In front of his friends.

He thought about praying, but he didn't know if anyone would hear him from way down there in the underworld. Then again, with God gone, he'd never been really sure if anyone was even listening any more.

He prayed anyway.

"Hello, it's me, Angelo," he said into his pressed-together palms. "I'm in Hades, so this might be a bad line, but if you can hear me, please look after my friends. They're the only ones I've got. So, um, yeah. Love to everyone. Amen."

There was a sound of breaking glass from over by the front entrance. Someone big and heavy came crashing through the doors before they had a chance to swish all the way open. The monstrous figure landed heavily on its misshapen torso, dragged itself back up on to all four feet, then plunged once more into the club.

Angelo squashed himself further into the shadows as the sounds of battle rang out through the broken doors of Eyedol. He tried to think about Batman, lurking in the dark just like he was. Batman wouldn't be scared. Batman wasn't scared of anything.

But he wasn't Batman. And he was terrified.

"An. Gel. Lo."

His name came as a whisper, broken into three syllables by a voice that sounded parchment dry. Angelo froze exactly like Batman wouldn't.

"An. Gel. Lo."

The voice seemed to come from nowhere in particular. It was just there, loitering around his ears, up to no good.

"An. Gel. Lo."

"Um, h-hello?" he whimpered. "Who... who's there?"

"An. Gel. Lo. *An. Gel. Lo.*"

"Stop it. I'm w-warning you. I know karate."

There was a soft giggle from the darkness. "No, *An. Gel. Lo*," said the whispers. "You don't."

And with a rustle, the night snapped shut around him.

Zac stepped into the corridor and the door blew closed, cutting off what little light there had been. He heard the lock slide into place, and knew that there was no going back.

He took a moment to replace his lock-picking tools, before he went for another pocket and pulled out a short plastic tube about the size of a marker pen. It gave a *krik* as he bent it, and a weak green glow spread along the tube's length.

The walls on both sides of him blinked in the emerald light. Literally blinked. Hundreds of eyes, each the size of a marble, were embedded into the plaster. They stared at Zac, and Zac stared back. He brought the glow-stick closer to one wall and watched the pupils dilate in response.

"I can see you, Zac Corgan," said the voice from along the corridor. "Can you see me?"

The voice sounded like it was close to laughter. There was an accent to it too. Greek, probably, considering which underworld they'd ended up in.

Zac stepped away from the wall and peered along the corridor. The green light only extended a metre or two along it, leaving the rest behind a curtain of impenetrable black.

Watched from both sides by countless tiny eyes, Zac pushed on into the darkness until he came to a smooth metal door set into the back wall of the corridor. It opened with a *ding*, revealing a windowless metal box. There was a light mounted in the ceiling and a rectangular LCD display built into one of the walls.

"Going up," said the voice.

Zac took a look back along the corridor and found it still in darkness. He could hear the faint clicking sound of ten thousand blinking eyelids, and the distant din of fighting from beyond the door.

"Hurry, Zac Corgan. I do not have all day."

"All right, all right. Keep your hair on," Zac muttered, then he stepped into the elevator, turned round, and watched the doors slide closed. The number *666* flashed up in red on the display and the lift began to climb, slowly at first, but quickly picking up speed until Zac felt the G-force pressing down on him.

Just a minute or so later, he experienced a tiny moment of near-weightlessness as the lift came to an abrupt stop. He waited for the doors to open and, after what felt like a very long time, they did.

He stepped out of the lift and gazed around at the room he had arrived in.

It took up roughly the same amount of space as the dance floor downstairs had done, but it couldn't have looked more different. A luxurious red carpet covered the floor. Vast chandeliers hung from the high, domed ceiling, casting a twinkling glow across the antique furniture. Something classical and dreary was being played on a vintage gramophone over in the corner, and the thudding of the dance music downstairs felt like a dim and distant memory.

"Greetings, Zac Corgan. Welcome to the home of Argus."

"Where are you?" Zac asked. He looked over the room. "Show yourself."

"I am here, Zac Corgan," the voice said. Greek. It was definitely Greek. "I am behind you."

Zac spun round and saw the lift doors close. There were pillars on either side of the lift, each several times wider than he was. Something about them drew his eye, and it took him just a moment to realise that they weren't pillars at all. They were legs.

Slowly – ever so slowly – Zac looked up.

Angelo's heart was playing the bongos in his chest. His arms were pinned by his sides and he could now say with absolute certainty that he *definitely* needed the toilet.

He was wrapped in a tight cocoon, unable to move, barely able to breathe. He felt as if he were dangling from a great height, being buffeted back and forth on the breeze, and occasionally bumped against something solid and flat. He was absolutely correct in every one of these assumptions.

It was warm in the cocoon, and as panic tightened round Angelo like a noose, it began to get considerably warmer.

Zac didn't believe in giants. Or rather, he *hadn't* believed in giants, until now.

The giant sitting in front of him had changed his mind. He was perched on an enormous throne, into the base of which the elevator doors had been built. He sat forward in the chair, his metre-long fingers gripping the armrests, his shed-sized head lolling down almost to his chest.

The clothes he wore were musty and thick with dust, giving him the look of a long-neglected museum exhibit. His skin was blotchy and held together with stitches. They criss-crossed his face like a city-centre road map, and Zac would've sworn that the thing in the chair was long dead, had it not been for the eyes.

The eyes were open. And they were staring down at him.

"Hi," Zac said. "Almost didn't see you there."

"Hello, Zac Corgan," said that voice again. The giant on

the throne made no movement. "Will you bow before the all-seeing Argus?"

Zac gave the question all the consideration it deserved. "Doubt it," he said.

The voice suddenly brightened. "Good. I cannot stand a kiss-ass!" it cried, and Zac realised it was coming from elsewhere in the room.

He turned to find a man grinning at him from behind dark-tinted glasses. The man was a little shorter than Zac, but considerably wider. He was bare from the waist up, his bulging belly sagging down over a baggy pair of white shorts that were tied with red bows round his knees.

His head was bald, but partially covered by a small red fez that he wore at a jaunty angle. The centre of the man's chest was matted with thick black hair, and his top lip was weighed down by an equally thick, equally black moustache.

All these things registered just barely at the back of Zac's mind. The front of his mind, meanwhile, was fully occupied with just one thought: nipples.

Where the man's nipples should have been, there were eyes. Zac stared at them. He couldn't help himself. How could he not stare? After a moment, one of the nipples gave him a cheeky wink.

"*Yiassas!*" cried the man. He caught Zac by the upper arms, then leaned in and kissed him on both cheeks before he could pull away. The man smelled of death and olives. "I am Argus Panoptes. You have been looking for me, yes?"

Zac stepped back. "*You're* Argus?" He jabbed a thumb in the direction of the seated giant. "Then who's that?"

Argus laughed, making his bare belly jiggle like half-set jelly. "This? This is just a statue."

"It doesn't look like a statue."

"It is woven from the skin of my enemies' children," Argus said. He smiled again, and in that moment Zac was reminded that he was dealing with a demon. There were too many teeth in that mouth, all crammed in together, jostling for space. "Feel it, yes? Touch it."

"No, thanks."

"Please. Please, I insist," Argus said. "Touch my giant leg. It bring you luck."

"Right, well, if it'll make you happy," Zac sighed. He touched the nearest leg. The skin was disturbingly smooth.

Argus beamed. "Is nice, yes?"

"Not really my cup of tea," Zac said. "What about the eyes? I'm guessing they didn't come from your enemies' children. Unless, you know, your enemies' children are huge."

"Ah, no, no. The eyes, they belong to me."

With a quick flick of his wrist, Argus removed his sunglasses, revealing two dark holes. Zac gazed into the empty sockets, then up at the beach-ball-sized eyeballs in the statue's face.

"Those must've been a tight fit," he said.

Argus laughed again. "Haha! Yes. They are not my actual eyes, of course. Would you care to sit?"

"No, I'm fine."

"Please, I insist. Please."

"I'd prefer to stand," said Zac.

Argus's shoulders slumped, then a wry grin crept across his face. He placed his hands on his stomach and folded two rolls of flab together, giving the impression of a mouth.

"Pwease, Zac," Argus said, moving the rolls so it looked as if they were talking. "Pwease sit down on our lovely couch."

To their credit, even Argus's nipples got in on the act. They looked imploringly at Zac.

"Yeah… OK," Zac said. He pointed at Argus's belly. "If you promise to stop that."

Argus laughed again, then he jigged over to a cream leather sofa that stood off to one side of the room. Zac noticed his shoes for the first time. They were bright red with gold trim, curled up at the toes like a genie in a pantomime.

The shoes danced on to a leopard-skin rug that was spread on the floor between the couch and a roaring coal fire. The demon jabbed at the coals with a poker while he waited for Zac to sit.

"I know why you have come to see me, Zac," he said once Zac had positioned himself on the couch. "I have been following you closely for some time."

Zac raised an eyebrow. "You have, have you?"

"Please, please, do not take it personally," said Argus, giving the coals a final stab. "I follow everyone closely."

He set the poker back on its hook, then turned to face his guest. Zac wished the demon would put the glasses back on, but they were nowhere to be seen, and so he forced himself to stare into the hollow sockets and did his best not to flinch.

Argus slapped his belly several times. It jiggled hypnotically. "You are seeking the *Book of Everything* and you have come to ask for my help, yes?"

Zac didn't reply.

"You believe I can provide you with – how you say? – *information* as to its exact whereabouts."

"They've built a tenth circle on to Hell. I've been told you might know what's down there."

"I bet you have," Argus exclaimed. He gave a twirl, and Zac saw there was another eye poking out from the demon's hairy back. "I am the all-seeing Argus, after all."

Zac leaned forward slowly, making the leather couch creak. "So what *is* down there?"

Argus tapped the side of his nose. "Aha! All in good time, yes? Right now, I see we are about to have company."

With a wink of his nipples, Argus turned and gestured towards the elevator doors, just as they opened with a *ping*.

CHAPTER TWENTY-ONE

THERE WAS A momentary commotion within the elevator, and then Herya was bundled out. The bouncer shoved her forward, then stepped out after her.

"Here she is, Mr Argus. Like you asked," he said. "Gimme a shout if she gets out of hand."

With a brief nod to his employer, the bouncer stepped back into the lift. Herya glared after him as the doors slid closed.

"Yeah," said Herya. "That's right. You'd better run, if you know what's good for you."

She stood up and dusted herself down, then looked over to Zac and Argus. When she saw the demon, her eyes widened just a fraction.

"All right?" Zac asked.

"Yes," Herya said defensively. "Of course."

"Herya of the Valkyries," Argus said. He spoke her name grandly, as if announcing her arrival at a formal dinner party. "Such a beautiful girl, you no think, Zac? That hair. The wings." He adjusted his fez and smiled more broadly than ever. "Beautiful girl."

"Oh, yeah, I forgot you two know each other," said Zac.

Argus laughed as he skipped over to the Valkyrie. "Ah, but if only I had such good fortune," he said, planting kisses on both of her cheeks. "Today is the first day I have had the pleasure."

Zac looked to Herya. "But I thought you said...?"

"No, I didn't," she replied quickly.

"But you—?"

She gave him the same look Argus's nipples had given him just minutes before. "Leave it," she said, then she added, "please."

Zac gave an uncertain nod and leaned back into the couch. Argus took Herya by the elbow and steered her over to join him. "Please, sit. Little Angelo will be joining us..."

A squirming sack landed with a *thud* on the floor between them.

"...now."

An enormous man in a small loincloth thudded down on to the carpet from a large hatch in the ceiling. The man straightened up and groaned as his back went *click*.

"Ooh, that's better," he said. "I'm not as young as I used to be."

The man had one eye set in the centre of his forehead. It blinked slowly as it looked at Zac and Herya.

Zac stood up. "Who is this?" he demanded.

"Ah, do not worry, do not fret. This is my assistant, Steropes," said Argus. "Steropes is a Cyclops, yes? You see the irony? I have many eyes; Steropes has only one!"

Zac stared up Steropes. Aside from having just one eye, the Cyclops looked much like a man. A large, mean-looking man. With tattoos.

His hair was clipped short and a rough stubble covered his chin. He was stockily built, with a broad neck and bodybuilder arms. Although he wore no clothes aside from a worryingly small loincloth, his tattoos covered his skin like an all-over rash.

Despite his appearance, Steropes's voice was soft and quiet. "Afternoon," he said. He gave Zac a friendly nod, which the boy felt obliged to return.

"All right?" Zac asked.

"Yeah, not bad, not bad," replied the Cyclops. "Thanks for asking." As he spoke, he bent and tore open the sack, letting Angelo spill out on to the floor.

"Wh—?" Angelo spluttered, blinking frantically in the sudden light. He flailed around on his back for a moment, before scrambling to his feet. He screamed when he spotted Steropes – a high-pitched girly screech that made the glass in the chandeliers quiver.

"Whoa, easy, easy," soothed the Cyclops. "Sorry about the whispering and the bundling you up in the bag an' all that. Boss's orders. Hope you weren't too traumatised by it all."

Angelo screamed again in response.

"Angelo, Angelo, relax," Zac said. He stepped closer to the boy, then tried to pull back as Angelo threw his arms round him. Try as he might, though, he couldn't break the bearhug.

"Oh, it was horrible," Angelo gasped. "Just horrible!"

Zac could feel the boy's heart pounding inside his chest. He was uncomfortably warm to the touch, but he was still a few degrees away from being *hot*. "I thought I was never going to see you again," Angelo sobbed. "Can you imagine how horrible that would be?"

Zac hesitated. "Horrible. Yeah."

Angelo spotted the Valkyrie and yelped with delight. "Herya!" He detached himself from Zac and hurried over to her, his arms spread wide.

"Don't even think about it," she warned. Angelo faltered to a stop just a few steps away from her, but his smile didn't fade.

"You're alive. We're all alive!" He raised both hands triumphantly above his head. "Go, Superfriends!"

There was a moment of embarrassed silence. Angelo lowered his arms again.

"Nice, nice! Is very nice, yes? Happy reunion," said Argus. "Please, my apologies for the way you were all brought here. In my line of work I find direct approach is simplest. Besides, I have an image to maintain, yes?"

Zac looked at the belly, the curly shoes and the tiny fez. "I'm sure you do."

Angelo glanced nervously at Zac. "Is that... Is that him?"

"Argus the all-seeing," said Argus. He did another twirl. His flabby torso undulated like a lava lamp.

"Why do they call you that?" asked Angelo.

Herya answered for him. "Legend says he's got a hundred eyes."

Argus nodded. "Very good! It does say that, doesn't it? But legend, it is a fool. It knows nothing."

"You haven't got *any* eyes," said Angelo, who had no intention of looking at any part of Argus below the neck, thank you very much.

"Ah, not here, maybe," conceded the demon, tapping a manicured finger against his temple, "but everywhere else. Downstairs. Outside. All across Hades and all through the other Afterworlds."

"Nipples," blurted Herya. She was staring at them, apparently having just noticed them for the first time.

"Ah, yes!" Argus said. He puffed up his chest proudly. "You like?"

Herya faltered. "Not really."

Argus grabbed two rolls of flab and made the belly-face again. "Oh, that is not vewy nice," he said. Then he laughed, spun on the spot, and trotted over to an antique globe that stood just a little away from the fireplace. The lid flipped open and smoke billowed out from within.

Reaching inside the globe, Argus pulled out a foil-wrapped bundle. "Febab?" he offered. "My own creation. It is kebab meat and the Feta cheese, all wrapped together with chilli sauce." He gave his belly a rub. "Hot. Spicy. Very nice."

"I'm all right," said Zac. He glanced along the couch to the others. "I think... yeah, we're all OK for now, thanks."

Argus shrugged and dropped the foil bundle back into the concealed barbecue, before closing the lid. "Where was I?"

"You were telling us you see everything," Zac prompted. "All the Afterworlds."

"Aha! Not just the Afterworlds," Argus corrected. His empty eye sockets turned towards Zac. "Have you ever felt that tingle up your spine telling you 'Hey! What is this? I am not alone!'? Have you ever had the feeling that someone was watching you? Like when you were in your bedroom, let us say, just before the Monk killed you?"

Zac thought back. The rooftop along the street. He

thought he'd seen someone watching him just before he closed the curtains.

Argus saw the realisation spread across the boy's face. "Yes, yes. That was me. You see, no matter what legend says, I am not having a hundred eyes. No, no. I am having a hundred *billion* of them. Watching. Always watching everything and everyone."

Steropes leaned over him. "But not in a creepy way or that," he reassured.

"Oh no," said Argus. "Not in a creepy way." He slapped a drumbeat on his belly before speaking again. "This is how I knew you were coming. And I must say, your antics in Asgard made for most amusing viewing. And you," he said, fixing Angelo with an approving look, "you were the biggest treat of all."

"I was?"

"You are – how you say? – *remarkable*, do you know?"

Angelo grinned. "I am?"

"Enough small talk," interjected Zac, before the demon could give away what had happened in Asgard. "Can we get down to business?"

"Ah, yes, we must press on, I think," said Argus. "But

first, drinks. I have taken the liberty of preparing your favourites."

Steropes recognised his cue. He scuttled over to a bar at the back of the room, then returned carrying a tray. Two glasses sat on it, both resting atop little paper doilies.

"For you, Zac, lemonade, just the way your grandfather makes it. You like this, yes?"

"Ha!" laughed Herya. "Lemonade. You're such a child."

"And for you, Herya of the Valkyries, yak's milk, warmed to five degrees above room temperature."

It was Zac's turn to laugh. Herya blushed. "You've made a mistake," she told Argus. "I drink ale."

Argus frowned. "Oh. My apologies. I did not know this. I have watched you many, many times – almost every moment of your life – and I have not once seen you drink ale."

"Well, I do," she insisted. "Gallons of it."

Zac patted her on the arm. "You know, there are organisations who can help you with that. Admitting you have a problem – that's the first step."

"Funny guy," she said, and she flicked milk in his face.

"What about me?" asked Angelo. "I'm thirsty too."

"Ah, yes," nodded the demon. "We have a real treat in store for you, I think."

Steropes set down the yak's milk beside Herya, who made a point of ignoring it completely. He scurried over to the bar again. They all watched as he pulled a welder's mask over his head and slipped thick gauntlets over each hand.

"We cannot be too careful, yes?" Argus said. The Cyclops stalked slowly back towards them. He was holding a pair of metal tongs and using them to carry a small silver flask.

Zac turned to Angelo. "What do you drink? Plutonium?"

The flask was set carefully on the table beside Angelo. Steropes quickly backed away, visibly relaxing as he did.

"Holy water," Argus explained. "Lethal to demons. Your favourite, I believe, yes?"

Angelo's eyes lit up with excitement. "You're not wrong there." He unscrewed the lid of the flask and sniffed the contents.

"From eighteen seventy-eight. A very good year, I am told," Argus said. "Blessed by Pope Pius the Ninth himself, mere days before his death."

Angelo took a sip. He licked his lips, then smacked them together. "Yummy scrummy in my tummy," he said. He grinned at Zac, who rolled his eyes in response.

"You said you knew what was in the tenth circle of Hell," said Zac, steering the conversation back to more important matters.

Argus gave Steropes a nod as the Cyclops set a glass of dark red liquid down in front of him. "I did not say this. You said this."

Zac frowned. "What?"

"I do not know what is in the tenth circle of Hell."

"I thought you saw everything?" said Herya.

"I do," nodded Argus. "Or I did. I knew many moons ago that they were starting work on the new circle. I saw them cut the turf and lay the very foundations, watched them build it brick by brick."

"So what happened?"

"They did not build a door," Argus explained. "Or windows. They have it locked down tight, sealed so the eyes of Argus cannot see in. Whatever they are doing down there, they do not want anyone knowing about it."

"Wow," said Zac quietly. "That must really kill you."

Argus's head twitched, as if he were shaking off a fly. "Yes," he admitted. "It does. When you're used to seeing everything, having a blind spot is very... troubling. Which is why I have a proposal for you."

"What sort of proposal?"

"A – what is the word – a *collaboration* of sorts," Argus said. "If I help you get to Hell and tell you what I know of the tenth circle, can you find a way inside?"

"Yes," said Zac without hesitation.

Argus nodded. "Then I propose just that. I arrange for you to be transported to Hell, and give you some tools that may be of use. The rest is up to you. Once inside, you may retrieve your book and do with it as you will. It is of no interest to me."

"And what's in it for you?" asked Zac.

"Knowledge," Argus shrugged. "This is all. I would ask that you leave an eye or two of mine behind when you make your escape. This is not too much to ask, I think?"

Zac looked to his companions. Angelo shrugged. Herya glanced away.

"OK. We can do that."

"I am very glad to hear it," Argus replied. He held his

arms out to the side, dropped to one knee, then bounced back up again. "We celebrate with dance, yes?"

Angelo stood up. "Conga, conga, cong-a!"

Zac shot him a withering glare, and Angelo reluctantly sat back down again.

"We'll probably just shoot off," Zac said. "If it's all the same to you."

"Very well. But you should know, Zac," said Argus, "about Haures."

"The Duke of Hell guy? What about him?"

"He knows you are coming. He *wants* you to come."

Zac paused while this new information sank in. "Why?"

"That I do not know," Argus admitted. "But Haures is a monster."

"Says the man with the child-skin statue."

"Haha. There are different types of monster, Zac, some worse than others. Whatever Haures wants you for, I cannot imagine it is anything good."

"Right," said Zac. "I'll keep my eyes open."

"As will I," said the demon. Argus slapped himself on the belly. It made a sound like the cracking of a whip, and every part of him from his neck to his waistband rippled.

"Are you ready, Zac Corgan?" he asked. "Are you ready to mount your assault on the domain of Satan himself?"

Zac stood and looked the demon squarely in the nipples. "Yeah," he said with a shrug. "Why the Hell not?"

CHAPTER TWENTY-TWO

"GABRIEL, THERE YOU are. Have you brought news?"

"Not much, sir, I'm afraid."

"Has he got the book yet?"

"Alas, no, sir. Not yet. The operation is ongoing."

"Hang it all. What's taking them so long?"

"The methods they are employing are... unexpected, sir."

"Oh? How so?"

"They went to Asgard, for starters. Entered the Hall of Valhalla and had something of a falling-out with Odin. Young Angelo got... upset."

"How upset?"

"*Very* upset, sir. If you know what I mean?"

"Of course I do! I wasn't created yesterday. Has he calmed down yet?"

"Mercifully, yes."

"Well, that's something, although I don't see why you had to send the boy in the first place."

"He volunteered, sir."

"Yes. So I'm led to believe. Where are they now?"

"Hades, sir."

"Hades?"

"Yes, sir. Hades."

"Why are they in blasted Hades? What's in Hades?"

"Argus, sir. We believe they've asked for his assistance."

"Hrmph."

"We thought that was rather resourceful, sir."

"Hrmph."

"Rest assured, everything is continuing as planned, despite their unorthodox strategy."

"Really? You're not just saying that to make me feel better?"

"Oh, no, sir. Everything is unfolding as we anticipated. They'll be inside Hell within the hour. Whether they'll make it back out, of course... Well, that remains to be seen."

CHAPTER TWENTY-THREE

Z
AC AND ARGUS stood by a wide window, looking down through gaps in the cloud. The ground was a dizzyingly long way away, and it was impossible to make out many details. Even the River Styx was little more than a squiggly black pencil line on a vast black page.

"And that's it?" said Zac, when Argus had finished telling him how to get to Hell. "That's all there is to it?"

"This is all there is," Argus said. "This is all you need to do. It is only a few miles downriver."

"It seems too easy."

The hollows of Argus's eye sockets widened in surprise. "You would prefer difficult?"

Zac scratched his chin. "No, of course not." He shook his head. "It's just... nothing's ever that easy."

Argus clapped Zac on the back. "You worry too much, Zac Corgan," he laughed. "What you must remember is that no one has tried breaking into Hell before. No one has ever been so – what is the word?"

"Insane?" suggested Herya, who was standing by the child-skin statue, looking up at it.

"*Foolish*," said Argus. "Only a fool would try to break into Hell, so they do not worry too much about building defences, I think."

"Oh, well, thanks for that," Zac said. He had to admit, though, it did make sense. Only a fool *would* try to break into Hell.

"Steropes will take you to the Styx. I have a boat there you can borrow. Borrow, yes? I would like it back. It is not too big, but it can float very good. All you must do is follow the Styx and soon you will find the Hell you are looking for."

"That's all, eh?" Zac mumbled. He turned from the window to look for Angelo and found the boy standing right behind him. Angelo smiled eagerly. "You sure you still want to come?" Zac asked.

"I Scooby-dooby-*do*!" Angelo yelled. He caught Zac's expression. "That was a yes, by the way."

Zac nodded. "Fine." He looked over to Herya. "You ready?" he called to her. "We're leaving."

"*You're* leaving," said the Valkyrie.

"What?"

"I never said I was coming with you. I said I'd take you to Argus." She pointed to the bare-chested demon. "There's Argus. Job done. You're on your own from here on in."

"But I thought—"

"Well, you thought wrong."

Zac glanced at the others, then back to Herya. He strode over to her. "Can I talk to you in private for a minute?" he asked, ushering her towards the far corner of the room.

"There's nothing to talk about," she said. "I'm not coming. I never said I was."

"Maybe not," Zac admitted, "but you never said you weren't, either. I thought you were into this stuff – adventure and excitement and all that."

Herya folded her arms. "Yeah, well I thought you didn't want me coming along. You work better alone, you said."

"I did. I do," said Zac. "But, well, you've got experience of these places. You're our expert. You know your way around. You said so yourself."

"Ooh, liar, liar pants on fire!" called Argus from across the room. He slapped himself on the hand. "Sorry. I lip-read. It is a terrible habit."

"She wasn't lying. She does know her way around. She led us here."

"Oh, really?" said Argus. "You ask her yourself."

Zac turned back to the Valkyrie. "You do. Don't you?"

Herya sighed softly. She shook her head. "He's right. I don't know anything."

"What? Yes, you do. You knew about the Nether Lands, about Hades and Eyedol. You'd been to them all before, you—"

"I haven't been anywhere."

Zac blinked. "What? But..."

"I haven't been anywhere, OK?" The Valkyrie looked down at the floor. "I've never even left Asgard before today. I've barely set foot outside Valhalla."

"But... all those things you knew."

"People talk," she said. She shrugged, sending a stab of pain through her injured wing. "Especially when they're drunk. They talk. I listen. I hear them going on about all these... these amazing places, and they sound so exotic and exciting and... I never thought I'd get to see any of them. So I just listened. And I've been listening for a long time."

Angelo appeared at Zac's back. "That's OK," he said cheerfully. "We don't have a clue where we're going, either. She can still come, can't she?"

Zac searched Herya's face. "She doesn't want to," he said at last. "Do you?"

Herya met his gaze just briefly. She shook her head. "Guess I'm not as tough as I say I am. I've never even been in a real fight before. Some warrior, huh?"

Zac didn't quite know what to say. "What will you do?" he asked.

"Go back to Asgard," Herya said. "Face my punishment. Hope they take me back."

"We could still use you," Zac told her. "You knew about these places. It doesn't matter *how* you knew. You knew about them. We could use your help getting the book back." Zac glanced back at the others and lowered his voice. "*I* could use your help."

Herya drew in a shaky breath. "I'm scared," she admitted, and her voice cracked with the weight of the word. "I don't want to go to Hell. I don't want to die. Not for the sake of some book."

"It's not just *some book*."

She smiled sadly. "It is to me."

"But... the team," whimpered Angelo. "You can't break up the team!"

Zac leaned back and folded his arms. "Forget it, Angelo. She's made her mind up."

"But... but, *the team*!"

"There is no team," Zac snapped, suddenly angry. Angelo took a startled step back. "Don't you get it? There's me doing the work and then there's you tagging along and getting in the way."

He saw the wounded look on Angelo's face and felt that pang of guilt in his chest again. It wasn't the boy's fault, but there was no denying the facts. "I'm the one they picked to get the book back. I don't need anyone's help."

"You do need this, though," said Argus, holding up a small black rucksack and grinning like some demented clown. "It may be of assistance. Usually it is not possible to bring things with you in or out of Hell, but anything inside this bag will make it through. I have placed some eyes in there. Once you are inside, you know what to do, yes?"

"I know what to do," said Zac, swinging a strap of the bag over his shoulder.

"Are you sure I cannot tempt you with some weapons?" the demon asked. "A flaming sword or two, maybe?"

"They'll just get in the way," Zac said. "The plan is to sneak in and out. If we get caught, then it's game over. Swords won't help."

"You are wise beyond your years," Argus acknowledged. He lifted his tiny fez in salute, then replaced it on his head. "And you are right, of course. But perhaps you will take this, at least?"

He passed over a leather case about the size of a small laptop computer. A slim buckle held it closed. Zac unclipped it and the case fell open.

"A gun?"

"A tranquilliser pistol," Argus said. "The darts, they are tipped with a unique blend of draughts and potions. They will send a manticore to sleep for a week, and they will do the same for any demons you meet."

Zac took the pistol from the case and tossed it from hand to hand, assessing the weight. "How many darts are in it?"

"Eight," Argus said. "This is all I have. The materials required for the poison are not easy to come by."

Zac tucked the gun into a fold inside his jacket. "Right," he said. "And, well... thanks."

"Do not thank me, Zac Corgan," Argus said. "It is you who are doing me the favour, yes? Deliver my eyes. Find your book."

"I will."

"Well, *yiassas*," Argus said, then he leaned in and pecked Zac on both cheeks. "*Yiassas*, Angelo," he continued, moving to kiss him too.

"Ugh, get off!" Angelo yelped, ducking for cover behind Zac. "I'm not kissing a demon!"

Argus looked puzzled. "What? But you are—"

"Leaving," said Zac hurriedly. "He's leaving. We both are. Right now."

Herya was suddenly standing beside them. Zac turned to her.

"Changed your mind?"

"No," the Valkyrie replied. "I was just going to wish you luck."

"I don't believe in luck," Zac told her. "Come on, Angelo. We're going."

He turned and made for the lift. Angelo hung back. He started to close in on Herya for a hug, then thought better of it and just waved instead. "Bye, then," he said, then he scampered after Zac and ducked into the elevator just as the doors swept closed.

"Bye," whispered Herya, watching the lights above the lift door begin counting down.

"Do not feel bad, Herya of the Valkyries," Argus said. "Not everyone can be the fearless hero."

He turned and flashed her his toothiest of grins. "Now, are you going to leave quietly?" he asked. His hands went to his belly and he formed the folds into the shape of a mouth once more. The flab-roll lips wobbled up and down as he made them speak: "Or must we have you killed?"

Zac and Angelo stood at a ramshackle wooden jetty on the banks of the River Styx. The black water burbled and boiled, bobbing a small motorboat up and down on its surface.

Above them, the clouds were a ceiling of grey, and in all directions the monochrome landscape was empty and sparse.

"Turned out nice again," said Steropes cheerfully. He was crouching down on the jetty, pulling the boat in with one massive hand.

Angelo shuddered. "This is nice?"

"Well, it isn't raining acid, and we haven't got the old toxic fog hanging about, so, yeah, I'd call that a right result." Steropes hauled the boat up to the edge of the small pier and held it steady. "There you go. In you hop."

Zac jumped down into the boat, then watched as Angelo fumbled around on the jetty's edge.

"Come on, hurry up!" Zac urged.

"I'm coming, give me a minute," Angelo replied. He sat on the pier's edge, then twisted on to his front. His legs dangled just a few centimetres above the boat, his toes stretching and kicking as they tried to find purchase.

"You're there, just jump."

"Stop rushing me!"

"Stop being so hard on your friend – he's doing his best," Steropes suggested.

"He's not my friend, he's my colleague," Zac said.

Angelo's arms had been wobbling with the effort of holding him up. They gave out then and he fell, screaming, into the boat. It rocked violently from side to side for a moment, before Steropes managed to steady it again.

"There we go," the Cyclops said. "That's you in." He pointed downriver in the direction of the flow. "You want to go that way. There should be plenty of fuel, but if you see anything moving in the water, you'll be best cutting the engines for a while."

Zac's head snapped up. "Anything moving? What do you mean? What's going to be moving?"

"Who knows?" said Steropes. "The river runs through some nasty places. There are bound to be a few things swimming around down there."

"Great," Zac tutted. "It would've been nice if Argus had mentioned that when we were planning this whole thing."

Steropes shrugged. "It would, but then he's a demon. He's not supposed to be nice."

"You're quite nice, though," Angelo said. Steropes's face lit up.

"Well, *thank* you, Angelo," he said. "I really appreciate that. And sorry again about putting you in a bag. It was nothing personal, honest."

"It's fine," Angelo said. "I quite enjoyed it. Not at the time, but looking back, I mean."

"All this male bonding's great and everything, but we really should get going," Zac said.

Steropes frowned. "What?"

"I said the male bonding – it's nice, but we need to move."

"*Male* bonding?" said Steropes. His eyebrows rose and his voice took on a higher pitch. "What are you saying?"

"What do you mean, *what am I saying*?"

"I'm not male!"

"You're... You're not?"

"No!" Steropes yelped. "I thought that would've been obvious!"

Zac stared at the Cyclops's stubble and bare, muscular chest. A shudder travelled the length of his spine. "My mistake," he said.

Steropes released her grip on the boat. "Right," she said, suddenly sounding much less friendly than she had just a moment ago. "Well... off you go, then."

Angelo unfolded himself and slid on to a wooden bench at the front of the boat, just as it began to drift down the river. "Bye, Steropes," he called, waving enthusiastically. The firing-up of the boat's motor cut off the Cyclops's reply.

"You know," Angelo said, "I'm going to miss him."

"Her," Zac corrected.

"Her. Right." The same shudder ran down Angelo's back. "I forgot."

"I wish I could," Zac muttered, then he steered the boat towards the centre of the river and *chug-chug-chugged* off in the direction of Hell.

CHAPTER TWENTY-FOUR

THE RIVER STYX was one of those things that cropped up in all sorts of different religions and legends. It was first mentioned in Greek mythology, where the ferryman Charon would transport the dead to the underworld on his boat, provided they'd remembered to bring the correct change, and weren't too concerned about the lack of toilet facilities.

Later, the river appeared in Christian tales. According to these stories, sinners would be drowned in its murky waters prior to being sent into Hell itself, like a small starter portion of suffering before the main course of eternal damnation.

And on and on the waters flowed, through other tales of other underworlds from countless other faiths.

Although *flowed* probably wasn't the right way to describe

the river's movement. It oozed like treacle through the desolate landscape. The water – for want of a better word – clung to the sides of the boat, making progress slow and steering sluggish. Zac watched the surface closely, but the constant bubbling made it difficult to detect any movement beneath the waves.

"Hey, look, people."

Zac looked in the direction Angelo was pointing and saw a crowd lining the shore. They stood like zombies, their mouths hanging open, their arms drooping limply by their sides. They gazed at the boat and through it as it crawled along.

"Coo-ee!" yelled Angelo, giving the figures on the shore a wave. They didn't wave back, just watched with mournful eyes and groaned with mournful mouths until they were swallowed by the gloom.

"Well, they weren't very friendly, were they?" Angelo said as the boat continued down the river.

Zac grunted. "Can't imagine why."

"It's all right, this, isn't it?" said Angelo.

There was a moment of stunned disbelief from Zac. "Well, I've had better days."

"Yeah, but right now. It's all right. Just hanging out on

a boat. I've never been on a boat before." Angelo reached for the rudder. "Can I drive?"

"No, you can't. Sit down," Zac told him.

Angelo deflated with a sigh, then slumped back on to the bench. "I wish Herya was here," he said. "I liked her. Did you like her?"

Zac stayed tight-lipped and focused on the river ahead.

"I liked her," said Angelo again. "I know she wasn't a proper angel, but she was nicer than a lot of the ones I know." His face went pale. "I shouldn't say that, should I? I could get into trouble."

"We're already going to Hell," Zac said. "What's the worst that could happen?"

They chugged along for a few metres until Zac finally added, "And yes, she was OK."

"Do you think we'll see her again?"

"I don't know if we'll see anyone again," Zac said.

Angelo considered this. "That would be a shame. For you, I mean. People would miss you. I don't know if anyone would miss me. Not even my mum."

He didn't say it like he was looking for sympathy – just like it was a matter of fact.

"What about your dad?" asked Zac, trying to be as tactful as possible. "Have you ever met him?"

Angelo shook his head. "He'll be well dead by now. Humans don't live very long. Um... no offence."

"Right, right... humans," Zac said. "But don't you know anything about him? Anything at all?"

There was a pause before Angelo replied. "No one's told me anything about him, but sometimes... Sometimes it's like I can feel him. Like I can sort of sense him somehow, and it's like I *do* know him then, and he's... nice. And I can imagine him sitting with me, down at the end of my bed, reading comics to me while I fall asleep."

He coughed softly, then blushed. "Pretty stupid, huh?"

"Well... who knows?" said Zac, noncommittal.

Angelo took a deep breath, then blew it all out in one go. He turned away so he could wipe his eyes on the cardigan sleeves. Zac pretended not to notice.

"Do you think we'll find the book?" asked Angelo, changing the subject.

"I think we're supposed to," Zac said. "I have a feeling finding it isn't going to be a problem. Argus said Haures wants us to come."

"Why would he want that?"

"I don't know, but all I can think is that it sounds like a trap."

"So... why are you doing it?" Angelo asked.

"Because it might not be. And because I don't have any choice."

"I suppose. You can't save the world without making some sacrifices," Angelo said. "You know where I learned that?"

"Jesus?" Zac guessed.

"Well, I was going to say *Superman II*, actually, but Jesus as well, I suppose."

Zac laughed. This made Angelo smile. "Look, sorry if I've been hard on you," Zac said hesitantly. "I'm not really a people person."

"I hadn't noticed," Angelo said. "So are we friends now?"

"Let's just do what we're here to do," Zac said. "And we'll see what happens."

"So that's like *a date* to become friends," Angelo beamed. "That's like us making a plan to become friends once we've saved the world. *Best* friends, probably."

"Well, we'll see. I'm not really worried about the world. I'm worried about my granddad."

"Gabriel said he'd look after him."

"Yeah. That's what I'm worried about."

"What about your mum and dad?" Angelo asked. "What happened to them?"

Zac gave a disinterested shrug. "They left. Dumped me with my granddad when I was a few months old and went travelling. Never wanted kids, apparently. Left us alone in a dirty little flat with no money and no income. Haven't heard from them since."

Angelo shook his head sadly. "Parents, eh? Yours sound even worse than mine."

Zac paused. "Well, that's probably open to debate."

"Did you want to get back at them?" pressed Angelo. "Is that why you started stealing?"

"No. I started stealing so my granddad and I could eat. And so we could get out of that flat before the damp killed us both."

Angelo nodded. "Right," he said slowly. "It's probably still wrong, though."

"Yeah," admitted Zac. "Probably."

They carried on in silence, each lost in their own thoughts. Other figures stood dotted along the shores. Angelo waved to the first few, but when none of them waved back he stopped. Eventually he avoided even looking their way as the boat crept on through the sludgy, slow-moving Styx.

A cold wind whispered across the surface of the water, forcing Angelo to pull his borrowed cardigan tighter around him.

"Bit chilly, isn't it?" he chittered.

"Ssh."

"What? Why? What's the—?"

Zac put his finger to his lips and glared. Angelo silenced himself by clamping his hand over his mouth and the two of them sat quietly, listening for whatever Zac had heard to come again.

Eventually, Angelo moved his hand away. He was about to speak when—

DONK.

They both looked down at their feet. The sound had been faint, but it had been unmistakable. Something had bumped against the underside of the boat.

Zac cut the engine and it coughed to a stop. The boat slowed, but the oozing flow of the Styx carried it onwards. In the near silence that followed, the only sounds were the lapping of the gloopy waves against the boat's wooden hull, and the distant groaning of the people on the shore.

"What was it?" Angelo whispered as quietly as he could.

Zac shrugged and pressed his finger to his lips again. The sound may have been nothing. The boat could've bumped against a rocky outcrop beneath the water, or a particularly lumpy wave might've made the knocking sounds. But he wasn't taking any chances.

"What do we do?" Angelo mouthed.

Zac looked across to the banks of the river. On one side was a throng of ghostly figures, all gawping eyes and gaping mouths. On the other a vast tangle of tall trees all but blocked the way.

"Nothing," said Zac softly. "Let's just wait and see what happens."

Angelo nodded. "OK."

The boat kept moving along the river, the wood creaking and groaning as the currents pulled it on.

"Can you swim?" Zac asked.

"What? Why are you asking that?" said Angelo, his eyes widening a little in panic.

"Just in case."

"In case what?"

"In case we have to swim to shore."

"Swim? In that?" Angelo whimpered. "Are you crazy? We can't swim in that. *Aquaman* couldn't swim in that! Look at the way it's bubbling. It's too hot for a start!"

"Quiet," Zac hissed. "Calm down. It's not hot, it just looks like it is. I felt it earlier. And no, I don't want to swim in it, either, and hopefully we won't have to. I was only asking if you could swim *just in case* something happened."

"Like what?" asked Angelo.

There was a *thud* from below and the boat lurched wildly from side to side. A few metres ahead of them something frothed the surface of the water, then sank quickly out of sight.

"Like that," Zac whispered.

Angelo's face was the colour of snow. His hands were gripping the bench he sat on, his fingernails digging grooves into the old wood. "What was it?" he whimpered. "*What was that?*"

"How should I know? Just stay quiet. Shut up and let me think."

"Maybe we should pray."

"I am *not* going to pray, so get that idea out of your head right now," Zac growled. "Just... just shut up for a minute."

There was a low drone from under the water, like the blasting of a foghorn, or the mournful cry of a wounded whale. Something splashed behind the boat. Zac turned, but all that remained was an expanding ring of ripples on the water's surface.

"I'm going to start the engine again," he said softly.

"What? Why? If you do that, it'll know we're here."

"It already knows we're here."

Zac took hold of the motor's ripcord and braced his foot against the wooden bench. He yanked hard on the cable. The motor growled once, then fell silent. Zac pulled again. There was another growl, another splutter, then more silence.

A few metres off the boat's port side, the surface of the Styx began to froth. Cursing below his breath, Zac tore at the cable, yanking it sharply again and again, trying to force the engine into life.

"Come on," he hissed, pulling the cord again. "*Come on!*"

Over the sputtering of the misfiring motor he heard Angelo draw in a breath. His eyes went to where the water had been foaming, even as his arm pulled back once more.

The water was no longer frothing. Something that might have been a tentacle and might have been a neck coiled above the surface of the Styx. At its tip, claws or teeth snapped together as it snaked slowly towards the boat.

"*Now* should we pray?"

"No!" Zac bellowed as the squirming shape drew closer. He tightened his grip on the ripcord handle and pulled. "I am *not* going to—"

With a roar, the motor came to life. There was another groan from the thing down below as the boat shot forward, spraying gloopy black liquid in its wake.

"Hallelujah!" cried Angelo, clapping his hands with relief.

A spout of water erupted right ahead of them, forcing Zac to lean hard on the rudder. Angelo grabbed the bench and clung on tightly as the boat leaned left.

"I'm going to fall in!" he wailed.

"No, you're not," Zac hissed. Another tentacle or neck or whatever the Hell it was stabbed up through the froth, forcing Zac to put more weight behind the rudder.

"I am!"

"You're not!" insisted Zac. "Trust me, you are *not* going to fall in."

Angelo fell in.

A moment later, so did Zac, as a third appendage struck the boat from beneath, flipping it over.

The water wasn't hot, but it wasn't too cold, either. It didn't take Zac's breath away. It didn't make his limbs cramp up. It just clung to him like runny tar, thick and gloopy and dragging him down.

The mournful thing beneath them groaned once again. Zac felt the sound more than heard it as the sludgy Styx vibrated all around him. Angelo flapped and flailed his arms, and took deep, unsteady breaths as he fought to keep his head above the surface.

"You didn't answer me," Zac said, dragging himself closer to the boy. "Can you swim?"

Angelo shook his head. "Don't know. Never tried," he gasped, and then the ink-black liquid flowed over his face and he sank beneath the Styx with a soft, gloopy *schlop*.

CHAPTER TWENTY-FIVE

Z AC FILLED HIS lungs and ducked down under the waves. The liquid stung his eyes, forcing them shut. He reached out, grabbing at empty space as he tried to catch the sinking boy.

Deeper down, the creature gave another low moan. The pressure of the water seemed to increase. It poked at Zac's eardrums and pressed down on his head. He felt his lungs shrivel up and it was all he could do to reach the surface before his mouth forced itself open.

The waters of the Styx oozed lazily down his face and tangled his hair. His eyelids were stuck closed, and it was only a splashing in the water that warned him something was behind him.

He had no chance to take a breath this time. He tucked

himself up and pulled himself down under the water just as something stabbed at him. He heard the impact on the surface, felt something sharp tearing at his leg, but then he was off and swimming in what he hoped was the direction of the shore.

The sound of his crashing heart thundered around inside his head. He thought of Angelo, down there somewhere in the dark. But it was too late to help him now. Only survival mattered, and survival meant getting to shore.

As he broke the surface, a current caught him, whipping him downriver. Scooping away the worst of the watery goo, he managed to open his eyes. The roaring was still there in his ears as he watched four slinking tentacles snake across the water towards him.

"Angelo!" he shouted, although he knew it was pointless. "Angelo, where are you?"

He thrashed against the current, trying to turn and scramble for the shore, which was now just five or six metres away. That was the moment he realised the roaring sound wasn't in his head at all.

It was coming from downriver.

It was coming, he realised, from the waterfall.

Zac swore loudly. A waterfall. Argus hadn't mentioned a waterfall, and yet there a waterfall was. Zac could see the black gloop foaming and frothing as it flowed over the edge of what sounded like a very long drop.

Kicking wildly, he struck out for the shore. The sludge and the currents pulled him down like quicksand. The more he thrashed the faster he sank, and so he focused on every movement, concentrated on his technique, ignored the panic that threatened to overwhelm him.

And all the while the things that may have been necks kept coming closer.

Dark grey rocks jutted up from the water around the shore. They broke the flow, making it erratic and difficult to swim through. Still kicking, Zac grabbed for the closest rock. His fingers brushed by it as the current dragged him closer to the waterfall's edge. The sound was all he could hear now, the dark misty spray almost all he could see.

The creature in the water droned again. It was closer this time, close enough to vibrate his whole skeleton and make his teeth ache. Something brushed against his leg from below and he found the strength to grab for another jagged rock. This time he was able to hold on, and with a final, desperate kick, he dragged himself up on to the shore.

Winded and exhausted, he crawled across a ground of polished black until his arms gave way beneath him. His brain screamed at him to move further from the water. His body said it would take the suggestion on board, but warned the brain not to get its hopes up.

And Zac just lay there, breathing in the ground and listening to the fury of the falling water.

Then, despite his body's better judgement, Zac stood up. He looked back at the River Styx. Whatever had been trying to come out, had gone back in. Either that, or it had been swept over the falls. Whatever, it didn't seem to be after him any longer.

The boat bobbed on by, upside down and spinning lazily as the currents caught it and pulled it towards the edge. Zac watched it go past, heard it bump against the rocks, and then it tipped over the waterfall and was gone.

Zac kept staring at the falls, long after the boat had vanished. "Told him he shouldn't have come," he whispered, and he put the crack in his voice down to the fact that his body was still shaking with shock.

Cautiously, he approached the boulders over by the waterfall and peered down over the edge. A rainbow of blacks and greys arced out across the thundering torrent as it tumbled several hundred metres down a sheer cliff face to more rocks below.

Argus and Steropes must have known about the falls. They *must* have. And yet they hadn't said anything. Zac didn't think Argus had been sending them to their doom. What would have been the point? If he'd wanted to destroy them, he could've done it in person, without sacrificing his boat or the dart gun he'd handed over as they'd said goodbye.

So either they *didn't* know about the waterfall, which was unlikely given that Argus was apparently *the all-seeing*, or – Zac turned away from the falls and gazed across the landscape beside it – they'd travelled too far.

A path of polished onyx led from the shore towards a towering set of wooden doors. A signpost stood just off the path, its metal surface pitted with rust and stained with spots of dried blood.

Words were written on the sign in jagged black print. Zac wiped the last of the gunge from his eyes and read the text:

WELCOME TO HELL

And below that, in smaller writing:

TRESPASSERS WILL BE INCINERATED

Zac stared at the sign. He was staring so intently at it that he almost cried out in shock when something large and lumpy splattered against it at tremendous speed. Despite the force of the impact, the sign remained undamaged and intact, which was a lot more than could be said for the thing that had hit it.

The flabby body burst like a bag full of warm custard, spraying yellowish-green gunge in all directions. Attached to the body were eight or nine long appendages, which may have been tentacles and may have been necks. Whatever they were, they all stopped moving as everything that had been inside the beast exploded out through the nearest available exit.

From the shore behind him, Zac heard the hiss of rapidly evaporating water. An enormous figure with scaly red skin and lethal-looking horns and Hellfire burning where his eyes should have been, emerged from the River Styx.

Zac didn't know whether to be relieved or terrified. His mind was made up for him when the Angelo-demon began bounding in his direction, black smoke snorting from his nostrils, his face all knotted up with rage.

The demon's footsteps shook the smooth ground. *Badoom. Badoom. Badoom.* Zac fumbled inside his jacket and found the gun Argus had given him. He raised it smoothly and squeezed the trigger.

Nothing happened.

Zac stared into the barrel of the pistol. Scum from the Styx clogged up the hole, making firing the gun impossible.

Angelo howled and kicked out with both legs, propelling himself in Zac's direction. Leaping into a sideways roll, Zac barely avoided the demon's fists as they came smashing down, cracking the polished rock where he'd stood.

Scrambling backwards, Zac put his mouth over the end of the gun and sucked out the plug of congealed gunge. He lifted the weapon again and fired. There was a *thwip* as a dart cut through the air, then a faint *boing* as it embedded deep into the demon's neck.

Another leap. Another dodge. Another *crack* as Angelo missed with another punch. Two more darts buried themselves in his scaly hide and he roared with frustration more than pain.

The air around him was a ripple of heat. He lowered his horns and charged like a bull, his feet booming thunder across the obsidian ground. Zac opened fire as he retreated. A fourth dart hit the demon, then a fifth.

Before he could fire a sixth, Zac tripped on a jagged outcrop and hit the ground hard. His chin smashed against the smooth rock. A jolt of pain buzzed through his skull.

The last thing Zac saw before he passed out was the hulking shape of the Angelo-demon crashing headlong towards him.

CHAPTER TWENTY-SIX

Zac was awoken by a finger. It was poking him repeatedly in the face and was, he quickly decided, really rather annoying.

"Cut it out," he said, snapping open his eyes. Angelo was kneeling beside him, his index finger hovering just millimetres away from completing another prod.

"You're awake!"

"Well, I am now, yes," Zac said. He quickly stood up and looked around. The river was still churning over the edge of the falls, the tall wooden doors were still closed and the gun was still in his hand.

The smell, though, was different. It was the stink of fish rotting in an open sewer. It flooded his nostrils and snagged in gulps at the back of his throat. He put his arm across his mouth and nose as his eyes began to water and his saliva turned sour.

"That's disgusting," he coughed.

Angelo nodded. He was topless again, but thankfully his trousers continued to stay in one piece. "Yeah, it's that thing over there," he said, pointing at the soggy remains of the river monster, which were spread out across twenty or thirty metres. "I think it might be dead."

"You think so?"

"I'm not sure," Angelo said, missing the sarcasm. "Should we, I don't know, check for a pulse or something?"

Zac bit his tongue. "No," he said, his voice deliberate and controlled. "It's definitely dead."

"Right," Angelo nodded. "So how did that happen, then? In fact, how did I get out? The last thing I remember is sinking, and then I woke up over there." His face lit up with excitement. "You saved me! Didn't you? See, I told you we make a great team!"

"How would me saving you make us a great team?" asked Zac. "Anyway, you got yourself out."

Angelo frowned. "Oh. Did I? I don't remember that. Are you sure?"

Zac took off the backpack and slipped the gun inside. "Pretty sure."

"Well... OK," said Angelo, shrugging his bare shoulders. He stepped past Zac and studied the signpost. Some of the letters were hidden beneath monster remains, so the sign now read:

COME TO HE

"It says *Welcome to Hell*," Zac explained. "You know, under the gunge and monster bits."

He stared hard at the wooden doors, as if trying to see through them to whatever lay beyond. "You sure you want to do this?"

Angelo still didn't hesitate. Despite everything that had happened to him, he still didn't hesitate. Even Zac had to admire that. "Yep."

"It'll be safer out here."

The angel-demon glanced back at the Styx and shivered. "I'm not sure it would be."

"Well, clearly it would," Zac insisted. "Being outside Hell would be safer than being inside Hell."

"Yes, but would it?"

"Yes."

"Ah," said Angelo. "But *would* it?"

"Yes, it would! Obviously. I mean, think about it."

"That's as may be," Angelo said, nodding sagely, "but would it really be—?"

"Forget it," Zac snapped. He adjusted the rucksack on his shoulders as he stomped off towards the door. "You coming then, or what?"

"Yippee!" said Angelo, skipping on bare feet across the polished floor. He caught up with Zac just as he arrived at the doors. They both leaned back and craned their necks and looked up.

The doorway was fifteen, maybe twenty metres high, and wide enough to drive two tanks through side by side. The wood of the door was dark and smooth, with two handles made of grey crystal mounted at about Zac's head height.

Angelo whistled quietly. "That's a big door."

"It is."

"I wonder why they need such a big door."

"I'm trying not to wonder that same thing," Zac said. He reached for the handles, but neither one turned. He tried pushing the doors, then pulling them. Neither one budged.

"What now?" asked Angelo.

"Not sure," Zac admitted. He gave the door a final dunt, then turned his attention to the walls on either side. "Wait, look at this."

Angelo was at his back in a heartbeat, leaning over him, trying to see. "What? What is it?"

Zac studied the metal and plastic box attached to the wall. It had a button marked CALL, and what looked like a small speaker directly above it. "I think... I think it's an intercom."

"Oh," Angelo said. He nodded slowly. "What's an intercom?"

"It's like a telephone thing. Press the button and you can speak to whoever is on the other side."

Realisation spread across Angelo's face. "Right, one of those. Oh, wait! I just thought of something!"

"What?"

"*Star Wars!* There's this bit in *Star Wars*, right? When Luke and Han Solo are trying to rescue Princess Leia from the Death Star, but she's, like, being guarded and everything."

Angelo bounced up and down with excitement. "So to get in, they dress up as Stormtroopers and put Chewbacca in handcuffs and pretend to have captured him!"

"Right," Zac said. "And what then?"

"They rescue Princess Leia."

Zac hesitated. "OK. And how does that help us?"

Angelo smiled uncertainly. "What?"

"Han Solo and Luke Skywalker. They dress as Stormtroopers and put Chewbacca in handcuffs. How does that apply here?"

Angelo shrugged. "Well... it doesn't."

"What? Why the Hell did you tell me, then?"

"Just that it's one of my favourite bits," Angelo explained. "Han Solo uses an intercom. That's what reminded me."

Zac slapped himself on the forehead. "Oh, for f—" he began, before a crackle from the wall-mounted speaker stopped him. A not-unpleasant female voice addressed them.

"Welcome to Hell, dominion of the Dark Prince Satan and all his underlings. Your misery is our satisfaction. How may I be of assistance today?"

Zac's mind raced. They'd lost the element of surprise, so there was nothing to gain from keeping quiet. But what could he say? How could he explain who they were and why they were there?

"Hello?" said the voice on the intercom. Zac was about to reply when Angelo stepped past him and approached the speaker. He gave Zac an exaggerated wink, then began to talk.

"*Bg*," he said. "*Pk. Sshk.*"

There was a pause from the other side. "Sorry? I didn't catch that."

"*Brrrk. Tsst. Jb?*" Angelo said, then he bit his lip to stop himself laughing.

"Sorry, we seem to be having technical difficulties," the woman said. There was a note of irritation in her voice. "One moment and I'll come on out."

Angelo stepped back, put his hand over his mouth, and mimed laughing. There was a *clunk* and a *creak* and the doors began to swing slowly outwards.

A moment later, a woman in a grey business suit came through the widening gap. Two stubby horns poked up through her greying hair, and as she stepped on to the onyx ground her hooves clipped and clopped.

"Sorry about all that," the woman said. She smiled, but it wasn't a real smile. It looked as if she'd learned it from a book, and not a very good book at that. "Now, how may I help you, gentlemen?"

A dart from Zac's gun lodged in her cheek, just below a pointed ear. Her eyes glazed over at once. "Well, isn't that just marvellous?" she slurred. A second later, she was asleep on the floor.

The smile fell from Angelo's face and he pointed down at the slumbering demon woman. "You shot her!" he gasped. "You shot her in the face. I can't believe you shot her in the face!"

"I thought that was the point," Zac replied. "I thought that was why you lured her out?"

"I wasn't luring anyone out, I was just having a laugh!" Angelo yelped. "I didn't know you were planning to shoot her in the face the minute she stepped outside!"

"It's just a tranquilliser. She'll be fine."

"You hear that, missus?" asked Angelo, leaning over the woman and raising his voice. "It's just a tranquilliser. You'll be fine." He watched her motionless body for a few more seconds. "Oh, look, that's perked her right up, that has."

Zac turned away and made for the doors. "Come on," he muttered.

"Shooting a woman in the face," Angelo tutted, following behind. "You should be ashamed of yourself."

They stepped through the doors and found themselves in a small reception area. The walls were painted in shades of lilac and lavender. The carpet was lime green with a darker green zigzag pattern running through it. When Zac looked at it, the pattern seemed to move. The effect made him queasy, so he tried not to look any longer.

A tidy desk stood just inside the doors. A pair of knitting needles and some wool sat on top of it, alongside a glossy magazine called *Your Hellhound*. On the magazine's cover was a demonic child hugging what looked to be a bear with all its skin torn off. Magma drizzled from the animal's snout, much to the apparent delight of the child.

On the wall behind the desk was a colourful laminated notice. It read: YOU DON'T HAVE TO BE DAMNED TO WORK HERE — *BUT IT HELPS!!!*

"Well, I'll be honest," said Angelo, "this isn't what I was expecting."

"No," agreed Zac. "Nor me."

"I expected it to be... hotter. And, you know, more screaming and stuff."

"Give it time."

There were three doors leading out of the room. They had just walked through one, so Zac concentrated on the other two. The first was painted in gloss white, with a small black and silver sign attached to it that read ARRIVALS. He went to this door and pressed his ear against the wood.

"Hear anything?" Angelo asked.

"Yes, you. Shut up."

Angelo kept quiet while Zac listened. After a moment, Zac stepped away from the door and shook his head. "Nothing," he said. He gripped the handle. "I'm going to take a look."

He pulled the door open a few centimetres. The reception area was filled with screaming and wailing and the crackling of an endless fire. Zac quickly closed the door and silence returned.

"Let's try the other one," he suggested.

Angelo nodded. "Good idea."

The third door opened without the fanfare of horror. Zac peeped out and saw a long corridor curving away from the door on both sides. There was no wall across from him,

271

only a waist-high barrier of frosted glass, allowing him to see all the way round in both directions.

There was nobody in sight, so he stepped out of the reception area and into the corridor. It formed a complete circle, covering an area about the size of a football pitch. Doors stood along the wall at two-metre intervals, each one blank and unremarkable.

Music was being piped in from somewhere. It was soft and quiet and would've been completely inoffensive had it not been so irritatingly catchy and just ever so slightly out of tune. It reminded him of a tune he knew, but it was as if someone was playing all the right notes in the wrong order, and just a little faster than they should have been played. It was music, Zac thought, designed to drive people mad.

Angelo emerged from the room and ran over to the glass barrier. The corridor was a ring with a vast circular space in the middle. Angelo leaned over the barrier and gave a low whistle of wonder.

"It goes down a long way," he said. Zac joined him in looking over the edge. He counted eight more ringed corridors below them. At least the next four had a similar number of doors to this one. After that, the angle made it impossible to see more than a few centimetres of floor at the edge of each storey.

On the ground floor the space in the middle of the ring was carpeted in the same jarring zigzag pattern. A gargoyle-shaped fountain stood slap bang in the centre, spewing red liquid from its mouth and eyes.

"Nine circles," Zac said. "It's the nine circles of Hell."

"It's nicer than I thought," Angelo said. "You know, apart from the fountain."

"Where's the tenth?" Zac asked himself. "There's supposed to be ten."

From below they heard the sound of someone whistling along with the muzak. Quietly, they leaned out over the edge and looked down at the corridor beneath the one they were on. They couldn't see much from where they were, but they spotted a leathery green arm and part of a clawed foot striding along on the second circle.

The hand carried what looked like a battery-operated drill. The drill bit whizzed round a few times, then the creature stopped whistling. They heard him clear his throat, a door creaked open, and the muzak was drowned out by a chorus of wretched moans.

"Right then, you 'orrible little buggers," cried the demon with the drill. "Say hello to my little friend!"

The groans grew in volume, before the door slammed closed and silenced them. Angelo looked sideways at Zac.

"Well, maybe it's not *that* nice."

Zac turned away from the edge and looked along the corridors. "Still, this isn't what I expected," he said. "I thought Hell was all labyrinths and dungeons and lakes of fire, not... not... carpets and corridors and—"

"Escalators," said Angelo.

Zac paused. "What? Where?"

"Over there," Angelo said, pointing to a spot about a third of the way round the top corridor. Two sets of moving stairs stood side by side, one leading down, the other coming back up.

Zac's eyes followed the second circle round until he saw another pair of escalators connecting it with the floor below. A few dozen metres along from those, more moving stairs went between the third and fourth circles.

"No," Zac frowned. "It can't be that easy. Can it?"

"Why not?"

"Well, because it's Hell. Hell's not supposed to be easy."

"Stop complaining," Angelo grinned. "You always want things to be harder than they are." He pointed right down to the bottom floor. "The book's down there, isn't it? The *Book of Everything*?"

"Apparently so."

"Come on, I'll race you. Last one to the stairs is a Judas Iscariot."

"Angelo, wait!"

It was no use. The boy was off and running, his bare feet thudding on the zigzag carpet, his arms pumping furiously as he sped towards the escalator.

And then a door was opening just along the corridor in front of him.

And then a demon was stepping out, a blood-stained cleaver in his misshapen hands.

The demon looked up. Angelo stumbled to a stop. Their eyes locked.

And that was when the screaming started.

CHAPTER TWENTY-SEVEN

THE DEMON CONTINUED to scream for just a few seconds, then stopped almost as suddenly as he had started.

"What in here's name do you think you're playing at?" he demanded, clutching at his bare chest. He nudged the door closed behind him and shot Angelo a dirty look. "You nearly gave me a sodding heart attack!"

Angelo glanced at Zac, then back to the figure in the doorway. "Um... sorry."

The demon was short and squat with a big nose and pointed ears. His skin was a burned shade of brown, with red nodules growing from his cheeks like tiny mushrooms. He wore a very small, very tight pair of satin gold pants, and it was only as he glided slowly forward that Zac realised he was also wearing roller skates.

"So you should be. Running about like that, scaring people. It shouldn't be allowed." He wiped his nose on the back of his arm, and eyed the tattered remains of Angelo's clothes. "Here, you ain't escaped, have you?"

Angelo quickly shook his head.

"You sure?" He looked both boys up and down. "Where you come from, then, if you ain't escap— *Ulk!*"

The tip of a dart dug into the demon's flesh where his neck met his shoulder. A long green tongue unfurled from within his mouth and his eyes rolled backwards in their sockets. His feet slid out from beneath him and his forehead hit the carpet with a slightly hollow *thunk*.

Angelo stared accusingly at Zac's gun. "Do you have to shoot *everyone* we meet?"

"Well, maybe if you listened to me and didn't go running off, I wouldn't have to! In future, do as you're told, OK?"

"Why, what will you do? Shoot me too?"

Zac pushed past him. "Wouldn't be the first time," he

mumbled, stepping up to the slumbering demon. They both peered down at him.

"Maybe you should steal his clothes," Angelo suggested. "You know, so you're in disguise. That's what Indiana Jones does."

Zac's eyes went to the gold satin hot pants and skates. "Yeah. I think I'll leave it," he said. He turned to Angelo. "I think you should wait here."

"What? Why?" asked Angelo.

"Because I don't know what else we'll meet, and I've only got one dart left."

Angelo counted on his fingers. "You've got six left. You've only shot two and Argus gave you eight."

"I dropped some," Zac replied, thinking fast.

"That was clumsy, Mr Butterfingers," Angelo scolded. "It doesn't matter, I'm coming. Gabriel said I had to stick close to you, so that's what I'm going to do. Besides," he added, "I feel safer with you around."

"I wish I could say the same," Zac said. He sighed. "Fine. But remember, the lower we get, the more dangerous it becomes. Keep calm. The last thing I need is for you to freak out on me."

Angelo gave a little laugh. "I don't freak out."

"Yes, you do," Zac replied. "You just never remember afterwards." He stepped on to the escalator and began the descent to the circle below. "Now, come on. Stay close and stay quiet."

The second circle of Hell was virtually identical to the first. The carpet was the same. It had the same frosted-glass barrier round the inside curve. The only difference was the doors.

The doors on the floor above had been glossy white. The ones on the second circle were a sort of creamy brown colour. Aside from that small difference, and the fact that there was no unconscious demon lying on this floor, the circles were virtually indistinguishable.

They moved quietly, keeping low so the glass would hide them from anything that might emerge from one of the doors on the opposite side of the circle. Zac slipped the gun back inside his jacket. He wanted to keep the last dart until he really needed it. If something stepped out of one of the doors ahead of them, he'd have to find some other way of dealing with it.

Fortunately, nothing did. They made it to the second

escalator in under a minute and let it carry them down to the floor below. The third circle looked just as empty as the others. The doors were a coppery shade of brown and the muzak sounded just a little louder and more grating, but otherwise it was nothing they hadn't seen before.

"See," Angelo grinned. "Easy. I told you you worry too much."

As if it had been standing in the wings waiting for its cue, an alarm began to ring. It was an old-fashioned *clang-clang-clang*, like someone was repeatedly striking a bell. The sound drowned out the muzak and carried all the way from the first circle to the last.

On every floor, doors began to open. Demons and monsters and things Zac couldn't describe stepped into the corridors, grumbling in annoyance or looking around in confusion. It was only a matter of time before—

"Oi!" shouted someone by the door on their left. "You two. What you playing at?"

"Run!" Zac cried, grabbing Angelo and powering along the corridor. They clattered past another door, then the next one along swung open and something large and heavily armoured ducked out and blocked the way.

"What do we do?" Angelo yelped. "What do we do?"

Zac turned and grabbed for the handle of the door they had passed. "In here," he said, throwing open the door and shoving Angelo inside.

"No, no, what are you doing?" the boy squealed, but Zac leaped in behind him and pushed the door closed with a *slam*. He jammed his foot and his shoulder against it, trying to stop the demons from coming in. But no demons came. The door did not move.

Still keeping his weight against the wood, Zac turned and looked into the room they had entered. It was dark in there. The only light came from an illuminated EXIT sign directly above his head. It threw a weak glow down the door, and in a faint puddle round his feet.

"Angelo," he whispered into the darkness. "You OK? Where are you?"

The only reply was a soft hissing, like static on a radio or rain falling on a window far overhead.

"Angelo?" he said again. "Stop mucking about. Where are you?"

The darkness kept hissing, but from Angelo there came no reply.

Zac dragged his foot a few centimetres from the door, ready to jam it again if anything tried to come through. Nothing did. Whatever the demons were doing, they weren't trying to get into this room.

"Come on, Angelo," he said, raising his voice a little. "I swear if you're messing around I'll kill you myself."

He opened the backpack and pulled out a slim black torch Argus had given him. It was waterproof, but not completely *Styx* proof, it seemed. The glow flickered erratically when he switched it on, sending shadows scurrying spider-like up and down the walls.

He turned the light towards the nearest wall. It blinked and flashed like the Morse Code of a madman, but the light was enough to let Zac see the wallpaper. In that first glimpse, he'd thought he had recognised it. Now he knew he did, and it made the blood become ice in his veins.

It was *his* wallpaper. Or rather, it *had* been. It was the wallpaper from the flat he and his granddad had lived in years ago, before Zac had scraped enough money together for them to rent a bigger place. The walls here were all mottled with damp and riddled with rot.

Around him, the hissing grew just a little louder. Zac

turned away from the wallpaper, pointed the flickering torch, and stepped onwards into the dark.

"Zac? Zac? Where are you?"

Even to himself, Angelo's voice sounded shrill and pathetic, but he was lost and afraid and he couldn't care less what he sounded like right at that moment.

He had been shoved through into a room that was in near darkness. Then the closing door had cut off all light from the outside and the blackness had swallowed him whole. He had been trying to find the door and Zac ever since, but whichever direction he reached out in he found nothing.

Eventually, when he realised he was completely, hopelessly lost, Angelo sat down on the carpeted floor and crossed his legs. There was only one thing for it.

He screwed his eyes tight shut, as he had been taught to do centuries ago. He gripped his knees and clenched his jaw and concentrated with everything he had. His face turned a worrying shade of purple in the darkness.

"*Hng*. Come... on..." he hissed through his gritted teeth.

It had been a long time since he had attempted this, and even longer since he'd succeeded. But it had to work now. It had to. "Do... or do not. There is... no... try! *Hnnnng.*"

A small circle of light fizzled into existence above his head, like a mini version of the neon *O* in the Eyedol sign. Angelo's body sagged as he let out a shaky breath. He reached up and touched the halo. It hummed faintly beneath his fingers. His hand moved down to his temple. He rubbed it gently and groaned as he stood up.

"I'm going to pay for that in the morning," he mumbled, but at least he could now see, even if it was only a few metres in every direction. What he saw was nothing. Nothing but carpet on all sides.

Angelo pointed north, south, east and west. "Eenie, meenie, minie, mo," he whispered, then he picked a direction and he began to walk.

The beam of the torch fizzled and flashed. Zac gave the lens a tap and the light settled for a few seconds. Not that he really needed it. His feet remembered the way all by themselves.

His bedroom led out into a narrow hallway – bathroom

to the right, everything else to the left. Six or seven shuffled steps took him to the other end of the hall. Four doors stood there. One led out on to the communal stairway. Another was a cupboard crammed full of toys and other old junk.

The door directly on his right led through to the living room, which in turn connected with the kitchen. The door just ahead and on his left had been his granddad's bedroom. He shone the flickering torch at that door and saw the handle was still hanging limp and broken, just as it had been when they'd moved out.

The hissing of the static was louder on his right, and so that was where he decided to go. Gripping the torch handle tightly, Zac pushed open the living-room door and stepped through into a nightmare.

CHAPTER TWENTY-EIGHT

ANGELO STOPPED BEFORE a familiar white door. It was his door. The one that led into his bedroom. That much was clear. What wasn't clear, was why it was in Hell.

But it was his door, and in Angelo's mind that made it safe. Or safer than doors that weren't his, at least. With the glow of his halo lighting the way, he pushed the door open and stepped into his bedroom.

A demon waited for him inside. Angelo knew it was a demon because he was dressed like a demon. He wore what looked like red pyjamas and a red cape and he held a trident – also red – in one clawed hand. He had a tail with an arrowhead tip. It drooped down and touched the floor behind him. His horns were small, his stomach wasn't.

The bottom of it bulged out beneath the pyjama top and hung hairy and bare over the waistband of the pyjama trousers.

The demon wasn't much taller than Angelo. What was left of his thinning hair was scraped across a head that looked to be around twenty per cent larger than it should have been. All in all, he would've just looked like a slightly odd, middle-aged man in an ill-fitting Halloween costume, had it not been for the tiny flickering flames at the centre of each of his eyes.

"There you are," said the demon, more cheerfully than might have been expected. "At last. I've been wondering when you'd turn up."

Angelo screamed and turned to run, but there was no door behind him, just a blank bedroom wall. Pressing his back against the wallpaper, Angelo faced the demon.

"Wh-who are you?" he gulped. "What are you doing in my bedroom?"

The demon glanced back briefly over his shoulder. "What, me?"

"Yes, you!"

"Right, yes," said the demon. "Sorry." He drew himself

up to his full, unimpressive height. "I am Murmur, Earl of Hell, and I have been tasked with—"

"My poster!" Angelo cried sharply. He stared in horror at his poster of Jesus. A moustache and beard had been drawn on to Christ in black marker pen. "Who did that? Was that you?"

Murmur's eyes went down to the pen in his hand, then back to Angelo. He quickly hid the hand behind his back. "Uh... nope."

"It was so! You drew a beard on Jesus."

Murmur looked mildly embarrassed. "OK, yes. Well, I'm a demon. I had to do *something* to it. What would everyone else say if I'd passed up a chance like that?"

Angelo shook his head in dismay. "But, I mean... why did you draw a beard? He's already got a beard."

"I know, I know," Murmur said. "Well, I mean, I didn't want to ruin it, did I?"

"Didn't you?" asked Angelo, surprised at that.

"Course not," said Murmur. He leaned in closer, forcing Angelo to press himself harder against the wall. "Between you and me, I think it's one of his better ones. He's usually all crucified and that. Nice to see him cracking a smile for once."

Angelo looked the demon up and down. So far, he didn't appear very demonic.

"What do you want? Why are you here?"

"What? Oh, yeah, right," Murmur said. He raised a clawed finger, then began patting across the front of his pyjama top. "One sec. I know it's here somewhere. Aha, here we go."

There was a rustle of paper as the demon unfolded a yellowing sheet of A4. He gave a shy smile as he positioned a pair of reading glasses on the bridge of his nose.

"Here we are now," he said, leaning his head back and squinting down at the paper. "By order of Lucifuge Rofocale, Grand Governor of Hell, upon encountering an intruder I am instructed to tear their flesh asunder and rip open the very..." Murmur's voice trailed off. His lips continued to move as he read in near silence. "Disembowl," he mumbled with a frown. "Feast on..."

The demon's puffy red skin paled a shade. He brought the page closer to his face, as if unable to believe what he was reading. "That's a bit much," he concluded, and he quietly refolded the paper and slipped it back into his inside pocket. Next he took off his glasses. The arms gave a *click* as he folded them together. "No, don't think we'll bother with that," he said. "Not really got the stomach for it these days."

Angelo was still pressing himself flat against the wall. His legs were beginning to ache from the effort. "So can I go, then?" he asked.

Murmur gave a long, sad sigh. "No, 'fraid not." He glanced up and around, as if checking they were alone. "I don't have much time. I'm not really supposed to be here, but, well, there's something I want to talk to you about." He lowered himself down on to the end of Angelo's bed, idly picked up a comic from the bedside table and flicked quickly through it. He put the comic back down, then quietly cleared his throat.

"Tell me, Angelo," the demon said. "Gabriel and Michael. What did they tell you about your father?"

"What's it got to do with you?" Angelo asked.

"Please," said Murmur. "What did they tell you?"

Angelo faltered. "That he was human. They told me he was human."

Murmur stood up. He nodded, as if a lifetime of suspicions had just been confirmed. "Yeah, I thought they might have said that. But, well, you see, they were lying, Angelo," Murmur said. He opened his arms wide and smiled in a way that looked like an apology. "*I* am your father."

Zac had been right. The hissing was static from a radio. Specifically, it was static from his granddad's radio, which sat on the coffee table in the centre of the small living room.

In the flickering glow of the torch, he saw his granddad's armchair. It faced away from the door, as it had always done, angled so the old man could sit and look out of the window at the world beyond. But the window was gone. In its place was a rectangle of grey bricks, the mortar between them crumbling away.

The light dimmed, but before it did, Zac caught sight of the top of his granddad's head, visible just above the chair's high back.

"Granddad?" he said, but the word came out as a croak. "Granddad, it's me. It's Zac."

The old man in the chair did not move. Zac shook some life back into the torch and stepped further into the room.

"This is a trick," he reminded himself. "This is not real."

And yet it was *so* real. Almost too real, as if everything that had happened since the days in this flat were a dream from which he was only now waking, like they'd never moved to the new house, never escaped this grotty little place.

The goldfish bowl sat on the table beside the radio. The water was grey and murky, with green scum on the glass. The fish was no longer zipping through the water, but floating limply near the top instead.

The dead fish made horrible sense. Of course it was dead. It had to be dead. In the other world, the fish had been alive for Zac's entire life, and that was impossible. Unless the other world was a dream, and *this* was the real one.

Zac saw his granddad's hand, withered and frail on the arm of the chair. His fingers were hooked round his little blue and green stress ball. Zac stared at the globe pattern for a moment. He felt a tingle at the back of his head, as if there was something significant about the ball that he couldn't quite put his finger on.

Before he could dwell on it too much, the ball slipped from the old man's fingers. It bounced once on the threadbare carpet, then rolled to a stop by the table. Zac followed it with the torch and carried on staring at it for a few moments, as if the answer to everything was written across its surface, if only he could see it.

He took another step forward and his granddad was revealed in profile. The old man looked even more ancient than usual. His grey hair had come out in clumps, leaving only a few wispy remnants behind. His skin seemed too tight for his face, but puckered and wrinkled at the same time, like an overripe fruit left out to rot.

Phillip's eyes were closed. His chest was still. Zac didn't expect any answer when he whispered, "Granddad?" into the dark. But he got one.

"Zac?"

The old man's voice was dry and brittle. It came out without help from his parched, unmoving lips.

"I'm here, Granddad," Zac said, but he hung back, unable to go to the old man's side. *This isn't real*, he told himself, but the voice in his head had lost all its conviction.

Phillip's eyes opened, revealing pupils that had turned milky and white. They gazed unseeing at the ceiling. "Why did you leave me, Zac?" he croaked. "Why did you leave me on my own?"

"I didn't," Zac said. "I didn't leave you. I mean... not like this."

"I waited for you, Zac. Why didn't you come back?"

Zac knelt by his grandfather's chair. The old man's skin felt like dry leaves as Zac took hold of his hand. "I did come back, Granddad. I am back. I'm here."

Phillip's head nodded slowly. His mouth flapped open and closed. "Stay with me, Zac," he wheezed. "Please don't leave me again."

"I won't leave you again," Zac promised. "I'll stay with you."

"For ever."

Zac tightened his grip on the withered hand. "For ever."

Angelo stared at the chubby demon in the ill-fitting clothes. He seemed to wilt beneath the boy's gaze.

"Aren't you going to say something?" Murmur asked. "I just told you I'm your father."

"No, you're not," Angelo said. "That's not true."

Murmur stood up. Angelo almost became one with the

wall behind him. "Search your feelings," urged the demon. "You know it to be true."

Angelo blinked. "That's from *Star Wars*. You nicked that from *Star Wars*."

Embarrassment darted across Murmur's face. "What? Um. Yes, well—"

"*The Empire Strikes Back*. The bit at the end."

"Yes, well, I wasn't sure how to break it to you. It's big news, let's face it. I thought I'd better do some research first."

Angelo stared in disbelief. "And you thought Darth Vader was a good role model to follow? *Darth Vader*? What's next? Chopping my hand off with a light sabre?"

"I haven't got a light sabre," Murmur said, shaking his head. He smiled at the thought. "Although, wouldn't that be brilliant?"

"It *would* be brilliant," Angelo conceded. "But can we get back to the point? You're not my father."

"Search your feelings, Angelo," said Murmur. "Oh, wait, I've done that bit, haven't I?"

"Yes."

Murmur nodded. "Right. Sorry, I'm not making a very good..."

He sat back down on the bed and words began to tumble out of him. "We were in Limbo. You know, on one of them team-building weekends? Archery, abseiling, goat sacrifice. The usual. I was sent to the Junk Room – that's where they keep all the equipment."

The demon's voice trailed off into a wistful smile. "And that's where I met Laila. That's where I met your mother." He gave himself a shake, snapping himself back to the present. "Turned out Heaven was having its own team-building thing, and she'd been sent to the Junk Room too. I was picking up some chainsaws; she was bringing back a canoe."

"A canoe?"

"Yes. Don't know why. No water in Limbo, but it didn't occur to me to ask. I was too busy staring. She was the most beautiful thing I'd ever seen. We started to talk, really hit it off, despite everything. We arranged to meet again later that night. One thing led to another and, well, I'm sure you can figure out what happened next."

Angelo's brow furrowed. "What happened next?"

Murmur's cheeks reddened. "*You know*."

"No, I don't," said Angelo blankly. "What happened next?"

The demon twitched nervously. "We, uh, well, we... had a baby."

Angelo drew in a sharp breath. "Me."

"You."

"No, that's not..." Angelo began, but he ran out of steam there. He stared at the demon. "Are you telling the truth?" he asked. "Are you really my dad?"

Murmur nodded. "'Fraid so," he said.

"No, but that means..." Angelo felt his stomach twist as the realisation hit him. "No, but that means I'm half... half..."

"Demon."

"*That means I'm half demon!*"

Murmur nodded again. "You are."

"But, but I don't want to be a demon," said Angelo. His jaw tightened as he fought against tears. "Demons are evil."

"Mostly," the demon conceded. "But you're only half demon. *You* don't have to be evil. You can be anything you like."

They looked at each other in silence for a long time. It was Angelo who eventually broke it.

"So what now?" he asked.

Murmur shrugged. "Wrestling?"

"*Wrestling?*"

"That's a suitable father-son activity, isn't it? Or fishing? You can catch some big ones in the Styx. Unless they catch you first. Or we could build a tree house? I don't know. I've never done this before. You're the only son I've got."

A low *creak* made the room vibrate. Murmur's eyes went wide. "No, no, no," he said. "Not yet. Not already."

"What is it?"

"They've found us."

"Who's found us?"

"*Them.* Haures and the others. I wasn't supposed to be here. I wasn't supposed to tell you any of this, but, well... I had to see you," he swallowed, "*son*. I had to see you just once."

The *creak* became a *rumble*. Half a dozen of Angelo's books vibrated off his shelves. "What's happening?" Angelo asked.

Murmur's voice was a whisper. "They're coming. Shout for your friend."

"What?"

"Your friend. Shout for him. You're safer together than apart."

Murmur gestured towards the wall. The door was suddenly back where it had always been. Angelo reached for the handle, but a sharp cry from Murmur stopped him.

"No! Don't go out there, you'll get lost. Call for your friend." He grabbed Angelo by the upper arms. There was fear flickering behind the flames in the demon's eyes. "You hear me, son? Call your friend. I know I've got no right to say this, but you have to trust me. Call your friend. Now!"

Angelo hesitated, then he turned to the door, opened his mouth and shouted Zac's name as loudly as he could.

Zac turned towards the kitchen door. "What was that?"

In the chair, Phillip shook his head. "Nothing. Ignore it. Stay here with me."

Another shout came, even more panicked than the last. "Angelo?"

Zac tried to stand, but his grandfather's hand clamped his like a vice. "Stay here with me," he said, and his wheeze became a menacing growl. "Don't leave me again."

Angelo was screaming, calling out for help.

"I have to check on him," Zac said. "I'll be back in one minute, OK?"

"*Don't you dare leave me*," Phillip warned, and now the growl had become a roar. Zac looked down at the chair, and panic made him yank his hand away. The person sitting there was no longer his grandfather. It had his grandfather's skin, but things wriggled inside it as if trying to force their way free. The withered hand grabbed for his again, but Zac was backing away, making for the door.

Phillip's mouth opened, and Zac saw poisonous shapes twisting there at the back of the throat. "Stay... with... me," a chorus of voices insisted. "I'm... your... grandfather."

"No," said Zac. "You're not."

The kitchen door was blocked from the other side. That didn't stop him. He powered a kick at it, driving his foot against the wood. There was a splintering *crack* and the door flew wide open.

He saw Angelo standing in what looked like his bedroom. A demon lurked right behind him. In one fluid movement Zac reached into his jacket. There was a *thwip* as he used up the last tranquilliser dart and the demon slumped down on to the floor. Angelo turned as he fell, and stood staring at him until Zac spoke.

"You all right?"

Angelo shook his head. "Not really," he said. "That was my dad."

"Oh. Right. Well, um, sorry I shot your dad."

"My dad's a demon," said Angelo, his voice trembling.

Zac looked down at the slumbering Murmur. "God, yeah. So he is. Who knew?"

"He got parenting tips from Darth Vader," Angelo continued. He turned to Zac, and Zac realised the boy was smiling. "How great is that? My dad likes *Star Wars*. He's just like me."

Angelo spotted the writhing shape in the doorway. It was squirming on the ground, black goo dripping from its nose and mouth.

"Ugh, what's that?" he asked, recoiling in horror.

"No one important," Zac said, pushing the door closed. There was a loud hammering on it almost at once. Angelo yelped in panic.

"Zaaaaaaac," wheezed a voice on the other side of the wood. "Heeeelp meeee, Zaaaaaaac."

Another low drone made the room shake. "What was that?" Zac asked.

"My dad said more demons are coming," Angelo said. "What do we do?"

"I have absolutely no idea," Zac admitted.

"Pleeeease, Zaaaaaac. Heeeelp meeee."

"Oh, cut it out," Zac said, thudding a fist against the door.

"Pray!" Angelo suggested. "We should pray!"

"I told you, *I'm not praying*." He grabbed the handle of the door and held it closed. He looked back over at Angelo, and that was when he saw the cat.

It appeared to step from thin air right beside Angelo. It looked lazily up at them both in turn. The animal's fur was ragged and filthy and coming out in clumps. It was the size of a kitten, but looked to have lived through at least eight of its nine lives.

Zac and Angelo watched the cat in silence as it sat down on the floor, wagged its tail and said, "Woof."

CHAPTER TWENTY-NINE

"H E'S FOUND 'EM," bellowed a voice from within the cupboard. "Toxie's found 'em. They're in here."

The bedroom around them went fuzzy at the edges. Zac felt the door handle melt away in his grip as the room became wispy like smoke. Far overhead a series of powerful lights flickered on, revealing what looked like a vast empty warehouse.

Where the poster of Jesus had been there now stood demons of assorted sizes. They ranged from around twenty centimetres in height to well over two metres, and they all carried ropes or nets or baseball bats with nails through them. The smallest demon seemed to be the brains of the outfit.

"There they is," he sneered, hopping up and down on spindly, frog-like legs. "There they is!" He scratched the cat behind the ears. It involved standing on tiptoes. "Who's a good Hellhound? Who's a good Hellhound? Toxie is. Toxie is!"

"Hellhound?" said Zac. "That thing's supposed to be a dog?"

The little frog-demon ignored the question. "Thought you could give us the slip, eh?" he asked, glaring tiny daggers at Zac and Angelo. "You're lucky we found you when we did or things could've gotten right messy."

The monstrous group parted as another figure stepped from thin air directly behind them. This demon was the largest of the lot. There was something different about him too. Something about the way he stood that said he was someone you really ought to be paying attention to. The smallest demon fired off a perfect salute as the newcomer stepped over him.

The stench of death and burning flesh caught at the back of Zac's throat as the demon stopped in front of him. "This is them?" the monster demanded.

"Yeah, that's them, Mr Haures, sir," nodded the little

one. "Told you we'd catch 'em. It was Toxie here what did—"

Haures clicked his scaly fingers. There was a brief scream and the little demon vanished in a plume of angry flame. "Shut up," said Haures absent-mindedly.

The big demon looked down at Murmur asleep on the floor, and shook his head in annoyance. He turned his gaze on both boys. His lips drew back into an approximation of a smile. "I've been waiting for you," he told them. "I've been waiting for you for a long, long time."

"Wh-who are you?" Angelo stammered.

Haures fixed him with a fiery stare. He said nothing for a while, as if contemplating the question.

"You will find out soon enough," he said at last. Turning away, he motioned to the larger members of the demon group. "Take them down to ten," he instructed. "*Carefully*. Anyone harms them and they will answer to me."

The other demons nodded hastily, bowing low as Haures swept past. There was a collective sigh of relief from them as he vanished into thin air. A moment later, he reappeared again.

"Oh, and notify the Master," he ordered. "He will want to see these insects for himself."

"Watch who you're calling an insect," Zac warned.

With a twitch of irritation, Haures snapped his fingers again. Something went *pop* inside Zac's head. He felt his ankles wobble, then his knees buckle. He probably felt the floor as he crashed down on to it, but he couldn't say for sure. Zac's eyes closed. The voices of the demons and the screams of Angelo sounded far away along a tunnel.

The last thing he heard before he surrendered to unconsciousness was the mad barking of the flea-bitten cat.

A jet of water woke him up. It was warm and smelled unpleasantly sour. He really hoped that it *was* water, but he had his doubts.

Spluttering, he looked up. A hunchbacked creature with too few eyes and too many teeth leered as it squirted murky yellow liquid at him from a plastic bottle. "He's awake," the demon said, in a surprisingly feminine voice.

She gave the bottle another squeeze, spraying Zac with more of the copper-coloured liquid. He tried to make a grab for it, but discovered his hands were shackled to a steel frame above his head. He tried to move his feet, but thick chains held those in place too.

He heard a whimper from his right and saw that Angelo was chained up exactly as he was. The boy's eyes were closed, but his head was moving, as if he were just waking up too.

Zac quickly glanced around the room, trying to get his bearings, but he was somewhere he had never seen before. The room was a stark, clinical white, with stainless steel worktops lining the walls on every side. There were no windows that he could see, and no doors, either. No way in or out.

A chair stood in the middle of the room, like something from a dentist's surgery – reclined fully back with a movable spotlight mounted above it. Zac wished he hadn't spotted the straps and buckles on the armrests, but they were the first things he had seen.

"Thank you, Eliza, that will be all."

A man just a little taller than Angelo stepped into view. He appeared human, more or less, with only two sawn-off stumps of what must once have been horns to suggest his true nature.

The man looked to be in his late sixties, with thinning grey hair and deep-set wrinkles. He was dressed in a black suit, which may originally have been tailor-made, but which now looked a size or two on the large side. His rumpled shirt was also black. He wore the top button open, with a blood-red tie hanging loosely round his neck.

His eyes were hidden behind a pair of designer sunglasses. He had rings on almost every finger and a gold watch on his wrist that was tarnished and scuffed. The man stared back at Zac and took a long, deep draw on a cigarette.

"Who are you supposed to be?" Zac asked.

There was a loud *crack* and pain tore across his back. He cried out with the shock and the heat of it. The old man puffed on his cigarette, unflinching.

"You do not address the Dark Lord," Haures snarled. He stepped into view, coiling his tail in his hands like a bullwhip.

Zac hissed through his teeth, breathing out the worst of the pain. "Dark Lord?" he frowned. "You mean...?" He looked the grey-haired man up and down. "Nah."

"Silence!" Haures roared. He flicked the tail and Zac felt a wasp sting across his cheek. "And bow your head before the Father of All Lies."

Zac groaned. "Dark Lord? Father of All Lies? What is it with you people having so many names? You're as bad as Odin."

Veins bulged on Haures's neck and forehead. "I said *silence*, you worthless little—"

"Haures."

The Dark Lord's voice was low and calm, but it stopped Haures immediately. The cigarette butt was dropped on the floor, then ground out beneath the heel of a well-worn leather shoe.

The Father of All Lies clapped his hands slowly three or four times. "Impressive," he said. "You succeeded in getting on Haures's bad side. That's something you may come to regret."

Zac said nothing. Despite the calm voice and the unassuming appearance, everything about the man screamed *danger*. Evil emanated from him with such force that Zac almost started to believe in auras. He could sense the Dark Lord's, all black and twisted and rotten and wrong.

"Wh-where are we?" coughed Angelo, fully wakening. "Where are we? What's happening? Who... who are you?"

"He's Satan," Zac said before Haures could start shouting again.

Angelo looked at the man in the suit. "Satan?" he said with a gasp. "You're *Satan?*" He looked the man up and down. "I thought you'd be taller."

The Dark Lord shrugged. "Not always," he said. "My associate here is Haures. He is one of the Dukes of Hell."

Angelo giggled sharply, then bit his lip. All eyes turned in his direction.

"Something funny?" asked Satan.

"Um, no," Angelo said.

"Well, clearly *something* made you laugh. Would you care to share it with the rest of us?"

Angelo swallowed nervously. "It's just... I thought you were going to say he was one of the Dukes of Hazzard."

There was a pause. Behind his sunglasses, the Dark Lord blinked. "I'm sorry?"

"*The Dukes of Hazzard*," repeated Angelo. From the expression on his face it was clear Satan was none the wiser. Angelo felt himself shrink beneath both demons' gaze. "It's an old TV show," he said meekly, "about some people who drive fast."

The Father of All Lies rubbed his teeth with his tongue. It made a rasping sound, like sandpaper. "*The Dukes of Hazzard*," he said slowly. "*The Dukes of Hazzard*. Is that one of ours?"

"No, sir," said Haures.

"Is it the one with the talking car?"

Haures cleared his throat gently. "You're thinking of *Knight Rider*, sir."

"Ah, yes, so I am. That was one of ours, wasn't it?"

"Yes, sir," confirmed Haures. "That was one of ours."

Satan waved a hand dismissively. "Enough. You asked where you are. You are in the tenth circle of Hell. Try not to touch anything, some of the paint's still wet." His eyes moved behind the sunglasses, looking at them both in turn. "You're here for the *Book of Doom*. Correct?"

"That's right," Zac nodded. "So if you'll just hand it over, we'll get out of your hair."

"Haha, yes," said Satan without mirth. "Very good. I'm sure you've already guessed that we had an ulterior motive for getting you down here. We've been watching you for a long time. Just between us, we never actually cared about the book. We just thought it might make good bait with which to draw you down."

"Well, it worked," said Zac. "But why? I don't understand. What do you want with me?"

The Dark Lord's head shifted just a fraction in his direction. "You?" he said. "Why would we want anything from *you*? I was talking to him." He turned his head towards Angelo.

Angelo and Zac exchanged a puzzled glance.

"Me?"

"Him?"

"Why did you want me?"

"You are unique, Angelo," Satan said. "One of a kind, almost certainly never to be repeated. And that makes you important. And it makes you fascinating." He gestured around at the stark walls and spotless worktops. "All this is for you, Angelo. We built the tenth circle for you, so that we may... get to know you better. Because you are special, my boy. Half angel and – drumroll, please – *half demon*."

"I know that," Angelo said.

Satan missed a beat. "Oh," he said. "Right. Do you?"

Angelo puffed out his pigeon chest. "My dad told me."

"Ah," said Satan. "Well, that's disappointing. I was looking forward to revealing that." He paced round the metal frames that held both boys, examining Angelo from all angles.

"You've spent such a long time up there," he said. "Now it's time you joined us down here for a while and indulged your dark side."

Angelo frowned. "What?"

The Dark Lord was interrupted before he could reply by the sound of a ringing phone. Eliza, the hunchbacked demon with the liquid bottle, flipped open a handset and pressed it to her ear.

"Yes?"

She listened intently, watched by the other four people in the room. After a moment, she moved the phone away from her ear.

"It's the fourth circle, sir. About the hot pokers. They're asking should they go through the eyes or up the bottom?"

Satan tapped a finger against his chin as he considered this. "Why not both?"

The hunchback nodded, spoke the instruction into the phone, then snapped it closed.

"Where was I?" Satan asked. He rocked back on his heels. "Ah, yes. Put him in the chair."

At that, everything seemed to grind into slow motion. Zac saw Haures lunge for Angelo, heard Angelo cry out in panic and fear. Shapes moved in the corners of Zac's eyes. He turned and saw a dozen or more demons in surgical clothing swarming towards the reclining chair. Had they been there the entire time, or was there a door behind him? A way out? An escape route? He twisted his neck, trying to see, but all he saw was white wall and silver worktop, and all he heard were Angelo's squeals as Haures unhooked him and carried him over towards the chair.

"What are you doing with him?" Zac cried. He pulled at his chains, but they held fast. "Let him go. Leave him alone."

Angelo was bucking and thrashing in Haures's arms, kicking out with his bare feet and biting at anything that came within reach. He shouted angrily. He pleaded and sobbed. He tried everything he could to stop them putting him in that chair, but then he was on it, and then he was strapped in, and then he was trapped.

The demons in the surgeon outfits chittered excitedly behind their masks. Their dark eyes swept over Angelo, appraising him even as their gnarled hands rubbed together with glee.

"The book."

Zac tore his eyes from Angelo. The Dark Lord stood beside him, a heavy leather-bound book balanced on the palm of one hand. A small padlock and strap fastened the pages closed. On the cover, the words: *THY BOOK OF EVERYTHING* glowed faintly in shades of gold.

"What, you're just giving it to me?" he asked.

Satan shrugged. "I don't want it. It has served its purpose. Keeping it would start a war, and that's the last thing anyone needs."

"You've already started a war," Zac told him. "If you don't let Angelo go, they'll send an army."

"Will they indeed?" said Satan. "We'll see."

He walked behind Zac and unzipped the backpack. The book was shoved roughly inside before the zip was fastened once more. Zac looked back at Angelo. Something like an oxygen mask had been slipped over his face, but the gas flowing in through his mouth and nostrils was a dark, brooding red. Angelo's eyes were bulging, staring up at the ceiling, but he was no longer fighting against the straps.

Satan appeared in front of Zac again. "Don't worry. We'll take good care of your friend." He tapped himself on the forehead. "Wait, I forgot – he isn't your friend, he's your *colleague*. Isn't that right?"

Zac didn't reply, just kept watching the boy in the chair.

"You have what you came for, Zac Corgan. You can return a hero and have all your sins washed away. Play your cards right and you'll never have to see me again." He smiled thinly. "And won't your grandfather be pleased to have you home?"

The mention of his grandfather made Zac look Satan's way. The Dark Lord's face became solemn. "Anyway, he was miserable up there. No friends. All alone. And that tattoo? Horrible. Who's to say he won't be happier down here with us? With his daddy and all his aunts and uncles and brothers and sisters."

Zac could feel the demon inside his head, twisting his thoughts and fogging his brain. "I'm... I'm not leaving without him," he hissed. "I'm not leaving him here."

The Dark Lord Satan, Father of All Lies, Angel of the Bottomless Pit, nodded. "Oh, but the thing is," he said, "you don't have any choice."

Then he smiled and snapped his fingers. The room around Zac began to fade. He saw Angelo's head loll sideways to look at him. "Don't go," the boy wheezed. "P-please."

"I'll come back!" Zac shouted. "I'll get help and come back. I promise!"

Then the room faded completely, and Angelo was abandoned to all the demons of Hell.

CHAPTER THIRTY

Z AC FELL FORWARD, the chains no longer round his ankles and wrist, and so no longer holding him up. He landed awkwardly on hard-packed sand and lay there, face down, until the inside of his head stopped spinning.

When he finally got up, Zac found himself standing beneath a pale blue sky. The sand stretched out around him in all directions, flat on his left, hills and dunes to his right.

There was no wind. Not a breath of air moved across the desert. He turned in a slow circle, sweeping his gaze out over the sand. There were no demons, no Angelo, no chair and no straps. He was, as far as he could tell, completely alone.

"Great," he muttered. "Now what?"

He walked a few paces in one direction, stopped and

walked back. He looked around again, but the landscape was still devoid of life.

Then he remembered the watch. Gabriel had said he could use it to contact Heaven once he had the book. He looked at the little screen. Where the time should have been was a question mark, and a basic animation of a stick man shrugging his shoulders.

Zac studied the watch more closely. It had four buttons along one side and two on the other. One of them, he imagined, would allow him to call for a rescue party. But which one?

There was a flash of light and a puff of smoke and the hunchbacked demon, Eliza, popped out of thin air. She stuck her tongue out at him, then smashed a little pointed hammer against the watch face. With a sharp giggle she vanished again, leaving Zac staring blankly at the broken timepiece on his wrist.

"Well, that's just great," he sighed, before a tennis ball hit him hard on the back of the head.

He turned, fists raised, head throbbing. The ball had come from the direction of the dunes. And now he was paying closer attention he could hear noises – voices, maybe – from behind the closest hill. He listened, and soon the voices were joined by the sound of heavy footsteps on the compacted sand.

A large man with a long, flame-coloured beard trudged into view at the top of the dune. He stopped when he saw Zac. There was a long moment in which he and Zac just stared at each other in silence, but then the man cupped his huge hands round his mouth and shouted, "Chuck us the ball back!"

Zac looked down at the tennis ball by his feet. It was grubby and weather-beaten. Someone had scribbled a large number 4 on it in black marker pen. Zac picked it up, then approached the man on the hill.

The closer he got, the bigger the man seemed. He stood almost as tall as Haures had. His beard was easily a metre long itself, and his muscles bulged beneath the leather armour he wore. The giant watched Zac impassively as he trudged up the hill.

"Who are you?" Zac demanded, stopping in front of the man.

"Who are *you*?" he replied in a thick Scottish accent.

"I asked you first."

The man reached over his shoulder. His fingers wrapped round a long handle, and there was a *shnink* of a blade being unsheathed.

"Well, I've got a big sword," the man scowled. "And it's dead sharp."

Zac weighed up his chances. He'd taken down plenty of adults before, but none as big as this one. He was holding the sword like he meant it too. It was not a fight Zac wanted to have.

"Zac Corgan," he said. "Now your turn."

The big man glowered down at him. "War," he said.

"War?"

"Aye," said the giant. "War."

"As in... battles and fighting and stuff?"

"As in the Horsemen of the Apocalypse."

Zac considered this. He looked War up and down. "Yeah," he said, willing to accept pretty much anything at this point. "Course you are. Where're the other three, then?"

"Coo-ee!" came a voice from beyond the brow of the hill. "Get a move on. We haven't got all day, you know?"

War sighed and closed his eyes. "You had to bloody ask."

A skinny man dressed all in white scurried the last few

steps up the dune. He wore a floppy sunhat on his head and thin rubber gloves on each hand. He gave a soft gasp when he spotted Zac. "Oh, hello," he said. "Who are you, then?"

"Zac Corgan, Pestilence," growled War. "Pestilence, Zac Corgan."

"Lovely to meet you," beamed Pestilence. "And I love the whole black-outfit look. Very mysterious."

War sighed. "Right, give us the ball back."

Zac handed it over. "What is this place?" he asked.

"It's Limbo," said War.

"Limbo?"

"Which probably means you've died, I'm afraid," added Pestilence. "So please accept our condolences."

"What's keeping you?" asked a voice a little way down the dune. A boy just a year or two younger than Zac marched to the top of the hill. He had an oversized plastic baseball bat in one hand. "I need to get back home soon or my mum's going to..."

The boy's voice trailed off. "Who's this?" he asked.

"Drake, this is Zac," Pestilence said. "Zac, Drake here is our latest Death."

"Latest?"

War grunted. "Long, boring story."

"Zac has recently died," Pestilence continued. "Isn't that a shame?"

"No, I haven't."

Pestilence smiled gently. "Yes, you have," he said. "I know it's hard, but the sooner you accept it, the sooner you can move on."

Zac shook his head. "No, I haven't. I was sent on a mission to find a stolen book. I was in Hell a minute ago, and now I'm here."

War and Pestilence exchanged a glance. "The *Book of Everything*?" Pestilence asked in a hushed voice.

"*Book of Everything, Book of Doom* – take your pick," Zac said. "I found it, but they kept my... colleague. It was all a trick to get him down there."

Pestilence's mouth tightened. "That's them all over, that is," he said. "Always up to something. I'm sure he'll be OK, though."

A snort of laughter came from War. "Oh aye, I'm sure he'll be just dandy. They're a right fun bunch down there, just ask anyone."

There was a moment of uncomfortable silence.

"That was sarcasm, by the way," War pointed out.

"Still, at least you found the book," said Pestilence. He clapped his hands. "Yay!"

"You brought it back to them yet?" War asked.

"No. I got stranded here. I've got no way of contacting them." He looked at the Horsemen in turn. "Unless you've got some way of getting in touch with Heaven?"

"We'll go one better," said Drake. "We'll take you there ourselves." He looked from Pestilence to War. "Um... we can do that, right?"

Zac stood in the shadow of a small wooden shed and gazed up at its jolly red roof. There was a *creak* from the door as Drake pushed it open. Zac hung back as War and Pestilence stepped inside.

"A shed?" he asked. "Why are we getting in a shed?"

Drake smiled. "Just trust me."

"No."

"Oh," said Drake, a little deflated. "Right. Well, the shed can travel across dimensions or... or something like that. It can fly you to Heaven."

"But it's a *shed*."

Drake shrugged. "Yeah, I said that at first too."

War's beard appeared round the doorframe, followed by the rest of his face. "You getting in or what?"

Zac looked from the giant to Drake, and then into the dark interior of the shed. He shrugged, sighed, then stepped inside. Drake pulled the door closed and they all squeezed into the narrow space.

"This is cosy, isn't it," breathed Pestilence.

Zac was too stunned to reply. He was looking beyond the Horseman at the chair behind him.

Something immensely fat slouched on the seat, wearing nothing but a sleeveless vest and a distressingly tight pair of flannel shorts. Sweat soaked his skin and dripped down on to the wooden floor. His face was red and blotchy and his breathing came in big, heavy gulps. Something brown was smeared across his blubbery lips.

Chocolate, Zac thought. *Let it be chocolate.*

"That's Famine," Drake explained. "He's, uh, having a rest."

Zac watched the fat man's chest wheezing up and down. "The game must've taken a lot out of him."

"What? Oh, no," Drake said. "That's just from getting changed. He hadn't started playing yet."

"Right," said War. "We're here."

Zac looked up at him. "We're where?"

The door swung open and Zac found himself gazing out at the vast palace Gabriel had taken him to earlier.

"How... how did you do that?" he asked.

"Techno-magic mumbo jumbo," War grunted, and then he shoved Zac out of the shed and slammed the door behind him. There was a muttering from inside it, then a *whoosh*. By the time Zac looked round, the shed was gone.

He waited a moment to see if it came back. When it didn't, he turned, pulled the straps of the backpack higher on his shoulders and strode purposefully towards the house that God built.

CHAPTER THIRTY-ONE

THE ORNATE FRONT door opened without a whisper and Zac stepped on to a marble floor.

"Gabriel?" he called, and his voice echoed around the cavernous hall. "Gabriel, you there?"

Almost immediately there came the sound of hard footsteps clopping across the polished floor. Gabriel entered through one of the many arched doorways at the back of the room. He appeared surprised to see Zac there, but his politician smile didn't waiver once.

"Ah, there you are," he said, spreading his arms wide. "We lost track of you and rather feared the worst. It is good to see you are in one piece." He stopped in front of Zac and the smile grew larger. "I trust you were able to retrieve the book?"

327

"I've got it. But they've kept Angelo."

Gabriel's smile slipped smoothly into a frown. "Have they? Have they indeed?" He gave a solemn nod, then the smile returned. "May I see it?"

"See what?"

"The book. May I see it?"

"Didn't you hear what I said? They've got Angelo. We have to do something."

Gabriel's eyes twitched. "All in good time. The book, please, Zac."

The force of the sudden realisation made Zac take a step back. "Wait... you knew. You knew they were going to keep him," he mumbled. "You made him wait outside the door. You knew I'd choose him over Michael. You knew I'd take him with me."

"The book," said Gabriel, his smile falling away completely. "Give me the book."

"So... what? You *swapped* him?"

"We made a deal," the archangel replied. "The boy for the book. His life for the lives of countless billion others. It was the right thing to do. It was the *good* thing to do."

"The *good* thing? You've sent him to Hell, and who knows

what they're going to do to him? That's not good, that's evil! I thought you lot were supposed to know the difference."

Gabriel held out a hand. "The book, Zacharias. Give me the book."

"No," Zac said. "I want to see the Metatron."

The archangel's eyebrows arched, but he said nothing.

"The voice of God. He's in charge now, right? Angelo told me all about it. I want to see him."

Gabriel chuckled. "What a strange thing to say. You don't see voices, Zac. You hear them."

"Well, I want to hear him, then. I want to talk to him."

"I'm afraid that's not possible," Gabriel said. "Now, while I appreciate your concern for Angelo, I am going to say this one final time. *Give me the book.*"

Zac shook his head. "No," he said. He turned back towards the door. He barely caught a glimpse of Michael standing there before the fiery blade of the archangel's sword was across his throat. Michael's flawless features fixed into an ugly snarl.

"Give me one good reason why I shouldn't cut you down," Michael growled.

Zac felt his strength leave him. His shoulders sagged and

his spirit sagged with them. "I promised him," he said quietly. "I promised him I'd get help."

Gabriel fished inside the backpack. He pulled out a small cloth bag filled with thirty or more little round balls. "Been playing marbles?" he asked, and Zac could hear the smirk on his face. Gabriel returned the bag to the backpack. A moment later, he took out the book.

There was a long moment of silence, broken eventually by Gabriel's clipped tones.

"Is this some sort of joke?" he demanded, catching Zac by the shoulder and spinning the boy round to face him. Gabriel's blue eyes were dark, his chiselled nostrils flared wide. "What is this?" he asked, holding up the leather-bound volume.

"The book," Zac replied.

"No, it isn't! This isn't the book. Look!"

He broke the clasp and padlock without any effort and the book fell open. Zac watched as the archangel flipped through the pages.

"See? Blank. There's nothing there. This isn't the *Book of Everything* it's a book of *nothing*." He turned and hurled the book across the room. It struck a pillar and sprayed plain white paper in all directions. Gabriel stepped in closer to Zac, visibly shaking with rage. "Where is it? Where is the real book?"

Zac shrugged. "That's the one they gave me."

"And you accepted it?" Gabriel snorted. "You're a bigger idiot than I thought."

"Send me back down," Zac suggested. "I'll get the real book and get Angelo at the same time."

"Oh, *Angelo, Angelo, Angelo*," Gabriel cried. "Stop talking about Angelo. Nobody cares about Angelo! Least of all you, if I remember correctly. The book is all that matters. Besides, for all we know they don't even have it. We're back to square one. This whole thing may have been a trick right from the start."

"Right," said Zac. "Which would make *you* the idiot."

Gabriel glared down at him. His jaw moved from side to side, as if chewing over his next few words. At last, he glanced at Michael. "Dispose of him," he said.

Michael's face cracked into a smile. "Now you're talking."

"Do whatever you feel necessary," said Gabriel. He turned and walked back towards the archway. "Just be sure to have someone clean up afterwards."

"By the time I'm finished there won't be anything left to clean up," Michael said.

Gabriel paused, but didn't look back. "I don't want to know," he said, then he continued walking. He was almost at the archway when a voice made him stop for a second time.

"Problems, Gabriel?"

Zac looked for the owner of the voice, but found no one. Then he remembered. You didn't see the Metatron, you only heard him.

Gabriel cleared his throat. Zac heard the silken rustle of Michael's sword sliding back into its sheath.

"Uh, no, sir," Gabriel said. "Or rather, yes, sir. We retrieved the book, but it was a fake."

"Bless it all," said the disembodied voice. It sounded to Zac like an old British military general. It was the type of voice that had a moustache and drank brandy and knew a lot about horses and cricket and impaling foreigners on bayonets. "So, what do we do now, then?" it asked.

Gabriel hesitated. "I... do not know, sir. We begin the search anew. Try to determine where the book is, then formulate a plan for getting it back."

Zac stepped away from Michael and looked into the centre of the room, as if that was where the voice was emanating from. "They're leaving someone down there in Hell," he said. "The boy, Angelo. Hell has him and they won't do anything about it."

Silence followed. Zac got the feeling he was being scrutinised. He stood his ground, waiting for a reply.

"Really?" said the Metatron at last. "Gabriel, is this true?"

"Yes, sir," Gabriel said.

"Was that your intention all along? Why wasn't I informed?"

"We, uh, thought it best to leave that part out, sir," Gabriel oozed. "In order to protect you from any fall-out. They wanted Angelo. We wanted the book. It seemed like a minor sacrifice to make."

"Ah, a sacrifice, eh? Haven't had a sacrifice in a long time. Ah well. Shame for the poor chap, of course, but these things have to be done, what?"

Gabriel's politician grin crept across his face. "My sentiments exactly, sir."

Zac shook his head in disgust. "You're just as bad as they are."

"Come on now, lad," spoke the Metatron. "The needs of the many and whatnot. Can't make an omelette without breaking some eggs." The voice addressed Gabriel. "What about him? What do you plan on doing with him?"

Gabriel glanced sideways at Michael. "We... weren't sure, sir. We had yet to decide."

"Send him back home."

"Sir?"

"You heard. Send him back home. Wasn't his fault the book was a fake. You know what they're like down there. Shower of wrong 'uns, the lot of them. Always up to no good. Not the lad's fault."

"But, sir, our concern was that—"

"I believe I gave an instruction, Gabriel," said the Metatron, and Zac felt the temperature in the room drop several degrees. "The boy completed his part of the deal, so he shall be returned home just as he was. Is that clear?"

Gabriel nodded. "Crystal, sir."

"Good. And you, lad. I believe the arrangement was that your sins would be wiped clean. Is that correct?"

"Yes," said Zac. "But I don't want it."

The Metatron snorted. "Pardon?"

"If being sin-free means coming here when I die, I want to keep them." He glared at Michael and Gabriel. "At least in Hell they don't pretend to be something they're not."

"Well... as you wish," conceded the Metatron. "Gabriel?"

Gabriel gestured to his fellow archangel. "Michael."

Zac recoiled as Michael's hand grabbed him roughly by the shoulder. He heard the man in the golden armour mutter, and then a burst of white exploded behind his eyes.

And then he was in his bedroom, sitting on the end of his bed, looking out through the open curtains at the bright summer's day just beyond the glass. He blinked. There had been a thought right there in his head, but it was gone, floating just out of reach.

He looked down at his clothes. They were filthy, stained with dust and soot and something dark and treacle-like. He was wearing a backpack he didn't recognise. He slipped it off and let it fall on to his bed, then he stood up, opened his bedroom door and went downstairs.

"Ah, Zac, you're back!" said Phillip as Zac shuffled into the kitchen. The old man smiled and gave his grandson a hug. "How was the trip?"

"Trip?"

"Yes, you know," said his granddad. "Your trip. You... you went on a trip."

Zac shook his head. "No, I didn't."

Phillip hesitated. His fingers pressed his stress ball against the palm of his hand. "Oh," he mumbled, his eyes glazing over, "didn't you? I'm... I'm sure you said something about a trip."

"No," replied Zac. "I don't think so."

His head felt full of fog, as if he'd just been woken from a deep sleep. His memory of the last few days was sketchy, but he'd have remembered going away. Wouldn't he?

"Sit down, Granddad, and I'll make you a cup of tea," he said, crossing to the kettle.

"Coffee would be nice," Phillip replied. "I was up half the night. I thought you'd come back. I was sure I heard that Albert's voice."

Zac flicked the kettle's switch. "Albert?"

"That is his name, isn't it?" Phillip said. "I forget sometimes."

A spoon of instant coffee went into a mug. "I don't know any Albert."

"Oh, maybe not Albert, then," fretted Phillip. "Angus? Adam?"

"Not ringing any bells."

Phillip squeezed his stress ball. "No, but... Oh, I wish I could remember. Kept hearing him all night. Sounded in a right panic. Scared too, very scared."

Zac smiled. "Don't worry about it, Granddad. It was just a dream or something, I wouldn't—"

"Angelo!"

Zac felt his legs turn to lead, but he didn't know why.

"Angelo, that was it," Phillip beamed. "I knew I'd remember."

"I... I don't know any Angelo," Zac said. A breeze blew around inside his head, swirling the fog that filled it.

His granddad tutted. "Course you do. Angelo. You had him here last night. Or was it the night before?"

Zac poured hot water into his grandfather's mug, and gave it a stir. "I'm telling you, I don't know anyone called Angelo."

"You do!"

"I don't," Zac insisted, picking up the mug.

"Don't be silly, Zac," Phillip sighed. "Stop trying to

confuse me, I'm bad enough as it is. You remember. Angelo. Your friend."

Zac's lips moved instinctively. "He's not my friend, he's my colleague," he said.

The mug slipped from his hand and smashed on the kitchen floor. The fog in his head thinned, offering glimpses of the memories that lay beyond.

He charged out of the kitchen and took the stairs two at a time. He tore at the zip of the backpack, then thrust his hand inside until he found the velvet bag. Cupping a hand, he tipped a few of the marble-sized balls out into his palm. He stared down at them, and they all stared right back.

"Eyes," he whispered. "Argus."

He looked down at the carpet and saw an inky black stain. He searched his bookcase until he spotted a slim, battered volume on the fourth shelf down. *The Strange Case of Dr Jekyll & Mr Hyde*, by Robert Louis Stevenson.

He remembered.

He remembered Heaven and Hell and everything else in between.

He remembered Angelo.

And he remembered leaving him down there, all alone with the demons and the monsters and who knew what else? He had told him he'd go back. He had promised.

He poured the eyes back in the bag, put the bag back in the backpack, pulled the backpack over his shoulders.

He's not my friend, he's my colleague.

Yeah, right. Who was he trying to kid?

Zac rummaged in his wastepaper bin and pulled out two small torn pieces of card. Then, with a final look around the room, he left, pulling the door firmly closed behind him.

CHAPTER THIRTY-TWO

Z AC HURRIED DOWN the stairs, along the hallway, where the goldfish was still splashing furiously in its bowl, and into the kitchen once more. His grandfather was mopping up the spilled coffee and looked up as Zac entered.

"Listen, Granddad, I have to go away again."

Phillip stopped mopping. He leaned on the handle and gave his grandson a withering look. "Again? I thought you said you hadn't been anywhere?"

"I know that's what I said," Zac admitted. "But I... forgot that I had."

The old man thought about this, then nodded. "Happens to the best of us," he said. "Will you be long?"

Zac nodded, and as he did he felt tears pricking the back of his eyes.

Phillip straightened up. "But... you're coming back."

It took all Zac's strength to shake his head.

"Oh," said his granddad. He rested the mop handle against the table. "What, never?"

"I... I don't know. I'm not sure, but there's a good chance I won't be."

Phillip nodded, as if not entirely surprised. "It's something to do with this Angelo," he said. "Isn't it?"

Zac nodded again. He knew if he spoke now his voice would betray him and tears would surely follow.

"You're going to help him," Phillip said. "Aren't you?"

"I'm the only one who can," said Zac croakily.

Phillip reached over and rested a hand on his grandson's shoulder. "You know, Zac, wherever they are, your parents would be very proud," he said. He smiled away tears of his own. "But not as proud as I am."

Zac put his arms round the old man and buried his face against his shoulder. "I'm sorry," he whispered. "I shouldn't be leaving you."

Phillip stepped back. "We all have to do what we have to do, Zac," he said, smiling again for his grandson's sake. "I'll be just fine. Right now Angelo needs you more. He's scared, Zac. He's so very, very scared."

Zac looked into his granddad's eyes. "How do you know?"

Phillip frowned. "I… I don't know. I hear him sometimes. Crying out. So very afraid. Help him, Zac. You have to help him."

"I'm going to. I will."

"But… but he seems so far away. How will you get to him?"

Zac's jaw clenched. "That bit I've got covered. I just have to make a couple of stops before I go."

Zac sat on a wall, his feet dangling over the edge. He tried not to think of his granddad. If he thought of his granddad there was a chance he'd turn back, and how could he turn back knowing everything he knew? How could he live with himself if he did?

The backpack was heavier now. He could feel it pulling him, holding him back. It had been a struggle to fit everything inside, and even more difficult getting the zip closed afterwards. But the man from the toyshop had been very helpful, and between them they'd got the job done.

The people in the church hadn't been quite so eager to assist. They'd been annoyed. Furious, even. But then religious people seemed to get furious at most things he did, and he'd long since decided not to care.

It was windy up there on the wall. He'd expected that. It was often windy up on the rooftops. The higher you went, the less cover there was from other buildings, and so the more the wind blew. Right now the wind was blowing very hard indeed.

He wished he could just jump. It would be easy if he could just jump. But he knew he never could. His instinct for survival would never allow him. That was why he'd had to make other arrangements.

"Hey, kid," said a voice behind him. *Right on time.*

Zac swung himself back up on to the roof and saw his reflection in the Monk's mirrored sunglasses. "You came."

"You called. I gotta be honest, kid, I've offed a lot of folks in my time. Not one of them ever phoned me up afterwards. That really takes the cake."

The Monk reached into his robe. A moment later, the gun came out. "You sure you wanna do this? You know what you're giving up, right?"

Zac clipped the straps of the backpack together across his chest. "I have to," he said. "I can't leave him alone down there. And he'd do it for me. He's... he's a good kid."

The Monk nodded. "That he is. Better than you an' me, anyhow."

"Better than you and me," agreed Zac. He straightened his back and held his head high. "Do it."

The Monk raised the pistol. "You got balls, kid, I'll give you that." He hesitated, his finger on the trigger. "Might not be any use to you, but you ever meet Gabriel again, you ask him about the Right of Enosh."

"The Right of Enosh?"

"The Right of Enosh," confirmed the Monk, and then his finger tightened and the pistol roared.

The force of the shot sent Zac staggering backwards over the roof edge. Clutching his bleeding stomach, he tried to scream. There was a faintly jarring *bump* as his body hit the concrete. His physical form stayed behind as a messy splat on the ground, but the rest of him just carried on falling.

The grey mists of the Nether Lands smothered him for a few seconds, then cleared to reveal a dark and barren landscape, spread out like a blanket at the world's gloomiest picnic. From way up high he was able to pick out some detail of the land below him. There was the River Styx. There was the waterfall. And there, way off in the distance was Hades and the flickering lights of Eyedol.

Zac fell. Down towards the sludgy water. Down towards the blood-stained welcome sign. Down towards Hell itself.

He fell.

He smiled.

And he kept on falling.

CHAPTER THIRTY-THREE

HE LANDED ON his feet and the ground rippled around him.

He had passed through the roof like a ghost and come to a stop in a cave-like room with lava flowing through gaps in the rocky floor. The wailing and the sobbing of the damned bounced like squash balls off the walls around him.

The worst of the wailing, though, seemed to be piped in through hidden speakers. There were only thirty or forty people in the room itself, and most of those were standing in small groups looking worried. Only two or three people were actually weeping, but the sound effects suggested thousands more of them were hiding round the corner.

There was demonic laughter too, and the crackling of deadly flames. Small log fires burned here and there around the cave, but the roar of the inferno was also coming from the speakers.

There was only one actual demon in the room, as far as Zac could tell. He wore gold hot pants and roller skates, and was bare from the waist up. The demon looked up from a clipboard and a flicker of recognition crossed his face. "Oi," he said. "I know you. You're the one what shot me."

The demon trundled awkwardly over on his skates. "Thought you were the big man, waving that gun about," he spat. "Thought you were the big *I am*. Not so tough now, are you? Not so tough n—"

Zac formed his left hand into the shape of a spearhead and jabbed it upward into the soft area just above the demon's right armpit.

"Ooyah," hissed the creature, and then half his face went slack, and half his body went limp, and all of him slumped to the ground in a whimpering heap.

Zac stepped over him and raced towards a door set into one of the rocky walls. He'd barely got his fingers on the handle when someone called out to him.

"Um... excuse me?"

He turned to find a middle-aged woman waving to him from one of the worried little groups. "We were just wondering... what should we do?" she asked. "It's just that we're all quite new to this and..." She ran out of steam then, and someone from another group took over.

"Should we just hang about here or what?" asked a man just a few years older than Zac. "Only no one's really told us anything since I arrived and, well, between you and me, I'm getting a bit sick of it."

There was murmured agreement from the rest of the damned. Zac sighed. He didn't have time for this.

"Well, I don't know," he said. "I mean, are any of you murderers or anything?"

A few questioning glances were exchanged. Then, at the back of the room, a solitary man in a long dirty raincoat raised a hand.

"Right, well, you stay here, then," Zac told him. The man tutted quietly, but sat down on a rock and did his best to make himself comfortable. "The rest of you do what you like," Zac shrugged. "Try to get out if you want. If you can make it upriver there's a nightclub. I'd imagine it's more fun than here. Tell the owner Zac sent you." He moved to open the door. "Oh, and tell him I said sorry about his boat."

The door led out into the reception area, where the secretary was sitting at her desk, knitting furiously and gazing down at a double-page spread in *Your Hellhound*. She looked up as Zac entered and the clicking of her needles stopped.

"All right?" he said. He set the backpack down on the floor, unzipped it and began rummaging inside.

"Um..." said the demon. "Um..."

"Sorry about earlier," he told her. "You know, shooting you in the face and stuff?"

"Um..."

"We were trying to be stealthy, that's why I did it." He took out a couple of small plastic guns and stuck them in his waistband, then he removed a much larger gun from the bag and set it on the floor. Next he removed the little sack of Argus eyes and put them in his pocket.

Finally, he took out the bomb. It was a simple thing. He'd bought it from Geneva Jones on his way to the toyshop. She'd agreed to give him a discount to make up for selling him out to the Monk. It was all just business in the end.

The bomb itself was relatively harmless. Relatively harmless compared to other bombs, at least. It contained only a very small amount of explosive. Four two-litre bottles of water were attached to it, making the whole thing awkwardly heavy. Zac slung the strap of the large gun over his shoulder, leaving his hands free to carry the bomb.

"But I'm not trying to be stealthy any more," he said, kicking the now empty backpack into the corner of the room. "You've got an alarm system in here."

The demon nodded. "Um..."

"You'd probably better press it."

The demon nodded again. Her finger slowly went to a button beneath her desk. Zac kicked open the door just as the alarm bells began to ring.

All round the first circle, doors began to open, and the alarm was briefly drowned out by the screams and howls of the damned. A green and purple demon with ape-like arms was unlucky enough to step out from the closest door.

"What's all the racket?" he demanded, before the tip of

Zac's shoe came up sharply between his legs. The demon clutched his groin and dropped to his knees, then he toppled sideways, groaning, on to the floor.

More demons poured from more doors up ahead. Others still emerged from the rooms behind him. Zac looked down at the floors below and saw that they too, were brimming with monsters, all gesturing angrily in his direction.

With a flick of a switch, Zac primed the bomb and a three-second countdown began. He tossed the thing out over the frosted-glass barrier and into the big space in the centre of the rings. The bomb flipped twice, then began to fall.

It had barely travelled three or four metres downwards when the explosive charge detonated. The bottles ruptured, spraying a rain of holy water in all directions. Those demons unlucky enough to be hit by the spray began to scream as their hides sizzled and blistered.

"Wow," said Zac. "So that's what it does to them."

The din of the demons' screams echoed round the corridors of Hell. The spray had only hit a small percentage of them, but their thrashing and howling and begging for help had quickly plunged the whole place into chaos.

The demon he'd kicked was still lying on the ground, holding his crotch and trying not to vomit on the carpet. He gave a high-pitched whimper when Zac hauled him to his feet.

"The tenth circle. Can you take me there?"

The demon shook his head. Zac took one of the smaller water pistols from his waistband and jammed it in the demon's mouth. "Holy water," he explained. He cocked his head and listened to the screaming from the lower floors. "But then you probably guessed that. I'm going to ask you again. The tenth circle. Can you take me there?"

The demon shook his head again. Zac squeezed the trigger, just enough for a single drop of water to dribble into the monster's mouth. The demon's eyes went wide as his tongue began to sizzle and burn.

"Tenth circle," Zac urged. "Yes or no?"

"'Es!" the demon squeaked. "'Es!"

Zac glanced around the corridor. Those demons who hadn't been hit by the spray were shoving past the others, making their way around to him. They'd be on him at any moment.

"Then do it," he growled. "*Now!*"

There was a *blip* and Zac found himself standing in the room he'd been in earlier. There were the chains that had bound him and Angelo. There was the reclining chair. But it looked like a tornado had ripped through the place.

The chair was in pieces. The light that had been mounted above it lay smashed and broken on the floor. A gaping hole had been torn through one wall. From beyond it, Zac could hear shouts of anger and yelps of panic, and the roars of something monstrous.

The captive demon watched him, his eyes bulging, the gun still wedged in his mouth. Zac carefully removed the pistol. "Sorry about that," he said, then he drove a left hook across the demon's cheek, knocking him out cold. "And that."

He looked over to the hole in the wall. "Right, then," he announced to no one in particular. "I'm guessing this way."

Just as he reached the gap, something large and scaly came hurtling backwards through it. With a cry of pain, Haures smashed through a stainless-steel worktop and thudded hard against the wall. Black blood oozed from the duke's nose and mouth. He coughed violently, mumbled, "That's more like it," then slid sideways on to the floor.

Zac cautiously poked his head round the edge of the hole and peered into a room larger than the one he was in. It was filled with what was probably until very recently state-of-the-art medical equipment, but which was now little more than scrap metal bent into a variety of interesting shapes.

A large metal box, which may once have been a prison cell, stood in the centre of the room. One of its walls had been torn away, the others were scorched and black with soot. Sparks rained down from a broken electric light that hung from the high ceiling. The other lights flickered, more off than on.

Three of the demons in surgical masks chittered excitedly as they launched themselves into the shadows beneath the broken light. A bellow of rage rocked the room and two of the demons were hurled from the darkness at terrifying speed. Their spindly bodies went *krik* as they broke against the wall.

Zac looked on as the third little demon came darting out of the gloom, its eyes wide open with terror. It made it four steps before a hand reached out of the dark and swatted it to the floor. The demon screamed as the hand dragged it back into the shadows, and then the screams became muffled before abruptly coming to a stop.

Silence followed, broken only by a burp from the darkness.

Zac stepped through the hole in the wall. "Hey, Angelo," he said, doing what he could to control the shake in his voice. "Hoped I'd find you here."

Breath hissed in the shadows. A growl rumbled at the back of a throat.

"I came back. You know, to rescue you. Like I said. Because, well, I was thinking and—"

A jet of flame crackled towards him, forcing Zac to throw himself sideways. He rolled expertly and took cover behind the buckled remains of a metal wall. The flame had come from high up, somewhere near the domed ceiling itself. Zac raised his eyes. The ceiling was ten metres high, maybe more. Higher than Angelo's demon form had been. Much, much higher.

There was a clatter from the hole in the wall and Haures came staggering through. The Duke of Hell glowered gleefully up into the darkness and extended his arms out wide.

"Come, my boy," he cried. "Come to Uncle Haures!"

Zac kept out of sight. He ducked down low and watched as the shadows parted revealing the Angelo-demon in all his true horror.

"Oh, come on," Zac muttered as the monstrous shape stepped into view. "You have *got* to be kidding me."

CHAPTER THIRTY-FOUR

ANGELO LOOKED PREHISTORIC. Not like a dinosaur, exactly, more like the thing that had killed all the dinosaurs off. And probably without even trying.

He stood seven or eight metres tall, with his horns adding eighty or ninety more centimetres on top. The horns scraped along the ceiling as he lumbered forward, his scaly red knuckles trailing across the floor, each thunderous footstep shaking the room.

"Yes," cackled Haures. "Yes! What a specimen you are! What a specimen you— *Oof!*"

The back of Angelo's hand swatted Haures across the room. The Duke of Hell was laughing with delight as he crunched into the metal barricade Zac was hiding behind.

Both Haures and the barricade tumbled on for several metres, before rolling to a stop.

Suddenly exposed, Zac straightened up and locked eyes with the Angelo-demon. Bones grew like tusks from the monster's neck and jaw. The fire in his eyes burned with such ferocity it looked like the whole top half of his head was ablaze. He snorted like a racehorse after a sprint, and each time he did, rings of black smoke blew from his wide nostrils.

"What did they do to you?" said Zac softly.

"We set him free," said Haures, limping in Zac's direction. "Impressive, isn't he?" He looked the intruder up and down. "How did you get back down here, by the way?"

Zac didn't answer.

Haures shrugged. "They tried to neuter him," he continued. "*Up there*. They tried to smother his dark side, kill it off. But you can't kill *that*. How can you kill *that*? All they did was bottle it up. And all we had to do was take the lid off."

The Angelo-demon's fist swung down at them. Zac and Haures leaped in opposite directions and the knuckles shattered the floor where they'd stood.

"And this is what you're left with!" Zac shouted. "He's out of control. He'll tear the whole place apart."

"We'll train him," Haures smirked. "We'll *break* him, and we'll keep breaking him until he does exactly as we say."

"Then you're doing just what Heaven did," Zac said. He ducked as Angelo's Boa Constrictor-like tail whistled by above his head. "You're only letting him be one thing – but now you're bottling up his angel side."

Haures snorted. "So once in a blue moon he'll lose control and do some really impressive charity work. I can live with that."

The demon duke feinted left as Angelo's tail snapped down at him. "He's already learned some basic commands," said Haures, recovering quickly. "Watch this."

Haures stabbed a clawed finger in Zac's direction. "Angelo!" he barked. The Angelo-demon's ears pricked up. It gazed down at the much smaller demon, unblinking. Haures smiled. "Kill."

Slowly, like a shadow at sunset, Angelo's gaze went to Zac.

"Don't," Zac said. "Don't do this, Angelo. You know me. Try to rememb—"

A guttural howl drowned out the rest of Zac's words. The Angelo-demon charged, claws swiping, fire spewing from his cavernous throat. Zac rolled, ducked, turned, ran. All around him was the crackling of the flames and the cackling of demonic laughter and the steady *boom boom boom* of footsteps chasing him down.

The crumpled jail cell stood just ahead. Zac powered forward. If he could make it there, he could buy himself a few seconds. If he could buy himself a few seconds, he could come up with a plan. And if he could come up with a plan, then maybe this wouldn't have to go down as the most botched rescue attempt in the history of the human race.

The pointed tip of Angelo's tail streaked by him. There was a nerve-splitting screeching sound as the tail tore through a metal wall, and then the entire cell was jerked up into the air.

Zac saw the shadow of the metal box grow larger around him. He hurled himself out of the way just as the cell was brought smashing down against the floor.

Clambering back to his feet, Zac swung the large water gun into his hands. "I didn't want to do this," he said, taking aim. "But you're not leaving me any choice."

He squeezed the trigger. A jet of holy water hit the Angelo-demon square in the chest, but the monster didn't react.

"Immune to the effects of holy water," roared Haures. "This just gets better and better!"

Angelo brought a foot stomping down towards Zac's head. Zac avoided it, but only just, and with each miss he made, Angelo became angrier and more aggressive. If Zac was going to take the demon down, he had to do it now.

He ran from the giant demon, not trying to escape, but trying to make space. As he ran, he dug in his pocket and pulled out the little black bag Argus had given him. He heard the footsteps of the Angelo-demon thudding after him. He stopped. He emptied the bag into his hand. And then he tossed the contents towards the oncoming beast.

The eyes rattled like marbles on the hard floor. They began to roll just as one of Angelo's feet came down on them. The foot slid sharply forward and the demon became horizontal in the air. All ten circles of Hell shook when he hit the ground.

Zac and Haures exchanged a glance, then they both set off running. Zac reached the fallen Angelo first. He leaped up on to his bare chest and fired a spray of holy water towards Haures, forcing the duke to duck for cover.

"Get away from him! What are you doing?" Haures demanded, but Zac was no longer listening to him. He scrambled along Angelo's chest until he could look him in the eye.

"Angelo, it's me. It's Zac," he said. "I know you're in there. I hope you can hear me."

He paused to scoosh more holy water at Haures, keeping him at bay.

"This isn't you, Angelo," he said. "Not really. This is what they made you, up there and down here. This is what they turned you into."

A low growl rumbled from Angelo's throat, but he wasn't yet moving to attack.

"Up there they tried to make you an angel, and down here all they want you to be is a demon, but the real you is somewhere in the middle." He shot more holy water backwards over his shoulder. Haures gave a yelp of panic and leaped out of harm's way.

"Don't listen to him, boy! Listen to your Uncle Haures."

"I thought we were nothing alike, but I was wrong,

Angelo," Zac said. "You're *exactly* like me – not perfect, but you're not a demon, either. You're exactly like *everyone*." He stared deep into the fireballs that were Angelo's eyes. "The one good thing they did for you up there was give you those Hulk comics. Everyone thinks the Hulk's a monster, but he isn't. That's what you said. All he wants is for people to stop trying to hurt him. All he wants is a friend. Right? Just like you, Angelo. Just like you. That's why you love the Hulk, Angelo. You *are* the Hulk."

Angelo's breaths were coming more slowly now. The angry scowl on his face had relaxed just a fraction.

"*Enough!*" boomed Haures from down by the fallen giant's knees. The demon duke raised both hands and fire flew from his fingertips. Pain contorted Angelo's face again, and as the pain faded it was replaced by something savage. His eyes fixed on Zac. His mouth pulled into a snarl. A voice like a tropical storm roared out from within him.

"Angelo *smash*!"

He began to sit up, and Zac was forced to grab on to one of his tusks to stop himself tumbling to the floor.

"Yes!" bellowed Haures, dancing backwards. "Kill him. Kill the human! Kill him now!"

Zac had one chance. He gave the water gun a shake and listened to the liquid sloshing around inside it. There was a litre of the stuff left, possibly less. Even if it did work, would it be enough?

Angelo began to stand. Dangling from his tusk, Zac fired every last drop of the holy water into the demon's mouth. There was a sizzle, but a faint one. Angelo stopped rising. He looked past his nose to where Zac hung. He raised his eyebrows. And then he licked his lips.

"M-more," slurred Angelo, and the breath felt to Zac as if an oven door had been opened right in front of his face. He remembered the pistols in his waistband, thought about emptying the water into the mouth, then decided just to toss the guns in themselves. They cracked between Angelo's teeth, then he gave a low moan of satisfaction as the blessed liquid trickled down his throat.

"Y-yuummeeee..."

"That's it," Zac said. "Remember. Remember who you are, Angelo. Remember who you are."

"S-s-scrummeee..."

Zac finished the sentence for him. "In your tummy."

"*What are you doing?*" Haures roared. He raised his hands

again and his fingers glowed white-hot. "Whatever it is, stop or I'll—"

CRUNCH!

Angelo's tail sent him hurtling through the air again. This time Haures didn't laugh as he thudded against the far wall and slid down on to the floor.

"Z-zaaac," mumbled Angelo, his brow creasing as he struggled to form the word. Zac almost cheered.

"Yes! It's me!" he said. "Can you... can you understand me?"

Quaking with the effort, Angelo nodded his head. The jerky movement almost made Zac lose his grip, but he wrapped his other arm round the tusk and swung himself up on to Angelo's scaly shoulder.

He glanced down at what was left of the room. Over in the far corner, Haures was getting shakily back to his feet. "Want to get out of here?" Zac asked.

Angelo nodded again. He stood up, then squatted down low. "Yssss," he said, and then his legs straightened and his hands reached up and together they tore through the ceiling of the tenth circle of Hell.

CHAPTER THIRTY-FIVE

ZAC TUCKED HIMSELF in behind the Angelo-demon's head as a chunk of the ceiling collapsed around them. The clanging of the alarm bell and the yelps of panic from the demons above rushed down to meet them, and Zac felt Angelo's muscles tense in panic.

"Ignore it," he said. "They can't hurt you. Just get us out of here."

Angelo pulled himself through the hole he had created and they emerged on to the zigzag carpet beside the fountain of blood. The nine circles of Hell stretched up above them. From down there, the first circle seemed an impossible distance away.

At least, it did to Zac. Angelo was already on the move.

He crouched down low again and his legs fired like pistons, propelling them upwards. His huge hands reached out, smashed through the frosted-glass barrier, then caught hold of the edge of the seventh circle. The demons on that floor screamed and scurried for safety as Angelo reached a hand up to the sixth circle and began to climb.

"Stop them!" commanded a voice over the Tannoy system. Zac recognised the tones of the Dark Lord himself. He did not sound impressed. "The specimen must not be permitted to escape. Whoever stops them will be given the human to do with as they see fit."

Zac saw several hundred dark eyes turn to him and gleam. "Keep climbing, Angelo," he urged as the demon stretched an arm up to the next floor.

One of the larger and braver demons on the fourth circle hurled himself towards Zac, claws bared, teeth gnashing. But his leap was woefully misjudged. Zac watched the creature begin frantically flapping his arms as he fell past, then heard the distant *whumpf* as his face was introduced to the carpet.

The fourth circle was heaving with demons, all undeterred by the fate of their fallen colleague. They gathered near the edge, ready to hurl themselves on to Angelo's shoulders as he drew level with them.

"On three, lads!" one of them shouted. "One... two..."

Angelo opened his mouth and an inferno rolled across the corridor. The demons retreated, throwing up their arms to shield their eyes. They lowered them in time to see a foot passing by the corridor as Angelo stretched up to a higher floor.

His claws scraped against the edge of the third circle. He gritted his razor-sharp teeth and stretched further, until his fingertips found purchase on the edge of the floor.

Zac felt the muscles on the Angelo-demon's back contract, even as he felt the first stirrings of panic fluttering in his own stomach. He looked at Angelo's horns. They were several centimetres shorter than they had been just a few seconds ago. His neck and shoulders now seemed significantly less broad too, and his hard scales felt considerably softer.

"You're shrinking! Why are you shrinking?" Zac groaned. "Not now. Don't change back now!"

"S-sorry," Angelo groaned. He was looking more and more like his old self with each moment that passed – an enormous version, granted, but his old self all the same.

His skin was going from red to a flushed pink. His horns had all but retreated into his skull. When he reached for the next floor, his arm fell a metre short. He was barely twice the size of Zac now, and he was shrinking fast.

Demons swarmed along the floors above and below them, fighting each other to be the one who stopped the escape.

Zac searched desperately for a way out, for a way past the squawking, chittering hordes, but there was no time to plan, no time for anything as Angelo returned to normal size. Clinging to each other, they fell. Down through the circles of Hell. Down past the braying demons. Down towards the broken floor and the shadowy embrace of the tenth circle beyond.

A sound, like a ripple of applause, filled the air around them. Hands caught Zac firmly beneath the arms and their descent began to slow. He tightened his grip round Angelo and looked up. A pair of feathery white wings filled his field of view.

An angel, he thought, until he saw the bloody wound on one of the wings and instead thought: *a Valkyrie*.

"Stop squirming," Herya hissed, her face contorted in pain as she beat both wings as hard as she could.

"I wasn't squirming."

"Well, stop talking then!" she spat.

"Is that Herya?" Angelo asked.

"Yeah."

"Hooray! Hello, Herya! You came back for us!"

The Valkyrie hissed again. "Regretting it already."

Zac felt his toes brush against the carpet. He caught a glimpse of Haures's fiery eyes blazing in the darkness of the tenth circle, and then they were rising again, climbing, soaring up towards the upper floors of Hell.

As they passed the third floor, a chubby demon with a Mohican haircut took aim with something that looked worryingly like a bazooka. A door flew open behind him and another demon in red pyjamas emerged. The new arrival raised a particularly heavy hardback copy of *Jekyll & Hyde* above his head, then brought it smashing down on the back of the other demon's Mohican.

The demon stumbled forward and crashed through the frosted-glass barrier. His eyes went wide. "Ooh, bugger," he mumbled, and then he and the bazooka went down as Herya and her cargo went up.

"Go on, son!" cheered Murmur, punching the air in triumph.

"Thanks, Dad!" Angelo shouted back. He waved enthusiastically as they passed the third circle and carried on all the way up to the first.

A squadron of uniformed demons were ready and waiting for them. "Halt!" commanded the leader. "In the name of the Dark Lord, Satan, I command you to—"

He stopped talking as Herya's forehead met his nose. The rest of his platoon stood gaping in surprise. Many of them had dreamed of the day their commanding officer would be cut down to size, but now it had come they weren't quite sure how they felt about it.

Zac didn't hesitate. He cut through them, all fists and feet and elbows and knees. Herya mopped up what was left, and in moments the three of them were surrounded by little mounds of unconscious monsters.

Angelo gave a low whistle, then smiled. "Crumbs. That was exciting, wasn't it?"

Zac looked the skinny boy up and down. "What I want to know," he said, "is how have you *still* managed to keep those trousers on?"

Herya was staring down at the senseless demons. She drew in a deep breath. "A fight. My gods. I was in a real fight."

Zac laid a hand on her shoulder. "You OK?"

"Are you kidding? That was *brilliant*!" she giggled. "Let's find more of them and do it again."

"Let's not," suggested Zac.

"*Cretins*," crackled the voice of the Dark Lord. "Stop them! Stop them now! Do not let them get to the main door. *Do not let them escape!*"

"Main door's this way," said Zac, leading them towards the exit he knew led to the reception area. He yanked it open and they tumbled inside. "Now, out here and we're home and dry."

A small figure in a large suit sat on the other side of the reception desk, his hands behind his head, his feet resting on the table. He gave a vague wave of his hand and the double doors that led out of Hell melted away and were replaced with solid rock.

"Surprise," said Satan. There was a sound like inrushing air, and Haures appeared in the doorway behind them. The Dark Lord leaned in towards the intercom again. "*Oh, don't let them get to the main doors,*" he said in a falsetto voice. "*Whatever will we do if they reach the main doors?*"

Zac heard Angelo gasp. "This was a trap," the half-angel whispered.

"You think?"

"Who are you?" demanded Herya, eyeballing the Dark Lord.

Zac did the introductions. "Herya, Satan. Satan, Herya."

Herya dialled the eyeballing back a few notches. "Oh," she said, then said nothing more.

"And the gentleman behind you is Haures," Satan said. "He's one of the Dukes of—"

"Hazzard," said Zac and Angelo together, then they exchanged a quick high five.

The Dark Lord swung his feet down and emerged from behind the desk. "Very amusing," he said. He regarded Zac. "So you came back for your colleague."

"No," said Zac. "I came back for my *friend*."

"Ker-ching!" cheered Angelo. "Back of the net!" He tried to hug Zac, but was nudged away.

"Not now," Zac told him.

Grinning broadly, Angelo began body-popping. "*He likes me. He likes me. He really, really likes me*," he sang in a robotic voice.

The demons watched him in bemused silence. After several seconds, Angelo stopped dancing. He coughed quietly. "Carry on."

Satan hesitated. "Right..." he said a little uncertainly. "Angelo will be taken back down and restored to his true form, while you two are given to some of my more... creative staff to have fun with." He smiled thinly. "Fun for them, you understand? Not for you."

The Dark Lord returned to the Tannoy and began calling for reinforcements. Zac, Angelo and Herya stood back to back, allowing them to keep an eye on both demons at once.

"What do we do?" whispered the Valkyrie.

Zac's mind raced. "I... I don't know."

"Why did I come back for you?" Herya groaned. "I could've been in Vegas by now."

"Shut up and let me think."

"I've got an idea," Angelo said, "but you won't like it."

"Right now, I'm prepared to try almost anything," Zac replied. Satan looked up from the Tannoy microphone, a vague expression of amusement on his face. From out in the corridor, Zac could hear the sound of hurried footsteps approaching. "What's the idea?"

Angelo took a deep breath. "We pray."

"Pray? That's your idea? We pray?"

"Have you got a better one?"

"I told you, I'm not praying," Zac said.

Satan took a step closer. "What are you whispering about, little ones?" he asked them, and his forked tongue flicked across his lips.

"Come on, what harm can it do?" Angelo asked.

"Whatever you're planning, just do it," Herya urged. She had her fists raised, but it was clear from the way her shoulders sagged that she didn't fancy their chances.

"You said you'd try anything," Angelo reminded him.

"I said *almost* anything."

"Just do *something*!" Herya yelped.

"Oh, all right," Zac snapped. He pressed his hands together. "Dear God, please save us," he said. He turned to Angelo. "Happy now?"

"You didn't say *Amen*."

Zac sighed. "Oh, well I'm sorry," he said. "*Amen*."

And as the word left his lips, the air was filled with blinding light and a joyous chorus of *Hallelujahs*.

Zac rubbed his eyes.

Angelo and Herya and Satan and Haures all rubbed their eyes too. As did the little old man who was suddenly just there, sitting in his favourite armchair in the corner of his living room.

Zac looked around at the familiar wallpaper, the familiar carpet, the familiar everything. He looked at his grandfather, who was staring open-mouthed at the five figures who had suddenly appeared in his front room out of the blue.

"Granddad?" Zac muttered. Phillip turned towards him and an expression of relief crossed the old man's face.

"Oh, Zac, there you are," he said. His fingers squashed his globe-patterned stress ball over and over. "I heard you, Zac. In my head. I heard you calling for help. *Please save us*, that's what you said. I heard you."

Zac frowned. "What? I mean... you did?"

"Hey, look. It's like the song," chirped Angelo. He nudged Zac in the ribs and pointed at Phillip's stress ball. "Your granddad. He's got the whole world in his hands!"

Zac stared at the globe. Then he stared at the old man's brilliant blue eyes. All those voices his granddad had heard for all those years. Asking him for help.

No, not asking.

Praying for help.

He had heard their prayers, and as far as Zac had ever been told, there was only one being who could hear people's prayers. One *supreme* being.

"Oh," said Zac. He swallowed. "My God."

CHAPTER THIRTY-SIX

THE DARK LORD Satan, Father of All Lies, cleared his throat politely.

"Would someone care to tell me what's going on?"

Philip turned to look at Satan. A flicker of recognition crossed his face, and just then, just for a moment, it wasn't Zac's granddad sitting in the chair. It was someone older. Much older. As old, in fact, as time itself.

The air around him crackled in a blaze of light so blinding that Zac was forced to shield his eyes. Phillip spoke, and when he did, his voice seemed to roll in from every direction at once.

"*You*," he said, and the whole world shook with the power of it. "Don't I know you?"

Satan licked his lips, which had suddenly become very dry. "What, me?" he said, brushing his fingers through his hair and hiding the stumps of his horns. "Um... nope. Don't think so."

"Oh."

The light stuttered and faded, and Phillip became his old self again. Zac glanced at the others. Only himself and Satan seemed to have noticed the change that had come over his grandfather.

He quit. That's what Angelo had said. Almost one hundred years ago, he'd quit. And nobody knew where he went.

Phillip gazed across the group. "Zac, who are these people?" he asked. "Why's that one got wings? And why's he in fancy dress?"

"Fancy dress?" growled Haures. He lunged at Phillip. "I'll show you fancy dress, you old—"

As his hand touched the old man, the demon popped like a bubble and disappeared. Silence fell. Satan shuffled his feet.

"Well, this is awkward," he mumbled.

There was a faint *whoosh* from the back of the room. They all turned to see Gabriel and Michael step out of thin air.

"Who's this pair now?" Phillip frowned. "Where did they come from?"

"Good afternoon," said Gabriel, his smile as false as ever. He nodded in Satan's direction. "And look here, if it isn't the Prince of Darkness himself. We were informed you were on Earth, but we didn't believe it. And yet here you are."

"Gabriel. Michael," acknowledged Satan. "How's tricks?"

"Oh, can't complain," Gabriel shrugged. "Can't complain. Do you have the book?"

"What book?"

Michael growled and took a step towards the Dark Lord, but Gabriel blocked his path. "You know very well which book," Gabriel smiled. "Our book. The *Book of Everything*."

"Oh, the *Book of Doom*, you mean." Satan breathed on his black fingernails and brushed them against his suit jacket. "We never had it. It was all just a trick. We only wanted the boy, and you fell for it. Too trusting, that's your problem. Well, one of them, anyway."

Gabriel's eye twitched. He glanced across at Angelo, who immediately took cover behind Zac and Herya.

"Quite," the archangel said. "But of course you realise that if that's the case, then the deal is off. You did not give us the book, and so you do not get the boy. He shall return with us."

"No, he won't."

Satan and the archangels turned at the sound of Zac's voice.

"I beg your pardon?" said Gabriel.

"He's not going with you, and he's not going with him, either."

Angelo tugged him by the sleeve. "What are you doing?" he whispered. "You're going to get into trouble!"

Zac pointed at Gabriel. "You tried to make him an angel." He pointed at Satan. "You tried to make him a demon. But he doesn't belong in Heaven, and he doesn't belong in Hell. He belongs here."

Gabriel laughed falsely. "Here? Among humans? Don't be ludicrous."

"He's halfway between angel and demon. Halfway between good and evil. That sounds pretty much human to me."

Satan gave a low chuckle. "He's got you there, Gabe," he smirked.

"Oh, I think not," Gabriel sighed. He gestured to Michael. "Seize the boy."

Zac stood his ground. "You'll have to get through me."

"And me," added Herya. "Although I don't actually have any idea what's going on here," she admitted. "But I really enjoyed punching people in the face earlier, and I'd like to do it again."

"Twice the fun," said Michael, drawing his sword. His eyes shone as he lunged with the blade straight towards Zac's chest.

"*Don't you dare hurt my grandson!*" Phillip cried in that voice that boomed from everywhere. Michael's attack faltered.

The angel stared down at the object he was holding in his hand. It had been a sword. He was absolutely certain that it had been a sword.

"Michael," began Gabriel quietly, "why are you brandishing an ice-cream cone?"

"It's... it's a sword," Michael insisted, refusing to believe what the mounting evidence was telling him. "It's a big sword with fire on it."

"It's a mint-choc-chip ice cream," said Zac. "And I'd *really* advise against letting it drip on my granddad's carpet."

Michael stepped back. He looked around for somewhere to put the cone. Finding nowhere, he licked it instead, and discovered that he really quite enjoyed mint choc chip.

Gabriel shot Zac a questioning look. "How did you do that?" he asked.

"Trade secret," Zac lied. "Just a little trick I picked up on my travels."

The archangel looked at the ice-cream cone, then he looked down at Phillip, still sitting in his armchair. It was a long time before he met Zac's gaze again. "I see," he said almost inaudibly. "Very interesting."

"Angelo stays here," said Zac. "He stays here and you leave him alone." He looked over at Satan. "*Everyone* leaves him alone."

Gabriel and the Dark Lord exchanged a glance. "Very well," said Gabriel. "You win. The boy will stay here."

Angelo leaped out from behind Zac and began body-popping once again. "Oooh yeah, I'm staying, I'm staying, I'm staying here. I'm staying, I'm—"

"You, of course," continued Gabriel, directing his smile firmly in Zac's direction, "shall return with Satan to Hell, whereupon your punishment shall commence immediately, and continue for all eternity. I trust the Dark Lord will take a special interest in your case."

Satan shot Phillip a quick glance, but the old man didn't appear to be paying much attention. The Father of All Lies' forked tongue flicked hungrily across his teeth. "Oh, you betcha," he said, but he kept his voice low so Phillip wouldn't hear.

Angelo stopped dancing. "Wait... what?"

"You can't do that," gasped Herya.

Zac turned and looked at his granddad, but that shadowy confusion was back behind Phillip's eyes. Whatever had awoken within him had now gone back to sleep.

"They can," Zac said. "I died. That's how I got back into Hell in the first place."

Tears sprang into Angelo's eyes. "No, but... but..."

"It's OK, Angelo," Zac told him. "I knew this would happen."

"Wait... what's happening now?" asked Phillip.

Zac knelt beside him. "I'm going away again, Granddad."

"What, again?" said the old man. "Make up your mind, will you?"

Zac smiled and patted Phillip's hand. "Angelo's going to stay here. He'll look after you. Look after him too, will you?"

He stood up and turned to face the rest of the room. "Right, then," he said. "Let's get this over with."

"It's not fair," sobbed Angelo, throwing his arms round Zac and holding on tight. "There has to be something we can do. There *has* to be."

"Well, there isn't," said Gabriel quickly. "Satan will take you to the underworld. Off you pop."

"No!" Angelo wailed.

"It's tragic, I know," Gabriel agreed, "but there's nothing that can be done. Our hands are tied."

"Fair enough," said Zac. He held out his wrists, ready to be led away. Just as Satan reached for them, though, he pulled back. "Unless..." Zac said, watching Gabriel closely, "What's the Right of Enosh"

Gabriel's left eye twitched. Michael paused, mid lick, then lowered the ice-cream cone from his mouth.

"Never heard of it," said Gabriel. "Now if there are no further delays..."

"Wait!" Angelo cried. "The Right of Enosh! I've read

about that. The Right of Enosh. The right to challenge Death for your soul. Remember?"

Gabriel's eye twitched so violently this time it made his whole head shake. Satan let out a low groan.

Zac frowned. "What? You mean you can really challenge Death? I thought that was just in movies."

"No!" laughed Angelo. "It's real. It's real, isn't it, Gabriel?"

Gabriel glared raw hatred at Angelo. "Why, yes," he said, through his fixed smile. "The Right of Enosh. How could I have forgotten? Those who request it may be given the opportunity to challenge Death to a game of chess. Win and you will be restored to life."

"And if I lose?"

"Then you will be cast into Hell."

Zac shrugged. "Well, I'll do that, then."

Gabriel's brow furrowed. "Are you sure that's wise?"

"I'm already going to Hell anyway, so yeah. Why not?"

"Well, yes, there is that," admitted Gabriel. "But if you lose you'll... go for longer."

"What, longer than all eternity?"

There was a pause. "Yes," said Gabriel through gritted

teeth. He was trying to hold his smile in place, but it was a losing battle.

"Let's give it a bash anyway," said Zac, and he saw what little remained of Gabriel's grin fall away.

"Right, fine," Gabriel snapped. He clicked his fingers. There was a soft *pop*, and a school desk appeared in the middle of the living room. Zac recognised the boy sitting behind it as the one he'd met in the shed in Limbo. Drake looked up from the sheet of paper in front of him.

"Um. Hi," he said.

"I give up," mumbled Phillip, whose already slender grasp on reality was being tested to the limit.

Drake looked at the faces staring down at him. "Hey, you're that guy with the book," he said, recognising Zac.

"That's me," Zac replied.

Drake smiled weakly. "You all right?"

"Yeah, not bad, not bad," Zac replied. "Dead, though."

"What, properly?"

"Yeah."

"Bummer."

"Yeah. Listen, we were wondering, can you play chess?"

Drake shook his head. "Nah."

Gabriel tutted sharply. "Well, can you learn?" he demanded.

"When for?" Drake asked.

"Now, ideally."

Drake looked down at the paper in front of him. "Not really," he said. "I'm doing a maths test. Actually, that's a point. Does anyone know what the square root of—"

Gabriel clicked his fingers and the desk vanished again. "Right, you win," he sighed. "Your life is restored, the messy remains you left on the pavement will be disposed of and no one will ever remember finding them."

"And Angelo stays here," Zac reminded him.

"Yes, yes," said Gabriel vaguely. He made a cryptic gesture with his hand, and reality parted a few dozen centimetres. "Come, Michael," he scowled, "we must return and continue our search for the book."

"That you off, then?" asked Phillip. He still had no idea what was going on, but he knew where his manners were. "Safe journey home."

Gabriel paused at the gap in space. He turned and gazed at Phillip. For a long time, he just gazed.

"Indeed," he said at last, then he stepped through the

gap and Michael stepped through after him. There was a sound like a zip being done up, and the hole closed over.

"I suppose I'd best be off as well," said Satan brightly. "Getting a new kitchen fitted this afternoon. Right bunch of cowboys doing it. Don't trust them as far as I could throw them. Although I could actually throw them quite a long way if the wind was right."

"Are you sure you wouldn't like a cup of tea?" Phillip asked vaguely. Satan gave a throaty chuckle and winked at Zac.

"Never changes, does he? No, I won't bother. Some other time, maybe."

He looked Angelo up and down. "Shame," was all he said, then he clicked his fingers and vanished in a puff of red smoke.

And with that, silence fell on the living room.

"Right, then," said Phillip, finally breaking the spell. "Let's have that cuppa."

Zac, Angelo and Herya stood in the kitchen, their mugs in their hands. Phillip was sitting at the table, reading a newspaper as if nothing out of the ordinary had happened.

"Does he know?" Herya asked.

Zac watched his grandfather. "I don't think so," he said. "I think he's... forgotten."

"Forgotten what?" asked Angelo.

"How do you forget something like that?" continued the Valkyrie.

Zac shrugged. "I don't know. Maybe he forgot on purpose. Maybe he didn't want to remember."

"Remember what?" Angelo quizzed. "What are you on about?"

"Can he do that? Can he make people forget?"

"I suppose he can do anything."

"Don't be daft," Angelo said. "Only God can do anything."

Zac and Herya exchanged a glance. They all sipped their tea.

"So, what now?" Herya asked.

Zac shrugged. "Dunno. Get a job, I suppose." He jabbed a thumb in Angelo's direction. "Doubt he'll let me go back to stealing. Will you?"

"Nope," said Angelo.

"That's what I thought," said Zac. "What about you, Herya?"

"Going to travel a bit," the Valkyrie said. "Find some adventures. You can come if you want."

"No, thanks."

"Good, I didn't want you to anyway. You'd only hold me back." She smiled, then gulped down the last of her tea. "Well, see you around," she said, making for the back door. "Nice to meet you, Mr Corgan."

Phillip looked up from the table. "You too, dear. And I like your wings." A flicker of something that might have been recognition shadowed his face as he admired the white feathers.

"Oh, but look," he said, getting up and shuffling over to her. "You've got blood on one." He licked his thumb and rubbed the wing. Both the dried blood and the wound itself were wiped away. "There," he said admiringly. "That's better."

Herya flexed the newly healed wing. "Thank you," she said. With a final glance to Zac and Angelo, she opened the back door.

"Herya," said Zac.

The Valkyrie paused.

"Thanks. You know... for coming back. For saving us."

She shrugged. "Don't get used to it," she said, then

stepped through the door. There was the sound of applause as the Valkyrie leaped into the air. It faded as she soared off across the skies.

"Right, then," said Zac, setting down his mug. "I'll show you your bedroom."

"What?" asked Angelo, following behind him as he made for the door leading into the hall. "I thought we'd be sharing a room."

"Uh, no."

"But I thought we could get bunk beds. *Bunk beds*, Zac!"

They walked out into the hall and made for the stairs. "Well, you thought wrong."

"But *bunk beds*. Everyone loves bunk beds. Bagsy being on the top bunk!"

"You can't bagsy the top bunk because there *is* no top bunk," Zac said. "You can't bagsy something that doesn't exist."

There was a rattle from the letterbox and a black envelope fluttered to the floor. Zac grabbed it, then opened the door and looked out. There was no one there, but had he paid more attention, he might have seen something one-eyed and semi-naked lumbering along the street in a decidedly unfeminine way.

Zac closed the door and studied the envelope. His and Angelo's names were written on the front in silver script. He tore open the top, and two rectangles of plastic slid out into his palm.

"What is it?" asked Angelo, craning his neck to see.

Zac held up the cards. "VIP passes for Eyedol."

"Aw," smiled Angelo. "That was nice of him."

"Want to go?"

"No way," said Angelo firmly.

"Yeah, nor me," said Zac, and he slipped the passes back in the envelope, then tossed them in the bin.

"You know the only thing that still bothers me, though?" Angelo asked.

"Steropes being a woman?"

"No!" Angelo shuddered. "Well, yes, but something else too."

Zac stepped on to the bottom stair. "What?"

"The book. Where's the book?"

"How should I know? Does it matter?"

"Depends. What if someone dangerous *has* got it?"

"I doubt they'd be any more dangerous than Gabriel."

He moved to head up the stairs, but as he did, his eyes fell on the goldfish bowl. The fish inside was swimming around as fast and as frantically as ever, darting through the water in a blur of shimmering orange.

Zac stopped.

He stepped back down into the hall.

"What is it?" asked Angelo. "What's the matter?"

Zac looked at the fish, and for the very first time, he saw. Properly saw. As it swam it left a shining trail behind it, like someone drawing in the air with a sparkler. Before Zac's eyes the trails became shapes and the shapes became letters and the letters spelled out words.

"Z-A-C," he said aloud.

Angelo's lips moved silently. "Zac," he said. "That spells Zac! Give me another one."

Zac shushed him and kept watching. The letters sparkled in the bowl, each one visible for only a tiny fraction of a second, but leaving an indelible imprint on his mind's eye.

ZAC CORGAN LOOKED IN DISBELIEF AT THE
BOOK OF EVERYTHING.

AND IN THAT MOMENT HE UNDERSTOOD, AND KNEW

THAT HE COULD NEVER TELL

ANOTHER LIVING SOUL WHAT HE HAD SEEN.

"What is it?" asked Angelo. "Why are you staring at the fish?"

"He took the book," Zac said to himself. "He took the book with him and he hid it." He glanced through into the kitchen where his grandfather sat. "Just like I'd have done."

"What? What are you on about?" asked Angelo.

Zac shook his head. "Oh, nothing," he said, and he turned towards the stairs once more. The thing that looked like a fish continued its endless, eternal swim.

ZAC CORGAN WALKED UP THE STAIRS, FOLLOWED BY
THE HALF-BLOOD, ANGELO.
ZAC CORGAN SMILED, AND FOR THE FIRST TIME IN
ZAC CORGAN'S LIFE,
HE CONSIDERED THE POSSIBILITY OF BUNK BEDS.

EPILOGUE

"I BRING NEWS, sir."

"Good show, Gabriel. News of the book?"

"The... uh... the book, sir?"

"Yes. You know. The... the book. What's it called?"

"I'm not sure I know what you mean, sir."

"What? Of course you do, man. The missing, uh, the missing... thing. What's it called?"

"Missing thing, sir?"

"Yes, you know. With the... and the... and whatnot."

"If you've misplaced something, sir, I can have some of the angels look into it."

"Misplaced something? Who's misplaced something?"

"I thought you had, sir."

"Me? No. How could I misplace anything? I'm a disembodied voice, for Heaven's sake."

"Quite, sir. Forgive me for asking, sir, but why was it you wanted to see me?"

"I didn't. I thought you wanted to see me."

"No, sir."

"You had news, you said. About... About something or other."

"I don't seem to recall having any news, sir."

"I'm almost certain that you did."

"Then it must've slipped my mind, sir."

"What did?"

"Uh... I don't know, sir."

"What?"

"Sorry, sir?"

"Why are you here, Gabriel?"

"My apologies, sir, I think I may have hit my head on the way in. I am having difficulty recalling my reason for coming."

"For coming where?"

"To see you, sir."

"Did you? When?"

"Now, sir."

"Ah, right. Yes."

"Begging your pardon, sir, I have some duties to which I must attend. Michael has requested that we try to source him some ice cream."

"Ice cream?"

"Yes, sir. He has rather inexplicably taken a shine to the flavour mint choc chip. We don't know where he got the taste from."

"Well, whatever keeps him happy, I suppose. You may go. Good day, Gabriel."

"Good day, sir. And should I remember what I came in for, rest assured you shall be the very first to know."

"To know what, Gabriel?"

"…"

"Gabriel?"

"Nothing, sir. But I think perhaps I'd better have something of a lie-down."